PRAISE FOR S. G. BROWNE
and his brilliantly original novels

"Browne pulls out something so unexpected and pitch-perfect that it's obvious Creativity knocked him out of his chair and started typing herself."

—The Washington Post

"Riotously funny and brilliantly executed . . . Browne's prose will have you hooked from the very first word to the very last."

—New York Journal of Books

"It's not just satire; it's literature. . . . S. G. Browne is an author to be reckoned with, a voice from the void of humanity that begs to be heard."

—The Inner Bean

"Marvelous. . . . One of the best speculative humorists working the field."

—HorrorScope

"S. G. Browne continues his streak of entertaining and delighting readers with his humor-filled writing prowess and supernaturally infused creative storytelling."

—BookFetish

"Hilarious . . . an extremely strong narrative voice."

—Publishers Weekly

LUCKY BASTARD

"Wickedly sharp and wildly entertaining. S. G. Browne is one of today's very best writers."

—*New York Times* **bestselling author**
Jonathan Maberry

"Insightful, intriguing . . . With twists aplenty, this fast-paced adventure succeeds as both a hard-boiled homage and a paranormal romp."

—*Publishers Weekly* **(starred review and**
a Pick of the Week)

"Browne adds a whimsical layer of philosophizing about the fundamental noir themes of fate, chance, and luck. . . . Wisecracks punctuate the action."

—*San Francisco Chronicle*

"Browne hits the funny bone hard."

—*Kirkus Reviews* **(starred review)**

"Thoroughly enjoyable . . . In spite of all the laughs, *Lucky Bastard* contains some thoughts about how to hang on to your morality."

—*Peoria Journal Star*

"A real original . . . Wildly entertaining and uncommonly moving."

—*Pretty Sinister Books*

"Full of witty writing and hilarious adventures . . . I laughed out loud many times. Read the book: it'll be your good fortune."

—*New York Times* **bestselling author Kevin J. Anderson**

"The titular bastard may be in for a very bad day, but Browne's readers are the lucky ones."

I SAW ZOMBIES EATING SANTA CLAUS

"Readers with a certain seasonal sensibility—one that renders zombies appropriate fare no matter the date on the calendar—will be shouting Ho! Ho! Ho!"

"If your idea of 'heart-warming' involves an organ roasting on a stick, *I Saw Zombies Eating Santa Claus* is the perfect holiday tale."

"Hilarious, horrifying . . . a must for anyone who can't get enough of the undead."

"Dark, bizarre, very funny, and yes, with a bit of sentimentality thrown in, *I Saw Zombies Eating Santa Claus* is the perfect Christmas read for those who like VERY black comedy in their holiday reading."

ALSO BY S. G. BROWNE

NOVELS
Breathers
Fated
Lucky Bastard

NOVELLAS / SHORT STORIES
Shooting Monkeys in a Barrel
I Saw Zombies Eating Santa Claus

To Lloyd,

BIG EGOS

A NOVEL

Reality is overrated.

S. G. BROWNE

G

GALLERY BOOKS

New York London Toronto Sydney New Delhi

A Division of Simon & Schuster, Inc.
1230 Avenue of the Americas
New York, NY 10020

First Gallery Books trade paperback edition August 2013

GALLERY BOOKS and colophon are registered trademarks of Simon & Schuster, Inc.

For information about special discounts for bulk purchases, please contact Simon & Schuster Special Sales at 1-866-506-1949 or business@simonandschuster.com.

The Simon & Schuster Speakers Bureau can bring authors to your live event. For more information or to book an event contact the Simon & Schuster Speakers Bureau at 1-866-248-3049 or visit our website at www.simonspeakers.com.

Designed by Jaime Putorti

Manufactured in the United States of America

10 9 8 7 6 5 4 3 2 1

Library of Congress Cataloging-in-Publication Data is available.

ISBN 978-1-4767-1167-6
ISBN 978-1-4767-1177-5 (ebook)

For Jeff, aka Big Nerd.
Thanks for keeping me real.

AUTHOR'S NOTE

All celebrities, fictional characters, and public personas portrayed in this novel are used in a fictitious and satirical manner and are the product of the author's imagination.

We are what we pretend to be, so we must be careful about what we pretend to be.

—**Kurt Vonnegut**

Be yourself; everyone else is already taken.

—**Oscar Wilde**

BiG EGOS

CHAPTER 1

I'm at another party, this one in a Beverly Hills brick Colonial Revival mansion just off Wilshire Boulevard. It's not exactly Graceland and this sure as hell ain't Memphis, but I have to remember that I didn't come here to indulge my own fantasies.

It's a select crowd, lots of familiar faces and everyone wants to shake my hand. I get stopped by Dick Clark, Jackie Kennedy Onassis, Liberace, and Starsky and Hutch, among others. Fairly white-bread gathering, though I run into Richard Pryor every now and then, so chances are he'll make an appearance.

The party is a typical L.A. gathering, lots of pretty faces and everyone looking around to see who else there is to see. The DJ is playing seventies-era Top 40 and disco that everyone's heard on the radio at one time or another. I think about suggesting he spin "Jailhouse Rock" or "Hound Dog" instead, but I don't want to get too self-absorbed. It's bad form.

I wander through the house, offering an occasional smile and a wave and a "thank you very much" as I check out the other guests. Bruce Lee is hitting on Hot Lips Houlihan. Evel Knievel is attempting to jump over half a dozen of the Dallas Cowboys Cheerleaders. Daisy Duke and Farrah Fawcett are comparing their breasts while Andy Kaufman officiates.

A huge banquet table of catered food sits in the middle of the dining room. Cher and Deborah Harry, both apparently high on devil weed, are scarfing down petits fours, while John Belushi sculpts the pâté into the shape of a penis. Fonzie sits in his trademark leather jacket near the head of the table, alternately eating from a tray of puff pastries and sucking on a half-smoked joint. He looks at me and says, "Nice lamb chops," then laughs. He has crumbs and a yellow stain down the front of his white T-shirt.

I'm tempted to bring up the whole "jumping the shark" thing but my momma always taught me to take the high road, so I just smile and keep my thoughts to myself.

Belushi offers me some of his artwork on a cracker but I decline. Maybe if they had a platter of Twinkies or some deep-fried banana and peanut butter sandwiches I'd reconsider, but I didn't come here to indulge The King's appetite. At least not for food.

Deborah Harry breaks into a rendition of "It's Now or Never" as Cher stuffs another petit four into her mouth and laughs, spraying food across the table. Cher and Blondie don't belong here, at least not legally since they're both still alive, but neither one of them appears to be in any kind of distress, so I let it slide.

I walk up to Blondie, tenderly brush the hair off her fore-

head, ask her if she's lonesome tonight, then give her a kiss that distracts Belushi from his pâté sculpture. When Blondie's knees buckle, I catch her and lower her into a chair, then turn and walk into the kitchen.

Joey Ramone and Sid Vicious are doing shots of tequila while Andy Warhol raids the refrigerator, which looks more like a walk-in closet than a Frigidaire. I reach past Warhol and grab two bottles of Coors, then wander down the hall and head upstairs.

The mansion has half a dozen bedrooms, each of them bigger than my own and half of them occupied. In one bedroom, I find Vinnie Barbarino getting stoned with George Carlin and Freddie Mercury. In another room, Rocky Balboa is having sex with Annie Hall. Finally, in the last room, a bedroom so enormous I could park both of my cars and still have enough space to stage Jesus Christ Superstar, I find who I've been looking for.

David Cassidy stands naked in front of a full-length mirror singing "I Think I Love You." His head is shaved, along with most of the rest of his body—his hair in a pile on the hardwood floor at his feet. He still has his pubic hair and his eyebrows, but he removes the eyebrows in the time it takes me to uncap the bottles of Coors.

"That's an interesting look," I say.

He turns away from the mirror and regards me with catatonic indifference.

"Are you from the party?" he asks.

I assure him that I am.

He eyes the two beers I'm holding in my right hand and asks if he can have one. I figured he'd be thirsty, so I hand him a bottle. As he tilts his head back and starts to drink, I remove a single liquid-filled capsule from my pocket and drop it into my own beer. The capsule dissolves within seconds.

He finishes his beer and drops the bottle, then wipes a distracted hand across his mouth. "I was thirsty," he says.

I offer him my beer. He takes it without a word and drinks it down in half a dozen gulps. When he drops the bottle, it shatters on the hardwood floor.

"How about I find us a couple more brews," I say.

"Okay," he says, then turns to the mirror and starts to shave his pubic hair as he breaks into The Partridge Family theme song.

Come on get happy.

I walk out of the room and close the door behind me, then I find the nearest bathroom to take care of business. Out of vanity and because it still gives me the giggles, I check my reflection in the mirror. The sideburns and hair are mine. The white jumpsuit and glasses came from a vintage clothing store. I look enough like Elvis to have groupies. I walk like him. I talk like him. Hell, if someone brought out a karaoke machine I could probably even sing like him. And as far as the other guests at the party are concerned, I am The King.

Which is all that really matters.

Perception is reality.

And after taking care of business with David Cassidy, my reality has a yearning for some hanky-panky.

I check my reflection in the mirror one more time, then I walk back down the hallway toward the dining room to see if I can interest Deborah Harry in some burnin' love.

CHAPTER 2

The alarm goes off at 9:01.

Classical Nuevo drifts out of the wall speakers. One of Vivaldi's seasons blended with Tchaikovsky's *1812 Overture*. Or maybe Orff's *Carmina Burana*. It's hard to tell with my hangover. Before I can figure out which one it is, Delilah's hand reaches out from beneath the goose-down comforter and turns off the alarm.

"Coffee please," she purrs with her slight southern lilt, then turns away, her naked torso exposed and her red hair spilled across the pillow like a painting by Courbet.

Her wish is my command. I slide out of the California king and stand up, my feet hitting the hardwood floor, which is when I realize my hangover is worse than I thought. I need to remember to drink more water. And take the recommended mixture of glucosamine and vitamin E.

I step past the white jumpsuit, discarded on the floor like molted skin, and stagger into the bathroom, leaving the lights off as I empty the contents of my bladder. After chasing some ibuprofen with a glass of water, I check my reflection by the morning sun coming in through the bathroom skylight.

I need a shave. And I could do with some Visine. And the flesh around my eyes and the corners of my mouth are a little puckered, but nothing a little Botox injection won't fix. The hair and sideburns are still there, but they're the only holdover from last night. The rest is all me.

My nose. *My* eyes. *My* lips.

Truth is, I don't look anything like Elvis.

At least not in the morning, once the effects have worn off. Most of the time I don't experience any form of depression, but Elvis Presley is a tough act to follow, so I pop a serotonin capsule, then throw on a T-shirt and a pair of jeans and climb into my convertible 1959 T-Bird to go get some over-the-counter stimulants.

I own a coffeemaker. I even own an espresso machine and another contraption that makes lattes and cappuccinos. But I've never used them. First off, they're still in their boxes. Housewarming gifts and birthday presents I've never bothered to open. Second, I've never made particularly good coffee and I hate having to deal with the cleanup. And third, why bother making something for yourself when you can pay someone else to do it for you?

Truth is, I'm just a product of society.

A creation of my culture.

An identity inspired by convenience.

My kitchen is filled with everything you need to make home-cooked, gourmet meals, prepared and served in style.

Waterford crystal wineglasses. Villeroy & Boch china. Sterling silver flatware.

Vitamix blenders. Cuisinart ice-cream makers. KitchenAid mixers.

All-Clad fry pans and saucières and French skillets hanging above a Sterling gas range with a cast-iron griddle and dual conventional ovens.

All of it pristine. None of it used. Taking up space and collecting dust while I dine out, ask for delivery, and order to go.

Sometimes it seems like a waste filling up space with all of these things that I never use, but I like knowing I have them in case I ever need them. And it makes a good impression when people come over. After all, your home is a reflection of your status, and what you fill your home with is a reflection of who you are. It doesn't matter if you use any of your personal possessions. What matters is perception.

The drive through the Hollywood Hills on a late August Sunday morning is soundstage perfect, so I put the top down on the T-Bird and drop down Laurel Canyon to the Starbucks on Sunset Boulevard.

People often ask me why I insist on driving a car that's more than sixty years old when I can afford a new model with the latest hybrid or electric technology, but I like the style of the mid-twentieth century. Besides, why would I want my ride to be what everyone else is driving?

While I'm sitting at the signal waiting for the light to change, Bettie Page sashays past in the crosswalk with a black standard poodle on a leash. The guy walking in the opposite direction stops in the middle of the road and does a double take, then jumps and gives me the finger as the light turns green and I lay on the horn.

Once inside Starbucks, I scan my smartphone and place my order for a tall caramel macchiato with whipped cream and a triple espresso. The caramel macchiato is for Delilah, who likes her caffeine served up like a soda fountain confection, while I prefer mine straight up like a good, stiff drink. If it's beer, I'll drink a Guinness. If it's a cocktail, I want scotch on the rocks. And if it's coffee, give it to me pure and unadorned in an IV drip.

Anything else is a waste of my gustatory time.

The woman in line behind me, who looks like Lucille Ball on crystal meth, orders a white mocha from the barista, changes her mind and orders an Americano, then cancels her Americano and orders an iced latte. Small. When the cashier asks if she means a tall, Lucy doesn't seem to understand the question.

"No, I want a small," she says.

"We don't have smalls," says the cashier. "Do you want a short?"

Nearly a quarter of the way into the twenty-first century and people still get confused while ordering at Starbucks.

"Ma'am," says the cashier, pointing to the different container sizes. "Would you like a short or a tall?"

Lucy bites her lower lip, her eyes flitting back and forth from one container to the next, then up to the menu on the wall. Over the sound of the milk steamer, faint but unmistakable, I hear her humming the theme song to *I Love Lucy*.

Maybe it's just me, but Lucy looks like she could use some help.

"A tall!" she finally shouts, saliva exploding from her lips in a fine spray. Then she grabs some money out of her wallet, puts a pinkie in her mouth, and starts chewing on the nail.

As I wait for my order, I alternately keep an eye on Lucy and eavesdrop on Ernest Hemingway and William Faulkner, who are sitting at a nearby table discussing bullfighting and sportfishing. Faulkner listens with a bored expression as Hemingway dominates the conversation with bombastic conviction, speaking in short sentences like bursts of machine-gun fire.

"Give me a boat," says Hemingway. "And the open sea. Nothing else matters."

"What about complex sentences?" says Faulkner.

"Overrated," says Hemingway. "And overdone."

"Have you ever made use of any word that might actually send one of your readers in search of a dictionary?"

"Big emotions don't come from big words," says Hemingway.

Faulkner leans back in his chair and puts his hands behind his head. "You're just bitter because I won the Pulitzer before you did."

"The Pulitzer is for pussies."

"Face it," says Faulkner. "As a storyteller, you suck."

"Suck on this," says Hemingway, giving Faulkner the one-finger salute.

"Crass and simple," says Faulkner. "I wouldn't expect anything else."

Hemingway stands up. "You want to take this outside?"

As they continue to argue, I listen to them and think, not for the first time, how like-minded Egos have a tendency to gravitate toward one another.

Writers. Actors. Rock stars.

I don't know if it's a familiarity born of physical recognition or if there's something more significant involved. A genetic pull. A cosmic attraction. A spiritual connection. Though I doubt there's anything religious going on here.

No one's claiming any miracles.

No one's hearing Jesus on the radio.

No one's seeing the Virgin Mary in their cappuccino.

Truth is, I don't think God would approve.

Other than Hemingway and Faulkner and a spun-out Lucille Ball, the other caffeine addicts in Starbucks are themselves. College students and accountants and writers. Teachers and Web designers and bartenders. Maybe a guy who writes an online column for the *Los Angeles Times* and a girl who plays stand-up bass for a punk jazz band that rocks Molly Malone's one Saturday a month.

This is who they are. These are the roles they play. Most of them probably don't earn enough to afford the luxury of being someone else. Not legally, anyway. But that doesn't mean they can't find another way.

The barista calls out my order. I give Lucille Ball another glance, then I grab Delilah's caramel macchiato and my triple espresso and I head out the door as Hemingway says something to Faulkner about a bell tolling.

I climb into my T-Bird and sit behind the wheel, my Sirius satellite radio tuned to the BBC as I sip my triple espresso and watch the front door of Starbucks and listen to the latest world news.

A report about the crackdown on Ego raves in London.

An investigative exposé on Japan's psyche subculture.

A congressional committee on the spiritual implication of the id.

I find it ironic that Congress is debating the concept of the soul, considering that it doesn't even have one. But I suppose they can't just stand by and ignore the concerns of some of their constituents, even if it's just for show.

I switch the radio to another station, something with lyrics and music, and come across a familiar song that reminds me of college and spring break and cold Coronas. I don't even have to close my eyes and I'm there on the beach, the moment playing back in my head like a video clip.

This has been happening to me lately: random memories from my life popping up, invading the present, blending in with the here and now, brought on by a familiar song or a scent or a turn of phrase. Kind of like little acid flashbacks, except I've never dropped acid.

One moment I'm sitting in my car and the next, I'm on the beach with my best friend Nat. Another moment I'm having sex with Delilah and the next, I'm eating dinner with my parents.

It's like flipping through channels on the television and getting snippets of scenes.

Flip.

I'm at a Buddhist meditation center.

Flip.

I'm stuffing my own stocking on Christmas Eve.

Flip.

I'm at a fraternity party during college.

Part of me wonders if I should report these mini-flashbacks or if I should be concerned, but another part of me explains them away as a trivial side effect. After all, my flashbacks aren't affecting my cognitive functions or my ability to deal with the minutiae of everyday life, so until they start causing a problem, I likely don't have anything to be worried about.

A few moments later, Lucy comes out of Starbucks and walks across the street to her car, a BMW 900 series, which in this neighborhood means there's a good chance she's Beverly Hills or Bel Air material, so she's probably not hurting for money. And while Lucille Ball has been dead for more than thirty years, her estate hasn't agreed to license her Ego. Couple that with the erratic behavior she's exhibiting and it's obvious Lucy acquired her Ego on the black market.

Which is where I come in.

I wait until Lucy pulls out into traffic and heads west on Sunset Boulevard, then I crank up the song on the radio that reminds me of spring break and I start following her.

CHAPTER 3

"I'm not following you," says Nat.

"What part aren't you following?" I ask.

Nat takes a drink of his Corona and looks at me from behind his sunglasses as a couple of bikini-clad co-eds walk past us toward the surf of the Pacific Ocean.

"All of it."

Where we are is Newport Beach during spring break of our senior year at UCLA. This is five years ago, in 2016, a few months before I started working full-time at EGOS.

A late March storm has given way to a gorgeous Southern California afternoon, with four- to six-foot swells, a long, lazy break, and dozens of nearly naked bodies adorning the sand and surf. In the middle of all this, I'm trying to explain to Nat about the new product being developed at EGOS, the bioengineering company where I'm interning. I really shouldn't be talking about it since I signed a nondisclosure agreement, but I've known Nat since we were in kindergarten and I trust him not to share this with anyone.

"Okay," I say. "How about this? What if you could be somebody else?"

"You mean like in that old movie *Being John Malkovich*?"

"No. I'm not talking about a portal into someone else's head. This is completely different."

"Good. Because I'm not all that excited about being spit out into a ditch on the side of the New Jersey Turnpike."

"You're not going to be spit out anywhere," I say. "And the experience will last a lot longer than just fifteen minutes."

"So it'll be better than sex?"

Nat has had sex twice in his twenty-one years: the first time during his sophomore year in high school with Debbie Rivers, a cheerleader who had been passed around like a bong at a drum circle; and the second time during his freshman year in college with a woman who turned out to be a prostitute. So when it comes to something being better than sex, Nat isn't exactly an expert on the subject. Though I'm sure he could teach a class on self-gratification.

I motion with my beer toward a trio of teenage women lounging on the beach, their bodies young and ripe and glistening with suntan lotion. "Imagine that all three of these women find you irresistible. Imagine that when they look at you, they see Heath Ledger or Paul Newman or James Bond."

"But I don't look anything like James Bond."

"You don't look like Heath Ledger, either."

"Thanks for clearing that up, bro."

Nat's called me "bro" ever since high school. Considering we've been best friends since we were kids and that neither one of us has any close family ties, I suppose it fits.

"Who you look like isn't the point," I say. "The point is, you would be who these women desire. You would be who they fantasize about. You would be who you always wanted to be."

Nat studies the three women. "Can I be Captain Kirk? I always wanted to be Captain Kirk. Or maybe Indiana Jones. Or Sherlock Holmes. Or Aragorn. Women would be all over me if I was Aragorn."

Nat has never been a big fan of reality. He's always identified with fictional characters and still spends a lot of his nights immersed in role-playing games like Skyrim and World of Warcraft and Apocalypto, living behind the mask of an online avatar.

Which doesn't exactly help with the whole not-getting-laid thing.

"Isn't there anyone real you'd want to be?" I ask. "Kurt Cobain? James Dean? John F. Kennedy Jr.?"

Nat scowls in concentration and purses his lips. He's done that ever since we were kids. Even at twenty-one, he still looks like a little boy.

"Ryan Reynolds," he says. "I'd be okay with him."

"Well, that's a start. But we might have trouble getting the rights to celebrities and public figures who are still alive."

The problem with living celebrities is that you get into issues of invasion of privacy and false impersonations and identity rights. It's less legally complicated to replicate the DNA of someone who's already dead or of a fictional character, even though estates and copyright holders still want royalties or a suitcase full of cash in exchange for a license.

"I still don't understand how you're going to do this," says Nat. "Is it like *Jurassic Park*? Or *Blade Runner*? Or *The Boys from Brazil*?"

"Not exactly."

I explain to Nat that while the science and technology involved is somewhat complicated, the basic premise is simple: we're going to replicate the DNA of dead celebrities and fictional characters using molecular cloning and then mix the DNA with a cocktail of amino acids, potassium, sodium, chlorine, enzymes, proteins, and a dash of serotonin. The idea is to create an experience of being someone else for several hours.

No one's cloning dinosaurs.

No one's creating replicants.

No one's developing a master race.

We're just revolutionizing role-playing games.

When the U.S. Court of Appeals for the Federal Circuit ruled that human genes can be patented because the DNA extracted from cells is not a product of nature, it opened the door for the patents on the cloning and replication of genes that would eventually lead to the creation of Big Egos.

"The trick," I say to Nat, "is using the right combination of proteins and enzymes, which is essential for the synthesis of the DNA with the host."

"You mean like on game shows?"

"No. You're the host."

"I'm the host?"

I'm thinking I shouldn't have tried explaining this to Nat while we were stoned.

"Can you mix it with alcohol and drink it?" asks Nat.

"Sure. But that's not the point. Once the cocktail has a chance to calibrate with the DNA of the . . ."

"You want another beer?" Nat digs into the ice chest. "All this talk about cocktails is making me thirsty."

I sigh, then forge ahead: "Once the cocktail has a chance to calibrate with the host DNA, the experience will last for anywhere from six to eight hours, though the primary consciousness will remain just beneath the surface as a reality monitor."

"So even though I'm someone else, I'll still be me?"

I explain to Nat how that's an essential component of the product. After all, just because someone thinks he's Superman doesn't mean he won't break his neck jumping off a roof because he thinks he can fly.

Nat sits there staring at me, drinking his Corona, his head nodding slightly, his lips pursed, his expression contemplative, and I think I've finally managed to get through to him. Then he turns and looks out at the expanse of beach and all the half-naked bodies strewn across the sand.

"So I'd be able to have sex with any one of these women?" he asks.

"Well . . . that depends on who you're pretending to be."

"Okay, so if I'm someone famous, can I have sex with famous women?" he says. "Like Taylor Swift or Jennifer Lawrence or Megan Fox?"

"Probably not them, because they're still alive. But anything's possible. Theoretically you can have sex with famous women, but it's easier if they're already dead."

The mother sitting near us with her two young children picks up her towels and personal belongings and moves farther away.

Nat looks up and down the beach at the selection of potential conquests, drinking his beer and nodding his head. "I think I'd like to have sex with Hermione Granger."

Nat always did have a thing for Emma Watson.

We sit there for a few minutes, sipping our beers in silence, watching the waves roll in as the three young women I'd pointed out earlier get up and walk down to the water and wade into the surf.

"You said that even though I was someone else, I'd still be me?" says Nat.

"That's right," I say. "Your consciousness will still be there just below the surface, monitoring what's happening."

"Kind of like a security guard?"

"Kind of."

Nat nods and takes a sip of his beer. "What if my security guard falls asleep on the job?"

"What do you mean?"

"What happens if I stay below the surface?" says Nat. "I know you said it's not going to be like *Being John Malkovich,* but what if I get trapped inside someone else's identity and I can't get back out?"

"That won't happen," I say.

"How do you know?"

"Because there are safeguards in place to make sure of it."

"How do you know?"

"Because they've had extensive trials and testing and are putting together a customer support team trained in psychology," I say. "Plus they have some of the best scientific minds in the country behind the technology."

"But how do you *know*?"

When Nat gets hold of a question, sometimes he can't seem to let it go.

"It's not going to pose any more of a risk than virtual reality," I say. "The main difference is that you won't need to wear goggles to enjoy the experience."

"Yeah, but with virtual reality you're not putting genetically mutated DNA into your body."

Admittedly that's one of the PR issues the company faces, but considering that people eat genetically modified fruits and vegetables, as well as animals pumped full of genetically modified hormones and antibiotics, getting the general public to accept the idea of Big Egos shouldn't be too difficult. Especially once they get to experience the ride.

"What about Captain Kirk and Indiana Jones and Aragorn?" I say. "I thought you liked the idea of becoming one of them."

"I do," says Nat, taking another sip of his beer. "I just don't want to end up getting spit out into a ditch in New Jersey."

CHAPTER 4

I'm back in 2021, sitting on my couch wearing my Google 3-D glasses and watching my Super Hi-Vision plasma TV, surfing from twenty-four-hour news channels to relentless talk shows to ubiquitous reality programs. Surfing from infomercials about vitamins and natural foods and exercise equipment to advertisements about weight loss and male performance drugs and cosmetic enhancements.

All of these commercials about health and diet and fitness. All of these ads for waistlines and libidos and teeth whiteners. If you're not taking care of yourself or eating right or exercising, if you're overweight or you have a small penis or you don't have bright enough teeth, then there's something wrong with you.

Spiritually. Physically. Morally.

Instead of being defined by your actions, you're defined

instead by your smile. Your sexual performance. Your percentage of body fat.

On the Fitness Network, a celebrity health guru is showing how to burn calories and fat by using his patented exercise formula.

It's a lot to live up to. These pressures of achieving. From the moment you're born, you're pounded with the expectations of what you need to actualize in order to become a success.

Go to college. Get married. Raise a family.

It's what you're supposed to do. The plans you're supposed to make. The life you're supposed to live. Diverge from the norm and you're frowned upon. Questioned. Shunned.

There's something wrong with you if you're not interested in improving yourself. If you can't make a commitment of marriage. If you don't want to have children.

So people earn a college degree so they can get a good job. They work at a job they hate just to earn a living. They spend two months' salary on an engagement ring. They pop out a couple of kids they don't really want just so they can fit in. Because it's what their parents did. Because it's what society expects you to do. Because it's safer to take the same path everyone else has traveled.

Truth is, no one's listening to Robert Frost.

Now all of these cardboard cutouts, these people who have spent their lives following guidelines and adhering to the parameters of society, are looking for a way out of their monotonous, cookie-cutter existence.

Looking for something. Looking for anything.

I flip from an infomercial about how to maintain a set of six-pack abs to a news report on MSNBC about the increase in popularity of faux celebrity key parties. On *Here and Now* with Bill Maher, the panel of guests includes Salvador Dalí, Austin Powers, and Eleanor Roosevelt. And on MTV is a reality show pitting the fictional casts of *The Brady Bunch* against *The Addams Family*.

People don't want to be themselves anymore. They want to be someone else. Someone important. Someone famous.

A movie star. A household name. An icon.

On BBC *World News America,* a newscaster is reporting about a Virgin Atlantic flight that was hijacked by Benjamin Franklin.

It used to be you were stuck with your own personality, your own identity, and that any adjustments to your persona would only be as successful as your acting ability.

That all changed with the introduction of Big Egos.

Not everyone wants to alter who they are, to live a life that isn't theirs and pretend to be someone they're not. There are plenty of men and women who are perfectly content with their lives and their struggles and the comforts of their own identities. But for those who can afford it, for those who seek the thrill of experimenting with alternate personalities and temporary identities, Big Egos offers a respite from the mundane.

You know that phrase about how the grass is always greener? Well, the other side of the fence is now as lush and inviting as Shangri-la.

A Paradise of fantasies. An Eden of possibilities.

On CBS is an advertisement for Big Egos: Does your lifestyle not fit the person inside of you? Try someone else on for size!

For three thousand dollars, you can change who you are by purchasing a DNA-encoded cocktail of your favorite dead actor, artist, writer, musician, singer, athlete, politician, talk-show host, or television star—all legally approved by their respective estates, because if there's one thing estate holders love, it's money. You can even purchase an officially licensed fictional character like The Luke Skywalker, The Mary Poppins, or The Harry Potter. And for an extra fee, you can special order a custom Big Ego that isn't available to the masses.

Each Big Ego comes in ten-milliliter bottles. While I often double my own dosage, one milliliter is all you need for a complete experience, so you get ten uses per bottle. Each experience is essentially the same price you'd pay to go skydiving, take a hot-air balloon ride, or go on a private helicopter tour in Hawaii. Except with Big Egos, you get more bang for your buck.

While it's not something everyone can afford, it's definitely not targeted to the rich and famous. That would kind of defeat the purpose, considering my company offers the opportunity to become rich and famous. In a manner of speaking. At least for a few hours.

To show our appreciation to returning customers, follow-up orders run two grand, but you have to purchase the same Big Ego. You can't start off with The Billie Holiday and then expect to get The Whitney Houston at a discount.

On *The Lindsay Lohan Show* are a bunch of guests who are confessed Egomaniacs.

Although the altering of the consciousness is the primary draw of Big Egos, there are also minor physiological changes that take place during the process. This is made possible by adding an evolution gene to the DNA strand during the replication process.

While it's not exactly Dr. Jekyll and Mr. Hyde, a delicate morphing of features occurs. A thickening of the brow. A thinning of the lips. A shifting of the hairline. Changes in your physical appearance to help make your experience more transformative. So it's helpful to select an Ego that's within reasonable spitting distance of your own physical makeup. In other words, if you look like Alfred Hitchcock, then you might not want to purchase The Jim Morrison.

To complete the transformation, most customers purchase an accessory package that includes items such as wigs, facial hair, colored contacts, clothing, and, where applicable, beauty marks. Although most people won't look exactly like their celebrity doppelgänger, it's close enough to make you look twice. Sometimes you can't tell the difference, which is why Big Egos of living celebrities are banned.

Of course, that doesn't mean everyone plays by the rules.

The developer and manufacturer of Big Egos is the Los Angeles–based Engineering Genetics Organization and Systems, or EGOS for short—a bioengineering company that's been around for the past two decades refining nanorobotics, molecular cloning, and cell replication technology. While some of their nanotechnology has been used by government agencies and other bioengineering firms, their largest successes have come in the creation of consumer products, with Big Egos proving to be the pinnacle of their accomplishments.

While no one else has the legal right to manufacture a

competing product, knockoffs are available on the black market at a fraction of the price. But they come with a serious risk. Amateurs who don't know how to properly recreate nucleic acids encode their fraudulent Egos not with DNA but with RNA, which produces proteins that act as retroviruses, forcing the host brain to manufacture more viruses instead of the proteins required for proper cell function. Ultimately, the RNA takes over the brain, leading to psychosis and other irreversible damage.

Not exactly something that's covered by your health insurance.

Some people believe that Big Egos is just a fad that will be something everyone looks back on and laughs about, like fanny packs or Myspace or Crocs. But the desire to be someone else isn't anything new. From tabletop role-playing games like Dungeons & Dragons to live-action costumed role-playing games to massive multiplayer online role-playing games such as World of Warcraft, people have been pretending they were someone else for the past fifty years. And with the proliferation of Sims games and online avatars during the first two decades of this century, this was just the inevitable next step.

Big Egos *is* the ultimate role-playing game.

On ESPN is a story about a New York Yankee who is petitioning the league to play as Babe Ruth so that he can reclaim the career home-run record.

Naturally not everyone is a fan. Even before the first Big Egos store opened here in Los Angeles, there have been naysayers and doubters lining up to protest, arguing that replicating DNA is against the laws of nature or reality or

God, while others believe Big Egos poses a risk to society by providing people with the opportunity to live in a constant fantasy world.

And then there's the Food and Drug Administration, which is attempting to regulate Big Egos as a drug rather than as a consumer product, claiming that regular use can lead to extreme side effects—from paranoid schizophrenia to floating delusions of alternate egos. They even point to one case of permanent physical deformation.

I don't know where they're getting their info, but I've injected hundreds of Big Egos for more than three years and other than an occasional headache, I haven't experienced any adverse side effects. And while initial product testing revealed a risk of depression for a small percentage of users, that was resolved by adding serotonin to the Ego cocktail as a depression inhibitor for when you stop being famous and return to being yourself.

You ask me, this is just another example of Big Brother trying to regulate consumers rather than letting the market determine what the people want. If the government isn't careful, they're going to end up creating a culture of crime the same way they did with Prohibition during the 1920s.

So far, government intervention into the production and marketing of Big Egos has been minimal and any proposed legislation has stalled, so it doesn't look like the opposition will get the regulations or bans they want anytime soon. This might have something to do with the fact that more than half of the members of Congress own multiple Big Egos.

On Fox News, there's a report about the rising influence of Egos being used by lobbyists and special interest groups.

You ask me, the FDA should be focusing their efforts on black market Egos, which are inherently dangerous and easily accessible, especially the ones that come from Mexico. Still, in spite of the risk, illegally manufactured Egos continue to be popular among young people and the affluent-challenged.

While the main attraction is the lower price, there's also the fringe element. Egos of living celebrities can be easily obtained on the black market, in addition to Egos of infamous historical figures and fictional villains. It's bad enough to think that someone can walk into an alley and purchase The Charlie Sheen or The Paris Hilton, but it's only a matter of time before some twisted soul creates The Adolf Hitler or The Hannibal Lecter.

Fortunately, that time has not yet come.

On CNN is a story about the death of a Beverly Hills man who suffered a brain aneurysm at a party as the result of a black market Ego.

For a moment there's something about the story that seems important, a revelation that dances at the edge of my memory, the flicker of a shadow in my mind. Then the moment passes and I change the channel.

CHAPTER 5

"*Why don't you come over tonight and let me suck you dry?*"

I'm standing outside of Emily's workstation, but she's not the one inviting me over to her place for a little fellatio. Emily's never offered me a ride home, let alone a blow job. This voice is coming from the workstation two down from Emily's.

"*Then you can bend me over your dining room table and tie me up and spank me while you tell me I'm a bad little girl.*"

I look at Emily and wonder if she's ever been bent over a dining room table and spanked. With her conservative slacks and buttoned-up shirt and unadorned face, she's always struck me more as the type to spend her evenings alone with a good book and a glass of pinot noir rather than wrist cuffs and a paddle. But for all I know, Emily could moonlight as a dominatrix. After all, you never really know what someone does when you're not around and they put on a different mask.

Like Billy Joel said, we all give in to our desire when the stranger comes along.

"Morning, Emily," I say, imagining Emily in a catsuit and thigh-high stiletto boots with a riding crop.

"Morning," she says without looking up from her touch-screen monitor. A Cinnabon sits on her desk in its container, partially eaten. Every day Emily brings a Cinnabon with her to work and nibbles at it and picks at it until it's nothing but a corpse of a cinnamon roll, a pastry victim, gutted and left for dead on her desk like breakfast roadkill. And then she throws it away.

I've been working with Emily for five years and I have yet to see her finish one of her Cinnabons.

"You have those reports on The Buddy Holly and The Marlon Brando?" I ask.

"Just finishing them up." She pulls off a piece of her cinnamon roll and eats it. "I'll have them on your desk before the hour."

"Great," I say, watching her as the leather catsuit disappears and it's just conservative Emily again with her constant doughy confection companion.

I leave Emily and walk down to Kurt's workstation, where I find him sitting at his desk, pressing the NEXT button on his voice mail. While listening to his private voice mails on speaker could be considered inappropriate for the workplace, none of the women on my team have a problem with it and actually told me they find it helps to liven up the place.

"Hey lover boy, I'm still having orgasms from last night. Listen."

Kurt is out of shape, balding, and is in dire need of a nose hair trimmer. I've never understood how he gets so much action. I'm guessing he puts his Egos to good use. Either that or he's got a certain je ne sais quoi that only women understand because I sure as hell don't know what anyone sees in him.

"Morning, Kurt."

Kurt stops listening to the moans coming from his voice mail and turns to me, a smile stretching from ear to ear like someone sliced open his face and inserted a cartoon smile. "Hey boss. You ready for another week?"

That's what Kurt says every Monday morning when I see him, as if it's his only line in a scene for a movie and he does the same take with the exact same tone and the exact same inflection. Even his facial expression never varies.

"Ready," I say, to which Kurt gives a single, approving nod.

I've tried mixing things up, saying something different, like *You betcha* or *If it's ready for me,* but whenever I do, Kurt gets this confused look about him, as if he's forgotten his own birthday and is frightened by the thought that he might be losing his mind. So I stick with what he expects.

"What's the latest feedback on The Peter Pan?" I ask.

The Peter Pan is the latest addition to our newly launched line of Animated Egos.

"I'm on top of it," says Kurt.

"Good. We don't want another Cinderella fiasco on our hands."

The first women who tested out The Cinderella reported feeling like an indentured servant rather than a glamorous debutante, with no fairy godmother in sight.

"It's under control," says Kurt with his Cheshire Cat of a smile.

I half expect him to disappear, his disembodied smile floating in front of me for a few moments before vanishing along with the rest of him—which reminds me that I need to follow up on the special order for The Mad Hatter.

"Great," I say. "Then as you were."

As I turn to leave, Kurt resumes listening to his voice mail.

"Hi big boy, where have you been? I miss your other big boy. Call me."

On the way to my office, I say good morning to Chloe—a half Korean, half French twenty-three-year-old beauty who is our youngest and brightest investigator. Chloe graduated from UC San Diego in May, with a double major in literature and physics. She skydives, fosters cats, and always seems to look as if she's laughing at a joke that no one else gets because they've never read James Joyce or bothered to understand the intricacies of quantum mechanics.

"How was your weekend?" I ask.

Chloe shrugs and takes a sip of her grande whatever from Starbucks. "I spent most of it reading Dante on my new iPad Platinum. You ever read *The Divine Comedy*?"

I spent my first two years at UCLA majoring in English before I discovered Freud and Jung and ended up switching to psychology. So while I consider myself fairly well-read in

American and Western literature, I was never a big fan of epic poems.

"Can't say that I have," I say.

"It's not very funny," says Chloe, then she gives me a smile that makes me wish I didn't have a girlfriend.

And like I did with Emily, I imagine Chloe moonlighting as a dominatrix. Only this time, the leather catsuit and thigh-high stilettos fit like a monoglove.

We talk for a few minutes about religion and existentialism and allegorical literature, topics Delilah and I never discuss, and I find myself wishing for the second time that I didn't have a girlfriend. Still, I walk away feeling intellectually inadequate.

After leaving Chloe I check in on Neil, who waves a dismissive hand at me as he arranges everything in his workstation. Much like Kurt's greeting, the arranging of his workstation is a morning ritual with Neil. Everything has to be in its place. But unlike Kurt, who is something of an exhibitionist, Neil is obsessive-compulsive, right down to his manicured fingernails and his perfectly arranged desk and his monochromatic outfits. Today he's dressed all in dark brown, with matching pants, shoes, a tweed jacket, and a coordinating sweater vest. He almost looks like he belongs in a Sir Arthur Conan Doyle novel.

Which reminds me: the reboot of The Sherlock Holmes is coming out this week.

In addition to Kurt, Emily, Chloe, and Neil, the rest of my crew includes Angela, a short, bubbly blonde who loves live music and always seems to have a new dating horror story, and Vincent, who claims to be a descendant of ragtime composer Scott Joplin and who has an affinity for twentieth-century pop culture.

We're all a part of the Investigations Department at EGOS, where we track the purchase and refills of Big Egos, conduct user interviews, and follow up on any complaints or unusual reactions—in part to determine which Egos are the most popular and in part to verify that our customers are not only using the product properly but are happy with their experiences.

Call it a kind of glorified customer service.

However, one of the perks of being in Investigations is that we have access to every Big Ego available for purchase, including every custom Ego ever ordered. No one else in the company has that kind of access. That's because in order to do our jobs thoroughly and with an accurate level of discretion, we need to know how each Ego should perform, so we're encouraged to test out as many as we'd like.

That's not to say that we're allowed to take advantage of the company's generosity. And Ego-ing on company time is grounds for immediate dismissal, which doesn't mean it hasn't happened. More than two dozen employees were let go in the first week after product launch, but everyone in my department has been on their best behavior.

There are more than three thousand Big Egos currently on the market, with another two hundred and fifty currently in production. Whenever someone famous dies or when a blockbuster movie comes out with a memorable character, the demand for an Ego of that celebrity or character floods Central Processing. Once the demand hits a certain level and the rights are cleared, an order is placed to develop a new Big Ego.

If you have enough disposable income and like to be first in line or the front-runner of the latest fashion, you can custom-order an Ego of a celebrity who isn't dead yet so that when they do eventually kick off, you'll receive your Big Ego well ahead of the product release.

Some of the guys in accounting run an Egos Dead Pool for aging celebrities, with whoever guessing the celebrity death closest to the actual date getting the pot. The last one paid out over $2,500.

Of course, we can't green-light an Ego for production until we have all the legalities taken care of, which means getting permission from the appropriate estates and copyright holders. While some of them are content with a onetime, up-front payout, most of them opt to receive annual royalties from sales, which is actually a better deal for them in the long run. Kind of like taking your lottery winnings in twenty annual installments rather than a lump-sum payment.

Although some of the celebrity estate and creative rights holders aren't willing to license the images of their family members or fictional creations to us, more and more are jumping on board. Fortunately, not every Big Ego requires paying for licensing rights. Historical figures like Cleopatra and Abraham Lincoln, as well as fictional creations such as Tarzan and Sherlock Holmes, are in the public domain. We even managed to avoid having to pay for the rights to one of our most popular Egos: The Elvis Presley. Since there are so many Elvis impersonators just in Vegas alone using The King's image for profit, any lawsuits brought against EGOS for financial restitution ended up getting thrown out due to legal precedent.

When the technology was first created, it took up to six months to roll out a new Big Ego, so my first two years here were primarily spent helping to create policies and protocol and doing market research. But the process has been improved and refined to the point where it now takes less than a month for an Ego to go from the execution of the estate rights contracts to the store shelves. Skeptics are concerned that this is a result of cost-cutting procedures to meet market demand, but it's not like we're doing factory farming here.

No one's selectively breeding.

No one's injecting hormones.

No one's pumping anyone full of antibiotics.

All of the proteins and enzymes and other ingredients used in the production of Big Egos are created naturally, with no artificial ingredients or preservatives. No steroids. No antibiotics. No human growth hormones.

Just all natural identities. Renewable celebrities. Organic personalities.

We're the next generation of green.

CHAPTER 6

"Eat your green beans, dear."

I'm six years old, eating dinner at the kitchen table with my parents. Meat loaf with green beans and mashed potatoes. Only they're not really mashed potatoes. My mother didn't peel them and chop them up and boil them. They came out of a box of Potato Buds. Everything my mother cooks comes out of a can or a jar or a box.

Mashed potatoes. SpaghettiOs. SPAM.

Hamburger Helper. Rice-A-Roni. Campbell's soup.

Frozen burritos and chicken pot pies and TV dinners.

Even the green beans are frozen. All of the vegetables my mother cooks come out of the freezer or the pantry. They're either defrosted or served with a can opener. The only thing that's real is the ground beef in the meat loaf, but my mother used onion soup mix and ketchup for seasoning. Otherwise, nothing else is fresh. Nothing is real. Everything is fake.

My mother sits on my right, eating her dinner and drinking her wine. My father sits across from me wearing a tie with his sleeves rolled up while he tells me how to properly chew my food.

"Ten times for every bite," he says. "No more, no less."

He's told me this at almost every meal since I was old enough to understand. It's supposed to help with digestion. Not long ago, I noticed my father doesn't follow his own rules. When I ask him why he doesn't chew ten times for every bite, he tells me that the rules are different for adults than they are for children. Which kind of sounds like a double standard to me, but what do I know? I'm just a little kid who longs for his father's approval.

So I just nod and say, "Yes, sir."

In addition to teaching me how to properly chew my food, my father coaches me on brushing my teeth, tying my shoes, loading the dishwasher, and a bunch of other practical things every kid should know how to do. He's never taught me how to throw a baseball or a football or how to play any games.

"Life isn't a game, son," he always tells me. "It involves choices and sacrifices and commitments. No one gets to sit around and watch. Everyone has to get involved. Everyone has a role to play."

He tells me that it's up to me to figure out what my role is going to be.

"No one's going to figure things out for you or solve your problems," he tells me. "Not Santa Claus or Peter Pan or your fairy godmother. So you're going to have to figure them out for yourself."

Since I'm only six, I haven't figured out my role yet, but at least I'll know how to chew my food properly for healthy digestion.

My mother and father spend the rest of the meal talking about local news and national politics and a bunch of stuff that doesn't interest me. Occasionally I share my thoughts on something Nat said or about something that happened in kindergarten, but for the most part it's just my parents talking.

I'm not really part of the conversation.

After a few more minutes, my father gets up and throws his napkin on his plate, signaling the end of his meal and leaving most of his green beans untouched. Even though the question pops into my head, I know better than to ask my father why it's okay for him to leave food on his dinner plate when I have to finish all of mine.

My father kisses my mother on the cheek. "I'm taking a shower and then calling it a night. Early flight tomorrow."

Then he grabs his coat off the back of his chair and exits the kitchen, leaving my mother and me to finish our dinner.

My father travels a lot on business. I still don't know what it is he does for a living, but his work always takes him someplace for a few days a week.

Des Moines. Phoenix. Reno.

Always someplace I've never been. But since I've never been anywhere more exotic than Venice Beach, every place is someplace I've never been.

Every time my father goes away on a trip, I can't wait for him to come back. Even though he can be overbearing and distant, I miss my father when he's not around. The house just seems empty without him in it. Mostly, though, I keep hoping he'll bring me something from one of his trips.

But my father never brings me anything. No stuffed animals or stickers or baseball hats. Not even a postcard. Nada. Zip. Zero. My other friends, the ones at school, all have T-shirts and toys and memorabilia they bring to show-and-tell from the places they or their parents have gone on vacation. Places like Hawaii and the Grand Canyon and Disneyland.

My father never takes me with him. Me or my mother.

Whenever I ask my father about the places he visits, whenever I ask him what it's like in Sacramento or Portland or Las Vegas, he tells me they're all the same, just in different locations on the map.

"If you've seen one place, you've seen them all," he says.

But since I haven't seen any of these places, I have no idea what he's talking about.

I've asked my father if I could go with him on one of his trips, but he said I'd just get in the way.

"Besides," he always says, "the road is no place for small boys."

So I don't ask anymore. Instead, I just say *yes, sir* and eat my green beans.

My mother and I sit in silence for the remainder of the meal—eating the mostly real meat loaf and the prepackaged potatoes and the frozen vegetables. We spend a lot of time like this: my mother looking over at me and smiling with her mouth closed and me picking at my food, waiting for my mother to say something. To say anything.

How are things at school?

Would you like to go see a movie?

What would you like to do for your birthday?

This last question is the one I want her to ask me the most. And for the past two years my answer would be the same: I want to go to Disneyland. I want to meet Mickey Mouse and Donald Duck and Goofy. I want to eat cotton candy and watch the parades and visit the Enchanted Tiki Room. I want to go on the Pirates of the Caribbean and Peter Pan's Flight and Mr. Toad's Wild Ride.

Instead, every year we spend my birthday at home.

No Mickey. No pirates. No parades.

No balloons. No hats. No party.

Just the three of us eating a Duncan Hines chocolate cake with vanilla ice cream.

But my mother doesn't ask me about Disneyland or my birthday or anything else. Whenever it's just the two of us, neither one of us seems to know what to say to the other. We just sit there in an awkward silence, smiling at each other or looking away. It's as if without my father there, we don't know how to communicate.

And when my father's out of town, my mother spends most of her time curled up on the couch watching television or reading books. Romance novels, mostly. Sometimes she invites one or more of her friends over and they drink wine and eat cheese and crackers and talk about things I'm not allowed to know.

We don't go out to the movies or go shopping at the mall or play any board games. We don't even watch television programs together. There's not a lot of quality mother-son bonding going on.

So I spend a lot of time playing over at Nat's or reading in my room, which is probably what I'll end up doing tonight.

When my mother finishes her meal, she gets up and clears her plate and my father's, then she stands with her back to me at the sink while she scrapes the food into the disposal and puts the dishes in the dishwasher. All without so much as a question or a sentence or a word.

CHAPTER **7**

"What do you think about a new couch?" Delilah stands in the middle of the living room, wearing that look women get when they decide they want to change something. Like your haircut or your wardrobe or the way you show her that you love her. "I was thinking we could upgrade the entire living room to something with a European flair."

I take off my Google 3-D glasses and look at the black leather couch, upon which I happen to be sitting while watching the news. "What's wrong with this one?"

On CNN, someone is talking about the twenty-year anniversary of 9/11.

"It's just so pre-postmodern," she says, running a hand through her mane of red hair, which is nearly half the length of her five-foot, two-inch frame. "Oh, and I was also thinking we should repaint the master bedroom."

"What's wrong with the color of the bedroom?"

"White doesn't exactly lend itself to a sizzling sex life, sugar. Feng shui recommends soft colors of red for the bedroom to inspire a healthy sex life. Like brick or vermilion or rose."

"I didn't realize there was a problem with our sex life."

She walks up to me and leans down and kisses me on the lips. "Men never do, sugar."

Ever since we moved into this place in January, Delilah has been suggesting ways to fix it. To make it better. But I like it the way it is. This is the place I've always wanted. The home I've always imagined. It's as if someone plugged into my subconscious and designed a floor plan and an interior exactly to my specifications—right down to the hardwood floors and the decorative ceiling with crown molding and the walk-in shower with dual showerheads.

The bathroom is about the only room in the house Delilah hasn't suggested we paint, change, or upgrade. She does love the kitchen, though, even if she's not really sure what to do in it.

When I bought the house and moved into it with Delilah, I didn't realize I'd be getting a live-in interior decorator who wanted to remake my home in her own image with my money.

"You don't think it's a little too much?" I ask whenever she suggests buying the latest style or insists on the best designer brands.

"Darlin'," she always says, "nothing's ever too much."

Delilah appreciates the finer things in life and encourages me to do the same.

Personally, I prefer the classic look. Fashion with a timeless quality. Like white dress shirts and denim blue jeans. Converse All-Stars and Ray-Ban Wayfarers. Hamilton watches and 1959 T-Birds. Things that never go out of style.

Delilah, on the other hand, is a fashion trend addict, always reinventing herself to adapt to the latest style or fad. I should have known better than to think she would have been satisfied with keeping my place as is, even when she told me how much she loved it.

I remember how Delilah wandered through the empty house when I first bought it, oohing and aahing at everything. It was like watching a kid walk through Disneyland— if Disneyland was a three-bedroom ranch-style house in the Hollywood Hills and the kid was a twenty-six-year-old redheaded actress with a southern accent, a pierced tongue, and no panty lines.

While I never had any interest in being an actor, Delilah has always wanted to be in the movies or onstage or on a television show. That's her calling. How she defines herself as a person. The role she was meant to play. But when you think about it, one way or another, we're all actors and actresses. And everyone plays the role of the hero in his or her own story.

The devoted mother who takes care of her family. The hardworking husband who cheats on his wife. The star varsity quarterback who torments the freshman nerds.

The CEO. The factory worker. The aspiring artist. The drug addict.

They're all the main protagonists, starring in their own

sitcoms and dramas and made-for-TV movies. Me? I'm still trying to figure out the role I'm supposed to play. And over the past twenty-seven years, I've played more than my share.

Friend. Lover. Employee.

Athlete. Politician. Buddhist.

James Bond. Indiana Jones. Elvis.

Truth is, I've played more roles than I can remember.

Although Delilah hasn't landed any lead roles yet or done any feature films, she's made a small career out of doing television commercials and has a minor recurring role in a series on the CW. She plays a high school goody two-shoes from the South who is always preaching abstinence and encouraging the stars of the show to treasure their virginity.

It's not exactly typecasting.

"And I was thinking it might be nice to hire a maid or a cleaning service to help out around here," she says. "Maybe even a personal chef to cook us up some nice meals every now and then. What do you think?"

I hadn't thought about hiring a maid or a personal chef, even though I can certainly afford it. If someone had told me I would own a place like this before I turned twenty-eight and be making enough to think about hired help, I would have laughed and asked them where I could get my hands on the drugs they were taking.

Funny thing is, this still doesn't seem real to me. It's like one of the games Nat and I used to play when we were kids, only this time it's just me and I'm playing Grown-Up and leaving Nat on his own.

Nat and I lived together all through college and for the first four and a half years after we graduated, so he was more than a little disappointed when I told him I was getting my own place with Delilah. As a result, we haven't seen much of each other since I moved out nine months ago.

But even before I moved out, Nat and I hadn't seen much of each other the last two years we lived together. Between Delilah and my job, I just didn't seem to have any free time. On numerous occasions, Delilah suggested we get our own place, but I just couldn't bring myself to leave Nat on his own. Until finally I decided it was time to cut the cord.

Even though my job played a role in the decreasing amount of time we hung out, Nat and I started growing apart from the moment I met Delilah.

"Why don't we go out this Friday," I say, changing the subject from redecorating my house and hiring skilled labor. "We'll go to Spago."

"Ooh, I like the sound of that." Delilah climbs onto my lap with a thigh on either side of me. "Can we Ego?"

Delilah always wants to Ego. *Always.* That's another reason Nat and I started to drift apart. He felt I was spending too much time as an alternate persona and that more and more often, Delilah was encouraging me to be less and less of myself.

★

"How am I not myself?" I say to Nat near the end of last year, not long before I start looking for my own place.

"Hey, isn't that a line from a movie?"

"Yes, but stop deflecting." Whenever I call Nat on something he's said or when the conversation gets too complicated or uncomfortable, he always looks for the nearest exit. "How am I not myself?"

"I don't know. It's like your personality's not the same."

"Since when are people's personalities consistent?"

"Mine's always consistent."

"Is it?" I say. "How about when you're teaching versus when you're on a date? Drunk versus sober? Happy versus sad? Horny versus wanting to watch *The Seth MacFarlane Show*? In each situation, you're someone different. You act different. You have a different personality."

"Yeah, but I'm still me. I'm just me acting different under the influence of specific situations."

"So you're saying these specific situations cause reactions that alter the way you'd normally behave? That there's Nat and then there's Nat under the influence of various circumstances?"

"Yeah."

"In other words, there's a part of your brain that corresponds to *you,* or the default *you,* and your different emotions cause you to make different choices."

"Yeah," he says, not looking quite so confident. "Sure."

"Then explain how there can be a default *you* and a separate emotion or reaction," I say. "Take away your morality, your emotions, and your reasoning and what are you left with?"

Nat opens his mouth and then closes it, like a fish gasping for oxygen.

"I'll tell you what you're left with," I say. "Nothing. No Nat. No default *you*. Just a big, fat zero."

Nat purses his lips and nods once, then starts looking around for the nearest exit. "So what line was that movie from?"

★

"Hey sugar," says Delilah, still straddling me on the couch. "Are we going to Ego Friday night or not? I was kind of hoping to try out something new."

Since Delilah can't afford to buy her own Big Egos, I help out by supplying her with some of her requests when I bring home Egos to test. It's against company policy to share Egos with family or friends, but All-You-Can-Get Sex has a way of making men break rules they wouldn't otherwise break.

"Sure," I say.

Delilah claps her hands and bounces up and down on my lap like a little kid who just found out what she's getting for Christmas. And even though I know he's not likely to want to join us, because he's on my mind: "I was thinking I'd invite Nat."

Delilah stops bouncing and lets out a theatrical sigh. "Do we have to invite Gnat?"

Delilah always pronounces Nat's name with a hard *g* because she says he's bothersome and annoying. My dad used to say the same thing.

"I know you're not a fan, but he is my best friend," I say. "And I haven't spent much time with him since I moved out."

"Wasn't that the point?" she says, tracing a finger along my jawline. "To spend less time with Gnat and more time with me? Plus he's such an Eeyore when it comes to Egos."

Delilah has never understood my relationship with Nat. She's always thought of him as my needy, nerdy, socially inept friend. And, I have to admit, she's spot-on with her assessment. Nat *is* nerdy and socially inept, and he has grown to depend on me more than your average friend, but that's because he doesn't have anyone else.

While both of Nat's parents are still alive, he hasn't spoken with either of them since he graduated from college and they sold everything they owned and moved to India to join an ashram.

Nat's parents didn't really want to be parents. They just played the role until their obligation was fulfilled, then they went to do what they really wanted to do.

"I worry about him," I say.

And while I know it's likely pointless, I'd like to see if I could get him to change his mind about Egos. Maybe get him to try one out so he can see that they're not as bad as he thinks.

Delilah makes a pouty face. "You worry too much about Gnat. I think you should worry about me, instead."

"Why should I worry about you?"

"Because I'm sitting here on your lap and you're completely ignoring me. How do you think that makes me feel?"

Why is it that women are always asking about how things make them feel?

"Plus you've been spending all of this time working extra hours and coming home late," she says. "I think you need to start spending more time with me."

"Okay," I say. "What did you have in mind?"

Delilah gives me a sly smile and starts unbuttoning her shirt and I completely forget about what's-his-name.

CHAPTER **8**

"Hey Dee," says Nat as he walks in the front door.

Delilah hates it when Nat calls her Dee, and he knows she hates it, which is why he calls her that every time he sees her. I can almost see her pale skin turning red to match the color of her hair.

"Hey Gnat." She closes the door and gives him a fake smile, which he reciprocates.

It's always heartwarming to see how well my best friend and my girlfriend get along.

"So how's life as a public high school algebra teacher?" says Delilah.

"Things are great," says Nat. "How's life as a TV commercial actress?"

They've been like this ever since Delilah and I started dating our last year in college. It got worse after I told Nat I was moving in with her.

After a few more unpleasantries, Delilah retreats into the bedroom as Nat joins me in the kitchen.

"Well, Dee seems happy to see me," he says. "Did she dye her hair again?"

Delilah's not a natural redhead. To be honest, I'm still not sure what her natural color is.

"How about we all pretend to be grown-ups?" I say, reaching into the refrigerator for a couple of beers.

"Isn't pretending what tonight is all about?" says Nat.

The fact that Nat agreed to even consider trying Egos was a surprise, considering his concerns about getting stuck inside someone else's identity or getting spit out into a ditch in New Jersey. I guess the fact that neither has happened to me helped to sway him.

"Just play nice," I say, handing him a Guinness. "Please. It'll make me happy."

We take our beers and go sit down on the couch, which I'm planning to keep—though I did agree to let Delilah repaint the bedroom.

"I see married life is treating you well," says Nat.

"We're not married," I say. "Delilah is my girlfriend."

"You say tomato, I say manipulative succubus."

Nat's still a little bitter that I moved out. Among other things.

"You know, maybe this wasn't such a good idea . . . ," I say, standing up.

"Wait." Nat grabs on to my arm. "I'm sorry, bro. That was totally out of line. I'll behave."

"Promise?"

Nat holds up three fingers. "Scout's honor."

"You were never in the Scouts."

"And I don't have much honor, so it all zeros out."

I never could argue with Nat's logic.

"Okay," I say, sitting back down. "Then let's pick one out."

On the coffee table is my hand-crafted cherrywood box, which I open to reveal the first of two velvet-lined trays with individual compartments containing a total of forty-eight Egos. Then I lift out one of the trays and set it on the coffee table.

Nat lets out a whistle. "That's a lot of alternate identities to choose from."

I feel a little gluttonous having so many because I know Nat can't afford even one. Most high school algebra teachers don't typically earn enough to afford groceries, let alone drop three grand on a luxury item. But I feel guilty about not spending much time with him. And about the way we left things when I moved out.

Still, I wonder if this is such a good idea. Not because it's against company policy, but because I can't help worrying how it might end up impacting my relationship with Nat. I'm also wondering if he's doing this because he really wants to, or because he thinks it's the only way he can still be my friend. I'd ask him, but he'd just deny it. Besides, I always thought his complaints about me not being myself had less to do with Egos and more to do with all the time I was spending with Delilah.

Nat looks down at the trays, studying my collection of fictional and celebrity identities. His fingers run across the Plexiglas vials as if they were prized possessions. Or naked breasts.

While it's not the first time he's actually seen my collection, it's the first time he's shown any interest in my Egos, most of which I didn't have to pay for. As a perk to our job, we get to take home up to twenty Egos at a time for testing. The ones I did pay for I got at a 50 percent employee discount.

"Captain Kirk. James Bond. Indiana Jones." Nat names off my Egos one by one. "It's like a roll call of awesome."

While I enjoy being Elvis Presley and Kurt Vonnegut and Vincent van Gogh, my favorite Egos are fictional characters. They have fewer emotional hang-ups and tend to allow for a bit more moral flexibility than your real-life celebrities, who are limited by a reality inhibitor.

But then, there's not a whole lot of reality going on around here lately.

When it comes to real-life celebrities and historical figures, you're not becoming them, but their public personas. The genetic engineering strips away the undesirable aspects to the Egos, in part for legal reasons but also because no one wants to experience the insecurities or the neuroses of the rich and famous. Or the way they act when they're not on camera.

No one wants to have a Mel Gibson or a Christian Bale meltdown.

Nat picks up the Plexiglas bottle labeled INDIANA JONES and stares at it like an archaeologist who has just found the Holy Grail. "So . . . what's it like being Indiana Jones?"

"Exactly like you'd imagine."

I leave out the part about how having sex as Indiana Jones is about the most fun you can have in bed without a nineteen-year-old gymnast and a gallon of Astroglide. Which I haven't ever tried, but Delilah is always up for a challenge.

Nat stares at the bottle a few moments longer, then returns it to its compartment like he's handling a priceless artifact before he continues to peruse his options.

"So who's it going to be?" I ask.

Nat looks over the two trays of Egos, going back and forth from bottle to bottle like an indecisive kid at Baskin-Robbins trying to select a flavor of ice cream.

"I don't know. There are so many choices. I don't know which one to pick."

He never could make a decision, which is how he ended up in teaching.

"Pick the one you feel most connected to right now," I say. "And if there's more than one you want to try, we can always do this again."

"Seriously?"

"Sure. We can even make this a monthly thing if you want."

That's my guilty conscience talking, trying to even things out and make up for being a neglectful friend. Though I still question the wisdom of introducing Nat to a lifestyle he can't afford. Not to mention the fallout from Delilah when she finds out I've invited Nat to join in our fun on a monthly basis.

Nat looks over the selection of Egos again, then picks up the bottle labeled CAPTAIN KIRK.

"Good choice," I say. "I think I'll go with The Han Solo, which should make for an interesting night."

Nat watches as I pull out two sterilized syringes and set them down next to our selected Egos.

While most consumers either drink their Big Egos with

some form of beverage or inject them like insulin shots, neither one of these delivery methods provides the most complete experience. To get the best results, I inject the Ego cocktail directly into my brain stem, where it can go to work instantly on the limbic system, recalibrating hormones, mood, and DNA.

The limbic system is the more primitive part of the brain that supports a variety of functions, including emotion, behavior, and motivation.

"So who's Delilah going to be?" asks Nat.

"I don't know. She said she hadn't made up her mind."

"You know, you two wouldn't have even met if it wasn't for me."

"I know," I say. "You remind me of that fact every chance you get."

I grab a syringe and draw two milliliters of The Han Solo and set it aside, then I pick up the bottle labeled CAPTAIN KIRK and insert the other syringe.

"It's kind of weird, isn't it?" says Nat. "Pretending to be someone else?"

I watch the amber liquid fill up the syringe, thinking about the hundreds of Egos I've injected over the past three years. "You get used to it."

But when you think about it, people pretend to be someone else every day.

Gay people who pretend to be straight. Depressed people who pretend to be happy. Smart people who pretend to be dumb.

People are always pretending to be someone else to fit in. To be accepted. To be loved.

Men who pretend to enjoy their marriage. Employees who pretend to enjoy their jobs. Women who pretend to enjoy sex.

They all slip into a role. Put on a mask. Be whoever it is they need to be for an hour. A day. A lifetime. Then they slip out of that role and play another one.

People show you what they want you to see. Or what they think you want to see, not who they really are. The reality lies somewhere in between.

Truth is, everyone is just playing a role.

"After a few minutes, it feels natural," I say to Nat. "Like you were always this other person and you just didn't know it."

I hand Nat his syringe. He takes it like I'm handing him a used diaper that's threatening to leak. "Are there any side effects?" he asks.

"Nothing serious. You might get a slight headache or some initial nausea, but I'll be here to talk you through it."

Nat stares at the syringe in his hand like he's about to put a gun to his head.

"Look," I say, "if you don't want to do this . . ."

Just then, Delilah walks out wearing a red strapless dress covered with sequins, red high-heeled shoes, and red satin gloves running up to her elbows with her red hair falling down over her bare, pale shoulders. She stops and turns to look at the two of us, her dress slit all the way up to mid-thigh. Her lips look like she's kissed a candy apple.

"I'm not bad," she says. "I'm just drawn this way."

Nat looks Delilah up and down. "Holy Mother of God."

Not exactly. But we are releasing The Virgin Mary next Easter.

"You don't know how hard it is being a woman looking the way I do," says Jessica Rabbit, who then glides off into the kitchen like a wet dream come to life.

In addition to The Jessica Rabbit, some of the more popular Animated Egos include The Brian Griffin, The Peter Pan, The Betty Boop, The Popeye, The Sterling Archer, The Homer Simpson, and The Tinker Bell. I've never been a cartoon Ego, but I hear it's a little like dropping acid at Disneyland.

I glance at Nat, who looks like a cartoon character with his mouth hanging open and his chin on the floor.

"So what do you think?" I say. "Are you game?"

Nat holds the syringe up and looks at the two milliliters of amber fluid that will turn him into Captain James T. Kirk for the next six hours. "Are you sure this is safe?"

"Absolutely." I pick up my own syringe and reach around to the back of my neck. "You don't have anything to worry about."

CHAPTER **9**

"Y ou don't have anything to worry about," I say.

"You sure?" says Nat, his face turning red. "Because it sure seems like I should be worried."

"Yeah," says one of the two Neanderthals holding Nat upside down by his legs. "He should be fuckin' worried."

Where we are is out behind Round Table Pizza on a Friday night during our junior year in high school, with Nat being dangled over a puddle of vomit by the starting middle linebacker and the right tackle for the varsity football team.

I'm not sure how Nat got into this mess. A few minutes ago, we ordered a large pepperoni pizza and then I went to the bathroom. When I got back, Nat was gone, along with most of the other high school kids who had descended upon the place. Eventually I found everyone out back, crowded around Nat and his tormenters.

I have no idea where the vomit came from but I don't think it matters.

Nat's always ending up on the wrong end of things and I'm always having to figure out how to make them right. While negotiating with a couple of varsity football goons isn't something I've ever attempted, I'm hoping my letterman's jacket helps.

Last year, I got on a running and athletic kick and tried out for the soccer team on a whim. Turns out I'm a natural-born center fullback and I never knew it.

Funny how you can spend the first sixteen years of your life with no idea that you had a talent like that inside you. But at least now I know what it is I want to do with my life, though I never would have guessed that being an athlete would be my calling. After parlaying my newfound abilities into a starting roster spot on the varsity soccer team, a whole new world opened up to me. A world of sports and cheerleaders and popularity. Which, in a fortuitous twist for Nat, gives me some added cachet with the other high school jocks.

Still, I'm dealing with a couple of football players, not fellow soccer players or the number-one doubles tennis team. Football players are a different breed of jock altogether. And in high school, your status and your identity is a reflection of who you hang out with.

Just before adolescence, the prefrontal cortex undergoes a flurry of activity, leading to the formation of an identity and the development of the notion of a self. So high school is where burgeoning men and women often work out their identities for the first time. The problem is that in high school, labels and identities are more often thrust upon you than asked for.

Jock. Brain. Nerd. Druggie. Rah Rah. Outcast. Popular. None of the Above.

This last one is almost worse than being labeled a nerd or an outcast. At least then you know who you are. If you're labeled None of the Above, you might as well be invisible.

But in Nat's case, I'm thinking that being invisible would probably be in his best interests.

"So what happened?" I ask.

"What happened?" says the middle linebacker, a juiced-up troglodyte who's probably compensating for his genetic shortcomings. Let's call him Big Steroid, Little Penis. Just not to his face. "The problem is that asswipe here has a big fuckin' mouth."

"A big fuckin' mouth," echoes the right tackle, a throw-back to Paleolithic man with the IQ of a popular sexual position. Let's call him Sixty-Nine. Same rules apply about saying that to his face.

Though I'm guessing Nat didn't follow the rules.

"Kick his ass!" yells some guy from the crowd, which isn't helping the situation.

When faced with a couple of high school football players who together weigh more than a quarter of a ton, it's best if you deal with them the same way you'd deal with a couple of angry silverbacks.

First, avoid making a show of dominance or assuming the role of the alpha male. That's a common mistake. You don't want to beat on your chest or fling shit at them. That'll just make them angry. Instead, you should use reassuring and familiar vocalizations to avoid antagonizing them. Gorillas keep in contact using belch vocalizations, but I don't need to start burping to gain their trust. I just need to sound like them.

"What did the dumb fuck say?" I ask.

"Hey!" Nat reaches down with his hands to try to support himself without touching the pool of vomit. "I thought you told me not to worry."

"Shut the fuck up, Nat," I say.

You should also make sure you position yourself so that you're either below the football player or at the same height so they don't feel threatened, which isn't a problem considering they're each a good four inches taller than me.

I can already see their posture changing as they grow comfortable with my presence. But if the football players show any sign of agitation, you'll need to convince them you're not dangerous by casually dropping down to one knee to tie your shoe, turning your body sideways and looking at them out of the corner of your eye. Which I do, just to play it safe.

"So what happened?" I ask.

Apparently, the two silverbacks bumped into Nat and were very polite about the entire encounter, to which Nat promptly called one of them a douche bag and told the other that he had the vocabulary of a Dr. Seuss book.

Nat's brain doesn't always consider the consequences of his mouth.

"Bad idea," says Big Steroid, Little Penis.

Sixty-Nine nods and shouts his assent amid a spray of saliva. "Bad fuckin' idea!"

If the football players give a screaming charge, don't run away. They're just trying to assert their dominance. Instead, stay hunkered down, scratch yourself in a nonchalant manner, and remain calm. If they make contact with you, curl up in a ball. There's the chance you might get thumped or bitten, but chances are you'll walk away with a great story to tell your friends.

Sensing that the two silverbacks are accepting me, I stand up.

"Any chance we can work something out?" I ask.

I almost said *negotiate,* but when dealing with high school football players, you want to avoid using big words. It makes them defensive and more likely to channel their inner primate. So try to dumb it down. Stay away from any word that contains more than three syllables.

"What's there to work out?" says Big Steroid, Little Penis.

"Yeah," says Sixty-Nine. "Payback is payback."

You can't argue with that kind of logic. And clearly, my soccer letterman's jacket isn't throwing around enough weight. So it looks like I'm going to have to switch to bribery.

"What if he apologized and offered to buy your pizza?" I say.

The two silverbacks look at each other and then down at Nat.

"Kick his ass!" yells the same guy from the crowd, which, sensing a nonviolent resolution, has started to break up.

"Two pizzas," says Big Steroid, Little Penis. "Extra-large. With everything."

"And garlic Parmesan twists," says Sixty-Nine. "Twelve pieces."

"Done," I say.

The three of us all look down at Nat, his hands on either side of the puddle of vomit.

"I'm sorry," he says. "What I said was unmerited and inappropriate."

The two football players don't let go, so I hold my right thumb and index finger up about an inch apart, hoping Nat gets the message. He does.

"I'm sorry," he says. "I'm a dumb fuck."

"Okay then. Apology accepted," says Big Steroid, Little Penis.

Ten seconds later, Nat is standing next to me tucking his shirt back into his pants while the two gorillas follow the disappointed crowd back into Round Table.

"Thanks, bro. I owe you."

"No." I point to the two varsity silverbacks. "You owe them."

We stand there a moment, neither one of us saying anything, until Nat finally breaks the silence. "How did you do that? It's like you used Jedi mind tricks or something."

That's not too far from the truth. The mind of a high school football player is about as easily manipulated as that of an Imperial storm trooper.

"You just have to play the role," I say. "Be the person you need to be when the situation calls for it."

"Like when Han Solo comes back to save Luke so he can blow up the Death Star?"

Nat's always boiling life lessons down into Star Wars analogies.

"Not exactly," I say. "Let me put it this way: When you

look in the mirror, you see a reflection of yourself, right? Not just who you are on the outside, but who you are as a person. But other people probably see you as someone completely different. And that's just as real to them as what you see."

Nat just stares at me with a glazed-over look.

"Okay, how about this," I say. "What matters isn't how you see yourself. What matters is how others see *you*. The trick is to make them see what *you* want them to see."

Of course in high school, teenagers often get preoccupied with who they appear to be in the eyes of others as compared with who they think they are, so your identity is really a matter of opinion.

"Is this more of your dad's bullshit life lessons?" says Nat.

"Hey, I'm just trying to answer your question and explain why you never get laid."

"Great. Not only do I almost get my ass kicked by the goon squad, but now my best friend is capping on my non-existent sex life."

"FYI, I'm the one who saved you from the ass-kicking," I say. "Again."

That shuts him up.

"Any more questions?" I ask.

"Yeah. Can I borrow some money?"

CHAPTER **10**

*I*t's just past eleven o'clock in the evening, late September, with *the sky clear and the moon waxing its way to full and the look of a party that's waning when I walk in the door. I'm wearing my navy blue suit with a white shirt, royal blue tie, black oxfords, and black wool socks. I'm clean, trimmed, pressed, and polished. I'm everything the well-dressed private detective should be. Everything, that is, except I'm not holding a drink in one hand and a cigarette in the other.*

The problem with parties is that they're usually made up of people.

Not that I don't like people. I like people just fine. But when you gather a group of them together in one place and mix them with alcohol, there's bound to be trouble. And trouble and I are too well acquainted to just ignore one another.

I walk up to the bar—a modern, half-moon-shaped back bar with a sink, tap, hanging beer glasses, a full complement of liquor bottles lined up like soldiers in front of a beveled mirror, and four double cross-back brushed metal stools, three of which are occupied.

Frank and Joe Hardy are chatting up Nancy Drew at the bar, the three of them sitting close enough they could be conjoined triplets. Nancy is a cute little number definitely worth more than a glance or two. Speaking of glances, she gives one to each of her suitors, packaged with a coy smile as she plays with her hair and runs a delicate, pale hand along one of her thighs. You don't have to be a detective to know that before tonight becomes tomorrow, the three of them are going to end up investigating one another.

"Good evening, Mr. Marlowe," says the bartender, polite and proper in his black shirt and his black tie and his white smile. "What can I get for you?"

"Bourbon sounds good," I say.

"And how would you like your bourbon, sir?"

"Any way at all."

The bartender grabs a bottle of Jim Beam off the shelf and in the mirror I see myself and the reflection of the room behind me, where Columbo and Thomas Magnum play a friendly game of eight-ball on the billiards table while Kojak sits by, sucking on a lollipop and ribbing both of the other detectives in fun, waiting to challenge the winner.

Off in the corner behind the three sleuths, Mike Hammer and Harry Callahan are drinking beers and brewing up a batch of testosterone, their voices growing louder and their faces turning the color of ripe tomatoes. Though I'm betting it's more from their short fuses than from the alcohol. Both of them have the look of a man it would pay to get along with and right now, neither one of them is taking out his wallet. Sooner or later, one of them is going to take out his fists instead.

I'm guessing sooner.

The bartender sets my bourbon down in front of me, on the rocks. I thank him with a nod and go to see what the rest of the party has to offer when I notice movement out of the corner of my eye. I turn to look and catch Sherlock Holmes dressed in a camouflage of greens and browns disappearing behind two six-foot-high potted ferns. A moment later, I don't see any sign of him.

I never understood the English way of doing things.

As I walk down the hallway, the door to a bathroom opens in front of me and out stumble Shaggy, Fred, Daphne, and Velma in a cloud of smoke, laughing so hard they can barely stand up. I'm guessing they weren't smoking tobacco. They look at me and stop laughing, their faces contorting to suppress their mirth. Fred puts a finger to his lips, then they tiptoe past me back toward the bar, letting out an occasional snort of laughter along the way.

I don't see any sign of Scooby.

When I turn around, Monk is coming down the hallway toward me, wearing light brown tweed pants, a dark brown tweed jacket, and a plaid shirt buttoned up to his throat with no tie. He takes measured steps, avoiding the seams in the tiled floor, and reaches out with a single index finger to touch the top right corner of each piece of art as he passes.

When he reaches me, he gives a nervous smile and a single nod and presses himself against the wall until he slides past and slips into the bathroom, closing the door with his foot.

I stare at the door a moment, contemplating my next move,

then I take my drink and escort it the rest of the way down the hall.

In the great room, I find the rest of the guests, though as I suspected the party is either sparsely attended or running itself out. Or both.

Sam Spade is sharing drinks and cigars and a spirited discussion with Lord Peter Wimsey and Auguste Dupin, until Inspector Jacques Clouseau stumbles into the three of them, knocking their drinks from their hands and somehow managing to set Dupin on fire.

At least this party still has some life to it.

Miss Marple and Hercule Poirot sit in a pair of matching leather wingbacks, drinking brandy in snifters and reciting "Ten Little Indians" together and giggling like a couple of kids.

"Seven little Indians, all chopping sticks. One chopped himself in half, then there were six."

Over on the couch, Stephanie Plum is surrounded by a quartet of Ellery Queen, Joe Friday, Dick Tracy, and Charlie Chan, all of whom are vying for her charms. While it doesn't look like any of them has a chance of getting more than a good slap, I'd put my money on Tracy. One, I'm thinking he's more Plum's type. And two, he's got the right first name for the job.

The rest of the cocktail party guests include Spenser, Angel, Shaft, Sonny Crockett, and Rico Tubbs, the last two of whom are wearing suits and jackets that have no business being out in public. Meanwhile, Nick Monday, apparently the host, walks around the room shaking everyone's hand before he disappears down the hallway toward the bar.

I look around to see if I've missed anyone. Other than Nancy, Stephanie, Daphne, and Velma, this party is heavy on *five o'clock shadows and aftershave. Even if you throw in Miss Marple, who's old enough to be my grandmother, the odds aren't in favor of any man making good use of anything but the palm of his hand.*

Except for Frank and Joe Hardy, who just walked through the room toward the back of the house with Nancy Drew leading them like a couple of pet Labradors.

I wander over to give my regards to Spenser and Spade, my bourbon tagging along. After making some small talk and watching as Chan and Queen bow out of the Stephanie Plum Sweepstakes, I finish off my bourbon, then head back down the hallway to give the ice in my cocktail glass some more company.

The bartender stands alone behind the bar, looking polite and lonely. Kojak is now playing eight-ball against Magnum while Columbo walks around in his trench coat with a drink in one hand and the other hand pressed to his forehead like he feels a migraine coming on. Hammer and Holmes are wrestling on the floor next to an uprooted fern as Dirty Harry backs Monday into a corner with his fists and a sardonic grin.

"Do you feel lucky?" says Callahan. "Well do you, punk?"

I head over to the bar and hand the bartender my drink with the lonely ice and turn to see if Holmes can get out of the headlock Hammer has him in. My money's on Hammer. Logic and astute observation might be helpful when solving a crime, but they're not much good in a bar fight with a violent misanthrope.

Just as my ice returns with a full complement of bourbon, Ace Ventura walks into the room, sits down at the bar next to me, and orders a Pink Squirrel. When the bartender informs him he doesn't have any crème de cacao, Ventura asks for a Funky Monkey. Again, the bartender explains, no crème de cacao.

"Fine," says Ventura in a huff. "Just give me a Greyhound, then."

He turns to look at me with a big grin and shrugs. "What are you gonna do?"

"Maybe next time order a real drink," I say, holding up mine as an example.

"Whatever," he says, then holds his finger and his thumb in the shape of an L on his forehead and calls me a loser in twice as many syllables as necessary.

I'd put my drink down and teach him a lesson, but that's not my style. Plus I've grown fond of my bourbon. So I just smile and take a drink and wonder if Dirty Harry would consider redirecting his anger.

Ventura spins around in his chair to survey the room, then spins back to face me.

"So is everyone in here a douche bag?" he says. "Or did you just win an award?"

His pupils are dilated and his skin looks like it's stretched a little too tight across his cheeks. His left eye twitches once. Twice.

"Hmm," I say.

"What does that mean?"

"It means, hmm."

The bartender arrives just in time with the Greyhound, which Ventura proceeds to down in three gulps before slamming the empty glass back on the bar.

"All righty, then!" He wipes his mouth, gives me the finger, then turns around and bends over and says, "It was nice to meet *you," with his butt cheeks before he stands up and walks out of the room.*

Holmes calls out "Uncle" and Kojak scratches on the eight-ball as I watch Ventura disappear down the hallway. I turn back to the bartender, order another Greyhound, and take a sip of bourbon as I wait for the bartender to mix the drink. Once he's done, I palm a capsule into the Greyhound, then take it and my bourbon and go in search of the pet detective to see if he'd like another drink.

CHAPTER 11

"Do you have a second?" Angela stands just outside my office, leaning in as if she doesn't want to make a commitment. Which is the story of her life. She's broken up more times than Elizabeth Taylor and Henry VIII combined.

"Sure," I say. "My place or yours?"

"Mine."

"I'll be there in a couple of minutes."

It's the last week of September, which means it's the end of the quarter and everyone's putting in extra time writing up reports for the new releases, including me.

I turn back to my computer, where I'm reading some of the complaints we've had for The Fox Mulder, based on the character from *The X-Files*. While it tested well and was listed among the Top Television Characters requested among men aged 50–59, apparently it's causing some undesirable behaviors, including paranoia, obsessive behavior, obstinacy, self-importance, and a predilection for pornography. One customer apparently ran up more than five hundred dollars' worth of charges on Internet porn sites during his experience, claiming he just couldn't help himself.

It's not often we release a clunker. Each Big Ego goes through a testing phase that prevents something like a Fox Mulder from hitting the marketplace, but apparently this one managed to slip through. Still, for every Fox Mulder we have solid releases like The Dalai Lama, The Orson Welles, and The Princess Leia. When it comes to hits versus misses, our track record is better than most Hollywood movie studios.

Say what you want, but we've never put out anything as bad as *The Adventures of Pluto Nash*.

In addition to the rare miss like The Fox Mulder, we occasionally get complaints of headaches, blurred vision, separation anxiety, and nausea. Most people aren't prepared for the experience of being someone else and it can create a feeling of imbalance, not unlike being on the ocean or experiencing some airplane turbulence. It takes a bit to get used to. After the first few experiences, the nausea for most people goes away, though we have had an occasional report of vertigo. And while depression isn't as much of an issue as it used to be, we offer serotonin boosts and psychiatric customer support as part of every Ego package. You should see the legalese that's included in your purchase.

I've never personally experienced any of the side effects some of our customers have reported and, to my knowledge, neither has anyone on my team. When used properly, Big

Egos are a safe and effective way to have a reality-shifting experience without the long-term cumulative effects of hallucinogenic drugs like LSD or mushrooms or mescaline. And it's far superior to any virtual reality technology or role-playing game. You don't need a headset or 3-D goggles or a gaming platform. *You* are the platform. And unlike virtual reality, it's not a simulation.

Of course, part of the popularity of Big Egos is that we're offering something that people want. The ability to become someone else. To walk in someone else's proverbial shoes. To not only see what life is like through someone else's eyes but to feel it. To live it. To experience an existence that doesn't belong to you.

A lot of people aren't really who they want to be.

They live the lives they choose to live rather than the ones they imagined. They don't go confidently in the direction of their dreams. They eschew Thoreau's advice and instead live vicariously through the lives of others. Rather than talking about themselves, they talk about other things. Other people. People whose lives are more interesting and exciting than their own.

Celebrities. Movie stars. Professional athletes.

They sit around tables in coffee break rooms or outside office buildings smoking cigarettes and talking about television shows and movies and sports. Talking about them as if they had nothing else to talk about. Focusing on the lives of other people rather than on their own existence.

When they get home, they sit around and watch reality television shows and celebrity gossip programs. They read online magazines like *People* and *Sports Illustrated* and the *National Enquirer.* They surf the Internet for news and updates on all the latest entertainment and sports news, spending endless amounts of energy and attention on people they've never met.

When they get together socially, they talk about their favorite episodes or moments from television sitcoms. They quote their favorite movies and lines from their favorite shows and pearls of wisdom from their favorite characters. They listen to the rhetoric of talk-show hosts and regurgitate their ideas.

This is their idea of originality. This is how they define themselves. Not by their own actions and thoughts and deeds, but by those of people they see on television and hear on the radio and read about on the Internet.

Oscar Wilde once said: "Most people are other people. Their thoughts are someone else's opinions, their lives a mimicry, their passions a quotation."

Although his quote occurred during the death throes of the nineteenth century, it's as relevant today as it was back then.

We've become a society of voyeurs, coveting other people's lives to make up for the fact that our own lives are dull and uninspiring and filled with ennui. So it only makes sense that Big Egos would become so popular. It's the perfect product at the perfect time.

I finish reading the reports on The Fox Mulder disaster, then I walk out of my office to see what Angela wants to talk to me about.

"I want your hairy body on top of me."

Kurt is listening to his voice mail on speaker again.

Sometimes I wonder if these are women he's actually been with or if he's just getting callbacks from a sex-line number. Except I've seen Kurt in action. While he might have shopped in the bargain bin for good looks, when it comes to confidence, Kurt paid top dollar.

And like I always tell Nat, women dig confidence.

Slurp, slurp, slurp.

The sound is coming from Neil's workstation. Three slurps, then a short pause followed by more slurping. Which means it must be juice box time.

Every Monday morning, Neil brings in five organic, single-serving juice boxes and puts them in the refrigerator in the break room. He puts them in the same location, on the bottom shelf of the refrigerator on the far left-hand side, lined up single file front to back with the labels facing forward. No one is supposed to touch his juice boxes. Not even to move them in order to make room for something else. He's made this very clear.

Then, every morning starting precisely at 10:15, Neil drinks one of his juice boxes. It takes him ten minutes to drink most of it, then he spends another five minutes slurping the container until it's empty. And it always takes him exactly fifteen minutes. Not fourteen minutes and fifty-seven seconds. Not fifteen minutes and five seconds. But fifteen minutes on the dot.

Slurp, slurp, slurp.

I glance up at the clock. So far this morning, he's been slurping for two minutes.

My guess is he slurps the same number of times during those five minutes, but no one in the office has ever bothered to keep count. Vincent tried once but lost track and gave up. We all just assume it's the same number of times each day.

"How's it going, Neil?" I ask, stopping outside his workstation.

He doesn't turn around and say anything or even acknowledge my presence, just continues his ritualistic emptying of his juice box.

Slurp, slurp, slurp.

"Okay then," I say. "Good talking to you."

I walk past Vincent's workstation, where he's reclining in his desk chair with an *Entertainment Weekly* over his face. I don't always find him like this with a copy of *Entertainment Weekly*. Some days it's *Rolling Stone*. Other days it's *Sports Illustrated*. Every now and then, it's a *Playboy*.

At least he's keeping himself well-read.

"Vincent," I say.

He sits up so fast his glasses slide halfway down his nose before he pushes them back into place. It's a little Clark Kent, but Vincent is no Superman. He's more like Jimmy Olsen, if Jimmy Olsen was a black, thirty-one-year-old Ego raver with a photographic memory who lived on quinoa, seaweed, and Red Bull.

"What are you doing?" I ask.

"Research," he says, setting the magazine down on his desk and patting it for emphasis. "Boning up on late-twentieth-century pop culture."

Vincent claims he reads his magazines through osmosis and that his catnaps help him to think. I'd call bullshit, but he gets his job done, so I don't care how he does it.

"Don't forget about those reports on The Rat Pack," I say.

The Rat Pack is a new Ego concept in beta testing that allows the user to experience being Frank Sinatra, Dean Martin, Joey Bishop, Peter Lawford, and Sammy Davis Jr. over a six-hour period, with a little over an hour for each one. Initial testing indicates that Sinatra overshadows the others and Lawford feels like he gets blamed for everything. It's the first multiple personality Big Ego. In a number of departments, it's affectionately referred to as The Sybil.

"I'm on it," says Vincent, popping another Red Bull.

When I reach Angela, she's just hanging up the phone. I don't catch any of what she said, but she turns to me wearing a concerned expression.

"Hey. I think we might have a little problem."

CHAPTER **12**

"We've got a little problem," says Bill Summers, head of Applied Research at EGOS.

"How can I help?" I say, taking a seat.

Where I am is Bill's office at the end of May, four months ago. Bill is a forty-something guy with a crisp suit, a smooth delivery, and dimples. I never met the man until this moment, but whatever it is Bill does at Applied Research, he probably does it well and is used to getting results.

And I'd wager that goes for everything else he sets his mind to. It's just a look he has. A look that says he's confident and knows what he's doing. Plus, you know, the dimples.

"Can I get you a drink?" he asks.

"Just a bottle of water, thanks."

There's a wet bar over in one corner, with rock glasses and highballs and single bottles of top-shelf vodka, scotch, tequila, gin, and rum. I notice the bottle of tequila is more than half empty.

"You've been with the company, what?" says Bill, pouring himself a glass of tequila. "Five years now?"

I nod. "Not including the year of internship I did during my senior year at UCLA."

Bill opens a small refrigerator and grabs a bottle of water, which he hands to me before he sits down behind his island of a desk in his ocean of an office, a view of Beverly Hills floating in the late May sun behind him. If I were a woman and this were a date, I'd be flashing him a smile and playing with my hair.

He glances at his computer monitor. "You've made some impressive contributions since you've been here."

First a drink, now a compliment. This guy knows how to score points.

"Thanks. I just like to think I'm doing my job."

To be honest, I'm pretty good at what I do. When I first joined EGOS I was an entry-level investigator, earning an annual salary in the high five figures. After just two years, I was promoted to manager of Investigations and my income nearly doubled.

But my father taught me the importance of playing roles and right now, I'm playing the part of the appreciative employee.

"What attracted you to EGOS?" Bill looks at me from across his desk with his appraising eyes.

If I were a woman and this were a date, I'd be lightly stroking my neck right about now.

"Initially, the internship attracted me because of the experience it provided," I say. "But after less than six months, I knew I wanted the opportunity to be involved in something groundbreaking. To play a part in the fostering of a revolutionary technology."

While I didn't come here expecting to kiss anyone's ass, sometimes it's best to just hold your breath and pucker up. Plus, for some reason, Bill brings out the ass kisser in me.

"So would it be fair to say that you're invested in the company?" he says. "That you believe in what we're doing here at EGOS?"

"Yes," I say. "Absolutely."

"Let me explain why we asked you here today." Bill takes a sip of his tequila. "As you know, in the early stages of production, our competitors on the street were busy trying to replicate our technology, without much success."

The first year Big Egos hit the stores, knockoffs started showing up everywhere, and it wasn't uncommon to see some grocery store clerk or coffeehouse barista looking like a bad copy of Scarlett O'Hara or Sylvester Stallone. Though with Stallone, sometimes you couldn't tell the difference.

"But over the past twelve months, it's become apparent that the quality of their product has improved significantly," says Bill. "And with the availability of Egos of living celebrities and serial killers, black market Egos have begun to grow in popularity and started to take a bigger chunk of the market. Though that's not the problem I mentioned earlier or why we asked you here."

His use of the royal *we* makes me wonder who else knows about our meeting. And who it is Bill reports to.

There are a lot of departments at EGOS. Research. Product development. Accounting. Marketing. Customer support. Biotechnology. Testing. Investigations. And a few others I can't even remember. I've never met anyone from Applied Research and I'm not sure I understand what purpose they serve.

"So . . . what's the problem?" I ask.

"We've discovered that some of the black market Egos are using intellectual property stolen from EGOS."

That is a problem. "How was it stolen?"

"We don't know that yet. But the issue we're facing is that if this information gets out, not only could we be held accountable for any side effects caused by the black market Egos, but it could end up having significant ramifications to the public's perception of the safety of Big Egos."

"I don't understand. The knockoffs are unsafe because they're encoded with RNA rather than with DNA. Everyone knows that."

"I know that and you know that, but the general public doesn't pay attention to those kinds of details," says Bill. "All they'll hear is that black market Egos are using the same technology and intellectual property as our product and that will be the kiss of death for us. The public won't see any distinction between legally and illegally manufactured Egos. Except for the price."

I nod. "So what can Investigations do to help?"

"Not Investigations," he says. "Just you."

If this were a date, I'd want to feel his hand running up my thigh right about now.

"Technically, it's not *just* you." He takes another sip of

tequila. "We're bringing in several dozen employees from different departments to help."

Apparently this date just turned into a gang bang.

"But you're the only one from Investigations," he says. "Why's that?"

"We're just picking the most talented minds in each department. The best of the best, you might say. Plus we're looking for people like you who have a knack for understanding the intricate workings of our product."

Instead of stroking my thigh, now he's stroking my ego. And it's working.

"What exactly are we talking about here?" I ask.

"As you mentioned, black market Egos are risky because they're improperly encoded with RNA rather than DNA, producing retroviruses that take over the host brain, resulting in psychosis and other problems."

And by *other problems*, he means death.

"We've developed an antidote that counteracts the retroviruses and stabilizes the DNA." Bill produces a vial containing a clear liquid and hands it to me. "While the chemical structure of the formula is a little complex and requires a degree in biochemistry to fully comprehend, suffice it to say that this will essentially turn the black market Ego into one of our own."

I hold the vial up to the light.

"The problem we're facing is that we don't have the time to put the antidote through the regular channels to get it tested, approved, and patented," says Bill. "It took more than half a decade to get the patents on the DNA replication for Big Egos and we can't wait for that process to play out. Plus there's the issue of going public with this, which is something we'd prefer to avoid."

I hand the vial back to him. "So where do I fit in?"

"We need your help to test the product."

"Why don't you just bring in volunteers?"

"We tried that. But the results were corrupted by test subjects who were less than forthcoming about their Ego purchasing habits. Because of your familiarity with the product line, we need your help getting the antidote to the test subjects out in the field."

"How exactly will I do that?"

"By attending Ego parties and identifying black market Ego users and giving them this," says Bill, holding up the vial for emphasis. "We also have it in a powder form. Your job is to deliver the antidote to them in some manner unknown to them. That's the important part. They can't know what they're being given."

"How will you know who's received the antidote?"

"The antidote is encoded with some of our GPS-tracking-enabled nanobots," says Bill. "Once the subject has received the antidote, the nanobots will allow us to track him or her via satellite."

"Is that legal?"

"It's a gray area," says Bill. "It falls under the category of *what they don't know won't hurt them.*"

I don't know if I agree with that assessment, but I'm intrigued enough to keep the date going.

"So how would this work?" I ask.

"First, we'll have you go through some video testing to help you recognize the various symptoms most often caused by the use of black market Egos so you'll be able to better identify those who are using them."

Ego Dementia is the commonly used academic term for what happens from repeated exposure to the retroviruses created in black market Egos, though I've heard the media use a number of other euphemisms to describe the condition, including Ego Mania, Ego Trips, and Inflated Egos.

"There's a bit more to explain if you agree," he says. "And you'll have to put in some extra hours, work a couple of nights a week, maybe an occasional weekend, but as I mentioned, because of your expertise, you're an ideal candidate for what we have in mind."

I'm not sure I want to work nights and weekends, but Bill keeps saying all the right things. If this were a date, I would have asked him back to my place, though I wouldn't give it up right away. I'd make him work for it.

Bill flashes his dimples. "Naturally, if you agree to do this, we'd offer you additional compensation."

There goes my bra and sweater.

"What type of compensation are we talking about?"

"How does a six-figure bonus, an additional hundred shares of stock, and a corporate penthouse suite sound?"

And off come the panties.

I think about that 1962 Aston Martin I've had my eye on. And the upgrades to the house that Delilah wants. And how those extra shares of stock could allow me to retire even earlier than I'd planned.

I know I should probably take some time to think about this before I make a decision, maybe talk to Delilah first, but my father always taught me that you need to embrace the opportunities that are given to you if you want to get what you want out of life.

Plus Bill is really good at what he does.

"All right," I say. "When do we start?"

CHAPTER **13**

"Ground control to Major Tom," says Angela.

I'm standing outside Angela's workstation as Vincent walks past and gives me the thumbs-up before wandering off, looking industrious, while Neil continues his daily juice box ritual.

Slurp, slurp, slurp.

"What?" I say.

"You looked like you went out of orbit for a minute there," says Angela. "You okay?"

"Yeah, I'm fine," I say. "So what's the problem?"

Angela pulls up a spreadsheet on her touchscreen monitor. "Come here and take a look at this."

I walk up behind her and look at her monitor, which displays a spreadsheet of Big Egos and various side effects, including frequency of occurrence and complaints. The spreadsheet I'm looking at now is for a group of fictional

Egos we call The Icons, which includes The Holly Golightly, The Sam Spade, The James Bond, The Annie Hall, and The Captain Kirk, among others.

This is Angela's area of expertise. Fictional characters. She's the only member of my team who has injected more fictional Egos than I have. And out of the more than three thousand Egos in our product line, the bestsellers are typically fictional characters.

It's not that surprising when you think about it. Not only are some celebrities better known for the characters they portray than for their own fame, but fictional characters in Hollywood and literature and folklore are often more real to us than the people in our lives.

Peter Parker. Jane Eyre. Santa Claus.

Harry Potter. Buffy Summers. Superman.

Not only are these characters always there for us and never let us down, but they affect us and inspire us and have a profound impact on who we are and what we believe in.

They've changed our lives. Made us laugh. Made us cry. Given us hope.

What's more real than that?

I think we long to be them because they've been such an important part of our lives. And since they'll be around long after we're gone, being one of them allows us to become immortal, even if only for a few hours.

"So what's the problem?" I repeat.

"Well, I was going over some numbers from The Icons and came across a couple of anomalies that show up in certain Egos during the third year."

"What kind of anomalies?"

"It's not something we've encountered before." Touching the screen, she sorts the spreadsheet according to one of the columns. "But they show up in the interviews and voice scans of a large number of customers who purchased one or more of five specific Egos."

Voice scans are used by EGOS investigators when talking with customers to help identify and compile potential problems. You can learn a lot from a person's voice, especially when it's run through software with a state-of-the-art polygraph program. Voice scans are more cost-effective than brain scans and easier to obtain, since the subject only needs to be recorded over the phone. With their permission, of course.

We record their voices and run their responses through a software app that searches for inflections, inconsistencies, repetitive phrases, etc. It's also used to compare changes in voice patterns in a customer from one interview to the next. Most of those changes can be attributed to normal fluctuations in stress levels brought on by relationships, work, financial issues, menstrual cycles, and children, among other things. But if you're trying to hide something, or if there's something else going on other than the normal day-to-day challenges of being an adult, the voice scan software will pick up on it.

"Which five Egos did the anomalies show up in?" I ask.

Angela sorts the spreadsheet again and points to her monitor. The Egos highlighted at the top of the spreadsheet are The Indiana Jones, The Captain Kirk, The Rocky Balboa, The Philip Marlowe, and The Charles Foster Kane.

It's not lost on me that three of the five Egos on the list

are in my personal collection at home. And that I've been using all of them for going on three years now.

"During the first two years, everything was normal," she says. "No indications of any abnormalities for the sampling of customers we interviewed."

She keeps talking about speech patterns and inflections and vocabulary. I'm listening and nodding in all the right places, but I'm waiting for her to get to the point.

"So what are the anomalies?" I ask again.

"Nearly three-quarters of the customers interviewed over the past month who'd used at least one of the five Icons regularly during the last three years mentioned that the number zero seemed to come up a lot for them." Angela sorts the list to highlight her point.

"What do you mean it came up a lot?"

"In random conversations," she says. "On digital clocks or temperature readouts or roulette wheels. Symbolically. Metaphorically. Socially. Sometimes the combined numbers for the time or the date or an address always seem to add up to a number ending in zero."

In some cultures, zero is a powerful number that brings about great transformational change, often profound. And profundity is something I can get excited about. But zero is also the absence of all quality or quantity, the lowest point, nothing—which doesn't exactly give me the warm fuzzies.

"If it was just a handful of customers or even ten percent, I'd probably write it off to a subconscious fixation—people looking for numbers or symbols and attributing some significant meaning when the number or pattern keeps coming up," says Angela. "But when seven out of ten customers mention the same thing, then I think it's a little more than people looking for patterns in chaos."

"What's the other anomaly?" I ask.

"Regular users of multiple Icons over that same three-year period who were interviewed each repeated some unusual or specific phrase multiple times."

"The same phrase?"

Angela shakes her head. "Something unique to each customer that they would use repetitively."

"How many of the customers displayed both behavioral anomalies?"

Angela touches the screen again and pulls up another spreadsheet. "More than fifty percent."

"How often did they use their Egos?" I ask.

Angela pulls up another spreadsheet on her monitor. "An average of seven times per year. Though users of The Indiana Jones and The Captain Kirk reported an average of once per month."

Considering I've used both The Indiana Jones and The Captain Kirk more than three times the average over the same period of time, I'm wondering if I should be concerned.

I think about whether I've been exhibiting either of the anomalies. I don't recall the number zero showing up an unusual amount in my daily routine. At least not that I can recall. I definitely haven't been looking for it. And I'm pretty sure I haven't repeated any unusual or specific phrase over and over.

Truth is, I think I'd notice something like that.

"I called Diagnostics and they ran it through some additional tests, which confirmed our findings," says Angela.

"Then they ran them past Applied Research, which is who I just got off the phone with."

"And what did Applied Research say?"

"They said not to worry about it."

I nod, feeling a little better about the anomalies. After all, if Applied Research doesn't think it's a problem, then it's probably not.

"What do you think?" I ask.

Angela doesn't say anything for a few moments but just sits in her desk chair staring at her monitor, her right index finger tapping on her desk. I watch her face, looking for any signs of what she's thinking, but if Angela were a poker player, she could be holding four aces and I wouldn't have a clue.

Then she finally looks at me. "Honestly, I'm a little worried."

CHAPTER **14**

William Shakespeare stands on a milk crate out in front of the ArcLight Cinerama Dome, wearing a soiled doublet and torn breeches and needing a bath. Next to him is a shopping cart filled with a blanket and a pillow and other personal belongings. In front of him sits a battered felt hat containing a smattering of coins and a handful of dollar bills as he quotes from *Hamlet*:

"To be or not to be, that is the question . . ."

"Yeah!" yells some guy with a shaved head and a goatee who leans out the window of a passing Mustang hybrid and gives Shakespeare the finger. "And this is the answer!"

Laughter drifts out from the car windows as the Mustang drives off down Sunset Boulevard. Shakespeare watches them go, then makes a comment about something being rotten in the state of Denmark.

Just up Sunset, less than half a block away, a small group

of protesters marches back and forth out in front of the Hollywood Big Egos store, carrying signs and chanting slogans like

Just be yourself.
Big Egos = Small Minds.
Jesus does not have an Ego.

They're probably upset about The Jesus, which we plan to release this Christmas. If pre-orders are any indication, the Son of God is going to be an instant bestseller.

It's the first Friday in October, and Delilah and I are standing in line outside the Cinerama Dome waiting to buy tickets to the latest Leonardo DiCaprio film. At least I'm here. Delilah is Scarlett O'Hara.

"Oh fiddle-dee-dee," she says. "I wish Rhett were here. It's just not the same without him around."

We used to go out in public together as ourselves more often. Lately, it's just a couple of times a month, but Delilah is becoming less and less interested in being herself. She loves the attention she gets from being someone else and I'm finding it harder and harder to be me. But after my office meeting with Angela, I decided to play it straight for a night, just to prove to myself that I could.

Kind of like someone who thinks he's an alcoholic going to a party and not drinking so he can convince himself he doesn't have a problem.

"That poor man," says Scarlett, motioning toward Shakespeare. "How long do you think he's been out here?"

I just shrug.

"For in that sleep of death what dreams may come when we have shuffled off this mortal coil must give us pause," says Shakespeare. "There's the respect that makes calamity of so long life."

He offers a slight bow to phantom applause and the ghostly donation of a few lonely coins.

"I feel sorry for him," says Scarlett. "Do you think he was Shakespeare before he became homeless?"

"If I had to guess, I'd say no."

Either way, I'm betting his Ego isn't legal.

I watch him, looking for any of the telltale signs of a black market Ego. Twitches or tics, anything that might give him away, but he seems perfectly normal. Not that I could do anything about it. I didn't bring any of the antidote with me.

Even before college I read a lot of Shakespeare, especially in my high school Western lit class. I was always a fan of the Bard and wonder what he would think about his words being performed by a black market version of himself, who is now quoting from a different scene in *Hamlet*.

"This above all: to thine own self be true," he says, his right index finger sweeping across his captive audience. "And it must follow, as the night follows the day, thou cannot then be false to any man."

When he stops, he's looking and pointing right at me. I know it's ridiculous, but I can't help thinking that he's trying to tell me something.

Scarlett pokes me in the ribs with her elbow. "Why don't you be a dear and give him some money?"

"What? Why? He's just going to use it to buy booze or drugs." Or another black market Ego.

"Great balls of fire." Scarlett fishes a five-dollar bill out of her clutch. "He can do with it what he wants. What does it matter to you?"

"I just don't want to be supporting his bad habits."

She holds the money out to me. "Please darlin'? For me?"

I never can say no to Delilah, even when she's Scarlett O'Hara. Which is a problem.

"Okay." I take the money and walk up to Shakespeare and deposit the five dollars in his hat. He nods and bows and then breaks into a scene from *As You Like It*.

"All the world's a stage, and all the men and women merely players: they have their exits and their entrances, and one man in his time plays many parts."

When he finishes, he looks at me with a smile and nods again, as if we've just shared some great secret. This strikes an uneasy chord with me and I think again about his previous quote, about being true to myself, and I wonder if he's just quoting random passages from his plays or if there's something more to it than that.

"Are you talking to me?" I say. Not like De Niro in *Taxi Driver*. I'm not trying to be a tough guy. It's just a question.

Shakespeare just smiles and gives me a wink.

I look around to see if anyone else noticed, then I walk back to Delilah, who gives me a kiss on the cheek. "See. Now that wasn't so awful, was it?"

As we wait in line to get our tickets, Shakespeare continues his performance, quoting scenes and passages and lines from play after play. *The Merchant of Venice. As You Like It.*

Richard III. Julius Caesar. Macbeth. And he keeps quoting lines that make me wonder if he knows something he's not telling me.

Now he's saying it's the winter of our discontent.

Now he's saying to beware the Ides of March.

Now he's saying something wicked this way comes.

I'm not exactly getting a happy vibe here.

It doesn't help that I keep glancing over and catching him looking directly at me. As if there's no one else around. As if he's performing for me and me alone.

Part of me realizes I'm only imagining things. That he's just a crazy homeless person who bought a black market Ego and ended up spouting random quotes from Shakespeare. That it's just a coincidence I'm even here.

But another part of me believes there's no such thing as coincidence.

"Now thou art an O without a figure!" he yells. "I am better than thou art now. I am a fool. Thou art nothing."

I think about zeros and repeated phrases and Angela telling me she's worried.

I listen to Shakespeare until I start to feel as if there's something going on I should know about. Until I think he was sent here to give me some kind of message. I realize it's preposterous, but I can't seem to let go of the thought.

"I'll be right back," I say.

"Where are you off to?" asks Scarlett.

"To give him some more money."

I walk over to Shakespeare, who stands there on his milk crate in his dirty clothes wearing his knowing smile. He gives me a wink.

"Do you have something you want to tell me?" I ask.

"Oh, that way madness lies."

I look back at Scarlett, who watches me while she cools herself with a hand fan. I turn back to Shakespeare. "It's okay. You can tell me what it is."

"Chaos is come again."

Not the most promising of answers, but the Bard did write his share of tragedies. Still, I'm hoping for something a little lighter. Something uplifting. Something with a happy ending.

I know they're just words spoken by a street person strung out on a black market Ego, but I can't help thinking that this madness and chaos he alluded to are somehow related to me.

I step closer and whisper. "Tell me what I need to do."

"What's done is done," he says.

Great. I'm hoping for *Twelfth Night* and instead I get *Macbeth*.

"What on earth *are* you doing?" says Scarlett.

I turn around to find her standing right behind me holding the movie tickets. "Nothing," I say. "Come on, let's go."

As we walk toward the theater entrance, Shakespeare shouts out behind us. "But soft, what light through yonder window breaks? It is the east and Juliet is the sun."

We turn around and Shakespeare winks and bows to Scarlett.

"Well, isn't that just too sweet?" She pulls another five-dollar bill out of her purse and hands it to me. With a sigh, I take the five and walk back over to him.

As I put the five into his hat, Shakespeare looks toward

Scarlett, who smiles and waves, and he says: "She is a dish fit for the gods."

"You've got that right," I say.

"Misery acquaints a man with strange bedfellows."

I look at him and he raises his eyebrows a couple of times.

"Not a chance, pal."

"A plague on both your houses."

I turn away and walk back to Scarlett. Behind me, Shakespeare calls out:

"O! She doth teach the torches to burn bright!"

CHAPTER **15**

"Fire!"

Nat is running toward me wearing a look of terror, his hands waving back and forth in the air. His expression is pretty believable, especially for Nat. He's not much of an actor. He doesn't own a poker face and he tends to make fear look more like constipation. But this time he's got the expression nailed. Even the smoke alarm is going off. When I see smoke starting to pour out of his bedroom, I almost believe there's a fire. Either his parents finally caved in and bought him a smoke machine or else he's taking the game to a whole new level.

Where we are is Nat's house during the summer after sixth grade. We're playing Emergency, one of the games we've made up to entertain our twelve-year-old imaginations. Most kids our age pretend to be their favorite baseball or football or basketball player whenever they get together for some street ball or a pickup game, but Nat and I aren't much into sports.

So we invent games where we pretend to be firemen or secret agents or surgeons. Some of the other games we play include Rescue, Global Disaster, and Jehovah's Witness Protection Program. One of my favorite games is Reanimation, where we pretend to be a zombie in a society in which we don't have any rights and are abused by the living. Usually Nat gets dressed up like a zombie and I pelt him with expired food products, but sometimes I play the part of the recently reanimated and he pretends to be my therapist.

Emergency, what we're currently playing, is this game where one of us creates an emergency and the other one has to figure out how to solve the problem. And not just fires or natural disasters, but all sorts of emergencies.

Blackouts. Famines. Alien invasions.

Most of the time, we just flip some circuit breakers or empty the cupboards or put on an alien mask and let our imaginations do the rest. One time when we were playing Emergency, Nat went out and caught five dozen frogs and released them in the backyard, which was really more of an infestation than an emergency, so he decided that should be a new game called Plagues of Egypt.

Apparently, for this episode of Emergency, Nat has decided to actually start a real fire rather than a pretend one.

"What are you doing?" I ask.

"Fire!" he shouts as he runs past me and around the corner into the kitchen.

I look back down the hallway toward his bedroom,

where smoke continues to drift out of his open doorway to the wailing alarm of the smoke detector.

"Is that a real fire or are you just trying to trick me?" I ask.

"It's a real fire!" he shouts from the kitchen.

I hear the sound of a cupboard banging open, something metal hitting the kitchen floor, followed by running feet. An instant later, Nat is racing past me toward his bedroom with a fire extinguisher.

"I thought it was my turn to solve the emergency," I say, walking down the hallway after him, the calm yin to Nat's yang.

When I reach Nat's room, he's managed to put out the fire, which isn't really much more than a smoldering pile of paper and scrap wood and something that looks like it used to be a plastic garbage can, which has more or less melted and burned a hole in his carpet. The room smells like burned rubber and plastic and ammonium phosphate, so I open a window to help air it out.

"You know, you could have just lit a candle and we could have pretended it was a real fire," I say, waving my hands at the smoke and coughing.

"You're not helping," says Nat, emptying the last of the fire extinguisher on the charred and melted mess.

"I think it's out."

"Not helping!" he shouts, his pitch nearly matching the wail of the smoke alarm.

I understand his concern. This is, after all, his house and not mine. Still, Nat's my best friend and I don't want him to get into trouble. But as far as I'm concerned, this is just another game of Emergency and it's up to me to figure out how to solve the problem.

"Crap." Nat sets the fire extinguisher down and looks at the mess of melted plastic and burned carpet and dry chemical. "My mom's gonna kill me."

"Not if we fix it before she gets home."

"Fix it?" He gestures at the floor. "How are we going to fix this?"

I look around the room, sizing things up, considering possible solutions.

"Okay," I say. "Here's what we're going to do. First, we'll air the place out, then we'll throw some frozen pizzas in the oven and burn 'em to a crisp. Light some scented candles or spray a bunch of deodorizer to pretend like we're covering the smell of the burned pizza."

Nat looks at me, scratching his head the way he does whenever he's thinking something over. Either that or he has lice.

"But don't admit to burning the pizzas right away," I say. "Not before your mom asks. If you admit too soon, she'll figure something's up. So you have to act like you're trying to hide something, just not what you're really trying to hide."

"What about the carpet and the garbage can?"

"We'll replace the garbage can." I glance around his bedroom, thinking. "We throw the old one in the Dumpster out behind the 7-Eleven, then we buy a rug to cover the hole in your carpet. Maybe a bed pillow to match so it doesn't look so out of place."

"You think that'll work?"

"So long as we make it look like you're trying to cover something else up, she'll never know what really happened."

Nat stares at the melted sculpture on his bedroom floor, scratching at his head, not saying a word. The only sound in the house is the insistent wail of the smoke alarm.

"Okay," he says, nodding. "What do you want me to do?"

"Get me a fan," I say. "And some Febreze or a can of Lysol or some kind of deodorizer. Then throw the frozen pizzas in the oven. But first, shut off that stupid smoke alarm."

CHAPTER **16**

Nat sits on the couch next to me, drinking a Guinness as he looks over my updated selection of Egos, which includes The Mark Twain, The Kurt Vonnegut, and The Great Gatsby.

I've been in a literary mood lately.

Nat, however, tends to be more movie focused.

"What happened to The Luke Skywalker?" he says, checking the labels. "And The Bruce Wayne? That was pretty cool being Batman's alter ego. Hey, can you get The Batman? Or how about The Neo from *The Matrix*? Or The Dude? Yeah, I'd *love* to be The Dude."

I never should have introduced Nat to the world of Big Egos.

Not that I haven't enjoyed spending time with him. We've spent at least one night a week over the past month going to Ego parties and bar hopping, pretending to be

Luke Skywalker and Han Solo, Dean Martin and Frank Sinatra, Butch Cassidy and the Sundance Kid. I'd almost forgotten how much fun we could have together. Plus I've seen the positive change this has had on Nat, improving his self-esteem and making him more self-assured. It's as though by becoming someone else for a few hours, he's finally been able to become the person inside of him waiting to get out. The person he's always wanted to be.

The problem is, I get the feeling Nat's becoming dependent on Egos in order to maintain his newfound persona. While I'd hoped to convince him of their merits and get him to appreciate the experience rather than fear it, he's begun to develop a predilection for them. An almost obsessive compulsion. Over the past week, he's called me up to come over and try another Ego every other night.

Which doesn't exactly make for a happy Delilah.

"Is he coming over *again*?" she asked a couple of hours ago, complete with eye roll and exasperated sigh. "In that case, I'll make myself scarce."

So she did. And here we are, two childhood friends sitting in my living room drinking Guinness—one of us watching while the other one hovers over four dozen vials of alternate realities.

I don't know if it's the intense look in his eyes or the way his fingers caress the surface of each vial or how his tongue occasionally flicks out to lick his lips, but I decide it's time to share my concerns about his Ego usage.

"Hey Nat . . ."

"Yeah," he says, without looking up.

"How're you doing?"

"Great. Never been better."

"Good," I say, then I take a drink of my beer.

Neither one of us says anything for a couple of minutes. I'm trying to think of how to broach the subject, and clear my throat.

"Something on your mind, bro?" he says.

"No," I say. "I mean, yeah, now that you mention it."

Nat looks up at me. "Am I supposed to guess?"

I can hear the change in his voice. The cockiness. He's more sure of who he is, which is a stark contrast to the insecure Nat I've known since we were kids.

"No. It's just . . . I was thinking that maybe you . . . might have a little problem," I say.

"What kind of problem?"

I point to the trays of Egos on the coffee table with my beer and give my eyebrows a single raise that says: what do you think?

He stares at me without immediately responding, then takes a sip of his beer. "Let me ask you a question."

"Sure."

"Do you have a problem with Egos?" he says.

For a moment I think he's talking about the anomalies Angela found or about all the extra time I've spent testing the antidote for black market Egos, but then I realize that's ridiculous. Nat can't possibly know any of that. He's just throwing my own question back at me to throw me off.

"No," I say. "I don't have a problem. But that's not—"

"Then neither do I."

And that's it. That's the extent of our little heart-to-heart. That's the way some men share their feelings when they have something important to talk about. It's the way they communicate.

Show concern. Deny there's a problem. Go drinking.

None of the deeply involved, introspective, insightful conversations that women waste their time with. Talking about problems and issues and how to resolve them. After all, how are we supposed to get anything done if we spend all of our time talking about our feelings?

Still, the mood in the room has gone from anticipatory and charged to awkward and flat. Nat's no longer hovering over the trays of Egos but sitting back on the couch, drinking his beer and pouting.

Nat's always been a big pouter.

Whenever we would play one of our made-up games and Nat had to be the zombie or the bad guy or when things didn't go his way, he'd pout. Like the time we played Armageddon and he was Satan and I was the Messiah and he thought Satan was supposed to win, only to find out he had to spend a thousand years in a bottomless pit.

It's not my fault he didn't do his research on the Christian interpretation of the epic battle between good and evil.

But I can tell from the look on his face that he's settling into one of his *I don't want to play anymore* moods.

"What's the matter?" I say.

"Nothing."

"You sure?"

"Yes."

"So you're okay?"

"I'm fine."

Sometimes talking to Nat *is* like talking to a woman. What he says and what he means are two completely different things.

We sit there in silence for several minutes, drinking our beers, neither one of us making eye contact. Finally, Nat finishes his Guinness, sets the empty bottle on the table, then he stands up. "I think I'm gonna head out."

"Really? You don't want to Ego?"

"Nah. None of them really fit what I'm in the mood for, you know?"

I nod. Though I'm guessing I had more to do with his current mood and lack of enthusiasm than the selection of Egos.

"You want to hang out?" I say, trying to fix what I've broken. "Watch some Adult Swim?"

He shakes his head. "Maybe next time."

I watch Nat leave with a sense of remorse. I know how much he looks forward to coming over and I enjoy getting to hang out with him, even if he has become something of an Egomaniac. Or maybe I'm just projecting my own Ego use onto Nat and thinking he has a problem when, in reality, I'm the one with the problem. Maybe I should just appreciate my best friend's company without judging him.

So I grab another Guinness out of the fridge, pull out a pen and a pad of paper, think of some Egos Nat might like, then sit down at the dining room table and start making out a list.

CHAPTER **17**

I'm sitting at the kitchen table, making out my Christmas list while my mother watches *Jeopardy!* in the living room. I could be watching it with her, but this is too important to put off. And with the big day less than a month away, I want to make sure I don't forget anything.

I'm not complicated. I want the same things any seven-year-old boy wants for Christmas. Toys and a bicycle and books. Maybe an official Red Ryder carbine action two-hundred shot range model air rifle. What I want more than anything, though, is a video game system, like an Xbox or a PlayStation 2. And if not that, then I'd like the latest Harry Potter book, though I don't think *The Half-Blood Prince* comes out until next summer.

Last year I wanted more or less the same thing but last year I apparently wasn't a good little boy, so Santa didn't bring me what I wanted. Instead, I got pajamas and a backpack and coloring books.

My father told me Santa was being practical and to be grateful I got anything at all.

This year, I did my best to be extra good so that I might get one or more of the items on my list. I'm just hoping Santa's not in a practical mood.

My father walks into the kitchen and sits down across from me, his tie loosened and his face rough with a day's worth of whiskers. When I was four, I wanted to look more like my father so I gave myself whiskers by using my mother's mascara. When that wore off too quickly, I used a black Sharpie marker. I had whiskers for two weeks.

Even though he hasn't said anything yet, I stop writing my Christmas list and set down my pencil and give my father my full attention.

"How old are you?" asks my father.

I'm not sure if he doesn't really know or if he's testing me, but I answer because by now I know it's a bad idea to answer my father's questions with questions—especially with Christmas just around the corner and Santa keeping an eye on everyone.

I'm still not really sure how he watches more than six billion people all at the same time. That's a lot of customers. Even if we're just talking kids, that's at least a billion of us to keep track of. With less than ninety thousand seconds in a day, that's around ten thousand kids he has to keep track of every second, so chances are he's going to slip up somewhere. Maybe that's why he has elves. He must send them out as spies.

"Seven," I say to my father. "I'm seven."

"And what's that you're working on?" He nods at the single piece of paper next to me.

"My list for Santa," I say, with a certain amount of pride and satisfaction.

This isn't just some haphazard list I threw together on a whim. I spent a lot of time on it, adding and deleting items and moving them around. I'm only seven, but as far as I'm concerned, this is a literary masterpiece.

This year, my Christmas list includes, in order of preference:

1. Video game system
2. Bicycle
3. Books
4. BB gun
5. Toys

When it comes to asking Santa for presents, I've learned not to list brand names or models or to get too specific about color or style. According to my mother, Santa likes some flexibility. According to my father, Santa doesn't like to be told what to do.

Nat told me that Santa knows what you're thinking, even if you don't say it out loud. He says Santa's a mind reader. I told him if Santa were a mind reader, it would be in the lyrics to the song and it's not. Plus with more than a billion kids, even if Nat is right, I figure Santa doesn't have time to read *everyone's* mind.

My father reaches over and slides my Christmas list

across the table toward him, then he picks it up and starts reading. I watch his face and notice his eyes moving back and forth. I notice the pores on his nose and the hair on his knuckles and the armpits of his shirt stained with perspiration.

When he's done reading, he sets the list down next to him and looks at me over the pores of his nose.

"There is no Santa Claus," he says.

That's it. No warning. No gradual buildup. No gentle breaking of the news. Just a quick jab to the face. A kick in the crotch. Then he picks up today's newspaper and starts reading.

I stare at my father, not really sure I understand what he's talking about. Or maybe I'm just in shock. Of course there's a Santa Claus. It's like saying there's no Easter Bunny or no Tooth Fairy. It doesn't make any sense.

"What do you mean, Daddy?"

"Santa Claus isn't real," my father says. "He doesn't exist."

I look at my father reading the newspaper. I look at my mother watching *Jeopardy!* in the living room. Then I look down at myself. At my hands and my legs. At the chair I'm sitting on. At the table. At the floor.

If Santa Claus doesn't exist, then none of this can be real. But I know I'm sitting on the chair at the table in the kitchen. I can see the linoleum and I can feel the seat I'm sitting on. I can smell the onions on my father's breath and I can hear Alex Trebek on the television. So it has to exist. Everything. My father. Alex Trebek. Me. We all exist. We're all real. And so is Santa.

I look back at my father and I wonder if this is a test.

If he's trying to get me to do something bad so I won't get what I want for Christmas. I keep waiting for him to smile and nod and tell me how good I am and that I passed the test. Maybe even pat me on the head or ruffle my hair and make me a hot fudge sundae, then sit down with me and ask me about my Christmas list. He's never done that before, but I figure there's a first time for everything.

Instead, he keeps reading the news.

Finally I let out a little laugh to let him know I get the joke, to let him know I know it's just a test, but he doesn't laugh along with me. Or even give me a smile. And I start to worry that it's not a joke. That it's not a test.

"You're just kidding, right?"

"I'm not kidding, son," he says. "Your mother and I are the ones who buy your Christmas presents and wrap them up and put them under the tree and in your stocking. Santa Claus is just a story. And you're too old to keep believing in stories. It's time you realize that life isn't make-believe. Sooner or later, you have to grow up."

But I'm not even eight years old.

"What about the reindeer?" I ask, hanging on to my belief that is unraveling like a spool of Christmas ribbon. I can feel my eyes filling up with tears but I don't want to cry. My father always says real men don't cry. "What about the sleigh? And the elves?"

"There are no elves," says my father. "No reindeer. No Rudolph. No toy shop at the North Pole. No sleigh. No Santa Claus. I told you, he doesn't exist."

I sit there, staring at my father, fighting back tears. Then

I look down at my list, my hopes and anticipation for a merry Christmas crushed, and I'm thinking that things couldn't be any worse.

"And neither does the Tooth Fairy," says my father. "Or the Easter Bunny."

CHAPTER **18**

Chloe is on the karaoke stage singing "Like a Virgin." With her dark hair and exotic mix of French and Korean genes she doesn't look anything like Madonna, but she's nailing the performance. Or maybe I just think that because she keeps glancing my way during the chorus and I wonder if she's singing to me.

Touched for the very first time.

"She's good," says Vincent, sitting next to me and taking a drink from his pint of hefeweizen as he watches Chloe channel the Material Girl.

I get the feeling Vincent is thinking the same thing I'm thinking.

We're at the Blue Goose Lounge in Hollywood on a Thursday night a couple of weeks before Halloween. Not all departments at EGOS get together outside work, but when I was promoted to manager of Investigations, I thought it would be a good idea to promote team unity by having all of us go out socially once every couple of months.

"I like it here," says Angela, grooving to the beat of the song, looking around the bar, her mouth and tongue searching for the straw sticking out of her second margarita. "It's fun!"

Emily nods her conservative assent, enjoying the music somewhat less enthusiastically than Angela while using her fingers to guide the straw of her Cape Cod between her lips.

I seem to be fixated on mouths and straws this evening.

Like a virgin. Feels so good inside.

Up onstage, Chloe glances my way again, the lyrics coming out of her in a breathy purr. Next to me, Vincent takes another drink of his beer and nods along. Across from us, Neil sits next to Emily dressed in an all Dodger blue ensemble, which makes him look like a giant Smurf. In front of him sits a bottle of Newcastle, the label facing directly toward him. Neil cleaned off the top of the bottle with a sterilized hand wipe before he took his first sip, which makes me wonder what the flavor sensation of Newcastle and hand wipe tastes like.

"It's unsanitary to drink out of glasses in a public place," says Neil, pointing to Vincent's beer. "Do you have any idea how many people have had their lips on your glass?"

"Probably a lot more than have had their lips on yours," says Vincent before he drains the rest of his beer and heads to the bar for a refill.

On his way he walks past Kurt, who orders a drink while chatting up a brunette who looks so hot she should carry around a fire extinguisher.

"It's not only a matter of how many people use the same glass," says Neil, talking to whoever will listen. "But the bartender takes money from his customers, then he touches the cash register, which has been touched by other bartenders, who have touched money from all of their customers, then he touches your glass. So in effect, everyone at the bar has transferred their germs to *your* glass."

When it comes to loosening up, Neil is like a social corset.

"Which is why I only drink from bottles and cans," he finishes. "It's safer."

Angela and Emily look at Neil, then back to their glasses. Angela shrugs and sucks down half of her remaining margarita through her straw while Emily pushes her glass away, discarding it unfinished like her daily Cinnabon, and excuses herself to go use the restroom.

"Make sure to wash your hands!" Neil shouts after her.

Neil volunteers once a month at the St. Francis Center serving meals to the homeless. He told me it was a way to help others while helping him to tackle his fear of germs. I don't think it's working.

Angela holds up her empty glass. "I need another before it's my turn to sing. Anyone else need a refill?"

Neil and I shake our heads and Angela heads to the bar as Chloe finishes her song and exits the stage to applause and whistles, then makes her way back to join us, fending off several salivating drunks along the way.

While we've gone out before as a group for drinks, meals, and to the movies, this is the first time we've done karaoke. Chloe is the one who suggested it. And so far, she's the only one who's been brave enough to get up in front of everyone and sing.

Some local karaoke bars don't allow their customers to sing while using Egos, claiming it somehow defiles the history and tradition of the art of "empty orchestra." Other karaoke bars aren't so uptight and sponsor Ego nights or take a more relaxed position and allow anyone to sing, regardless of who they think they are.

The Blue Goose enforces a strict No Ego policy, which means that everyone here tonight is just being themselves. Or nearly so.

When you're onstage singing along to Madonna or Sinatra or Adele, channeling your inner Toby Keith or Lady Gaga or Neil Diamond, you're technically still pretending to be someone else, even if it's just for a three-minute, thirty-eight-second song.

"Nicely done," I say, raising my scotch on the rocks to Chloe as she sits down at the table. "Though I wouldn't have pegged you for a Madonna fan."

"I'm not. But for some reason I felt like singing that song." She takes a drink of her beer, staring at me over the rim of her pint glass.

Is it just me, or did it suddenly get warm in here?

"You missed a great conversation," says Neil. "I was just talking about how many people drink out of every glass at the bar . . ."

Chloe holds her hand up to Neil. "I don't want to hear it. What I want to hear is your voice coming out of those speakers."

"I don't sing," says Neil, as some guy with a wide grin

and narrow eyes gets up onstage and launches into an unfortunate rendition of "Desperado."

"Well, I already signed you up for 'I Will Survive,' so you better take your name off the list if you don't want to do it," says Chloe.

Neil gets an expression on his face like he just soiled his Smurf-blue briefs, then he gets up and walks toward the karaoke machine, taking the long way around to avoid as many people as possible, leaving just Chloe and me at the table.

"So . . ." Chloe leans on one elbow and places her chin in her palm, her eyes never leaving mine. "What do you think?"

"I think you were the best one tonight."

"I appreciate the flattery, but that's not what I'm talking about," she says, giving me a playful smile.

"What *are* you talking about?" I say, though I'm pretty sure I know the answer. I'm just not going to say it out loud.

"I thought the lyrics were self-explanatory," she says.

We sit there and stare at each other for a few seconds, neither one of us blinking. Literally or figuratively. And the image of Chloe in leather and thigh-high stilettos pops back into my head.

"As intrigued as I am by the thought of it," I finally manage to say, "I don't think it would be a good idea."

"Why not?"

"Because we work together," I say. "And because I have a girlfriend."

"I notice you didn't give that as your first reason."

"That doesn't mean it's any less important."

She gives me the slightest of smiles and I find myself staring at her lips and I can't help but wonder what it would be like to kiss her.

That's one of the problems with being a man. We're total idiots.

"Working together wouldn't be a problem for me. And I'm not looking for anything serious, so you don't have to worry about any awkward phone calls or text messages or messy entanglements," says Chloe. "Oh, and did you just refer to your girlfriend as *it*?"

Before I can respond, Vincent returns with two beers, one for him and one for Chloe, and she starts talking with him as if our conversation never took place. She's smiling and laughing, a stray hand reaching out and touching Vincent once, then a second time, her eyes never leaving him to dart over to see how I'm reacting.

Moments later, Emily returns from the bathroom, followed by Neil, who pretends to be amused by the joke Chloe played on him about signing him up for karaoke, then he tells Chloe that she should really wash her hands after having held the microphone, which more than a dozen people have touched since we've been here. Chloe ignores his suggestion, continuing to flirt with Vincent as Kurt arrives with the hot brunette who needs a fire extinguisher. He slaps me on the back and asks me if I'm ready for a big night, then introduces the brunette to the table as Ashley.

Before we have a chance to all shake hands, which launches Neil into another helpful tip about transferring germs, "Desperado" is done and Angela is at the microphone launching into Billie Holiday's "Me, Myself, and I."

We all turn our attention to the stage and applaud and let out a few shouts of encouragement. Occasionally I glance at Chloe to see if I catch her looking my way, but her attention is on Angela and Vincent and something Emily says. Anywhere but on me.

And I wonder if I imagined our entire conversation.

CHAPTER **19**

I don't remember the last time I had sex as myself.

You'd think you'd be able to remember something like that, but I've had sex as so many different people that I've actually forgotten what it's like to feel myself behind the overwhelming desire to fulfill my carnal lust.

Is it role-playing if you think you're someone else?

Right now I'm Indiana Jones, complete with felt fedora and trusty whip, standing at the edge of the California king with my pants around my ankles and Mary Magdalene naked on her hands and knees begging me to find the Holy Grail.

I never said I expected to go to heaven.

It's not like Delilah and I planned this out. I never would have picked Indiana and Mary to be compatible sex partners, but sometimes the most unlikely of combinations proves to be the most interesting.

The way this works is that one of us picks who they want to be first, and then the other one gets to choose. The idea is to challenge your partner to pick someone who has some sort of connection, the more ambiguous or bizarre the better. Kind of like playing the Six Degrees of Kevin Bacon, only we're looking for a game of connected sexual partners.

Since I have access to the complete line of Big Egos, the possibilities are endlessly erotic.

Elvis Presley and Marilyn Monroe.

Captain Kirk and Ellen Ripley.

Pablo Picasso and Jessica Rabbit.

But tonight we played Russian roulette, picking random identities and seeing what came up, though the way things turned out, it seems like our subconscious had a hand in the decision-making.

Freud said that the id is the dark, inaccessible part of our personality. A chaos. A cauldron full of seething excitations, striving to bring about the satisfaction of instinctual needs.

Truth is, we're just a slave to our instincts.

Men are genetically hardwired to have sex with as many different women as possible. Spread our seed. Ensure the propagation of our DNA. We're like the rhesus monkeys in that experiment where they put a male monkey in a cage with a female monkey and then let them go at it until the male monkey rolls over and starts snoring. Then they take out the female monkey and replace her with another female monkey. She taps the male on the shoulder and says, "Hi handsome." He perks up and says "Hey, you're new." And they go at it until he once more grows bored with her company. Then she gets replaced.

It goes on like this for hours, a revolving door of female monkeys.

Switch. Fuck. Repeat.

It's a regular primate porno.

Human men aren't much different. Given the opportunity and a free pass from consequences or complications, we'd have sex with as many women as possible. Marriage is an unnatural hindrance to our intended purpose.

So we cheat.

We watch Internet porn.

We pretend to be burglars or deliverymen or HDTV repairmen in order to spice things up in the bedroom. To keep the flame of passion from burning out. To maintain the façade of monogamy behind the personas we've adopted.

Sometimes we even inject the persona of an iconic film series character into our brain and have sex with a misunderstood biblical figure.

Mary glances back over her shoulder, her eyes half closed, and tells me she's about to ascend to heaven.

I consider telling her that I've already ascended without her, but I don't want to break the mood. So instead I think about ancient civilizations and priceless artifacts and getting chased by Nazis and that seems to do the trick.

When you've been having sex as someone else for as long as I have, you learn a few tricks, not the least of which is how to maintain some stamina.

Taking deep breaths.

Focusing on your sexual awareness.

Contracting your pubococcygeus muscle.

Problem is, when you're having sex with someone famous

or new or taboo, you tend to lose yourself in the experience. You forget everything you've learned and you just let go. You surrender to the pleasure. You lose yourself in the identity of someone else.

Antony and Cleopatra. Superman and Lois Lane. Ken and Barbie.

Sometimes I wonder if I know what I'm doing. If I'm still me. If I'm in control of this or if it's in control of me. But then I realize that I'm the one wondering about this, not Indiana Jones or Harrison Ford. These are *my* thoughts, *my* underlying current of reason that still exists. And I breathe a sigh of relief.

It's good to know I'm still in here somewhere.

But at the moment, I'm channeling my inner seeker of lost artifacts.

So I continue to bang away with Mary Magdalene, doing it doggie style with the alleged wife of Jesus, or at least his girlfriend, possibly one of his apostles, thinking about Judas and that blond German bitch from *The Last Crusade,* and I can't help but wonder if Mary is a Nazi spy.

CHAPTER **20**

I'm wearing an oversized, hunter green, Italian two-piece suit, which looks rain forest lush against my white collared shirt. A two-inch-wide coordinating tie nearly finishes off the ensemble until I bring my irises in line with colored contacts.

Tonight, green is my favorite color.

The clock on the wall indicates I'm approaching fashionably late. From a safe behind an original John Lennon drawing, I remove a small plastic vial filled with a fine white powder. After sliding the vial into my inside jacket pocket, I'm out the door and sitting behind the wheel of my 1962 Aston Martin on the way to an exclusive party in the Hollywood Hills.

"Thunderball" by Tom Jones pumps out of my stereo speakers as I pull out of my garage. Carly Simon sings "Nobody Does It Better" while I make my way up Laurel Canyon. Paul McCartney belts out "Live and Let Die" as I wind my way along Mulholland Drive.

There's nothing like having your own personal soundtrack to get you in the mood.

The entire time, I keep checking my rearview mirror to make sure I'm not being followed by any members of SPECTRE. You never know where Ernst Blofeld and his white Persian cat will show up.

After an all-too-brief drive, I arrive at my destination—a three-story sprawling monstrosity off Mulholland Drive with a 180-degree view of the San Fernando Valley. An eight-person gondola runs on a set of cables from the house to the automobile courtyard. I can tell the character of this particular gathering by the number of Bentleys and Rolls-Royces, though I spot a Porsche 911 and a 1957 Corvette, so not everyone will be pretentious.

I greet the valet with a nod and a Franklin, give him the keys to my car, then I step into the gondola. As the car lifts off and begins its climb toward the house, I case the grounds, looking for potential danger and alternate routes of escape, scanning for any sign of Hugo Drax, Dr. No, or Auric Goldfinger. And Oddjob. I hate that guy.

A few minutes later the butler lets me in the front door. A freshly groomed shih tzu with a purple bow on its head gives me the third degree, barking several times in an annoying, high-pitched yap before running off huffing and puffing. I watch the obnoxious, beady-eyed, walking throw rug disappear into the main room and wonder why anyone would choose a shih tzu over a Great Dane or an Old English mastiff. I guess some people lack the skills to own a real dog.

Morticia Addams appears in a black, form-fitting gothic dress with a hobble skirt and greets me with an alluring smile and a lingering handshake as she plants a kiss on my right cheek.

"Darling," she says. "So glad you could join us. Do come in."

Morticia leads me by the arm into the main room, which is large enough to accommodate one hundred people, though only forty-five, including myself, are in attendance. Tables of food line two of the walls. A string quartet is crowded into a corner playing something that sounds like an old television theme song, while a full-service bar takes up half of a third wall. I glide over to the bar and ask for a vodka martini, shaken, not stirred. I also ask for a small dish of pimento olives.

Three men nearest me at the bar are throwing out one-liners and making fun of the other guests. The tall one is Johnny Carson. The other two are Groucho Marx and George Burns. A dozen feet from them, Betty Boop is flirting with Winston Churchill. John Candy has camped out in front of the spinach dip while two women, both Annie Hall, are having an argument. Albert Einstein is talking politics with Pablo Picasso while Sammy Davis Jr. and Frank Sinatra smoke cigars and share a laugh. Henry David Thoreau stands by himself off in the corner, watching everyone, taking notes.

Edgar Allan Poe, Martin Luther King Jr., Billie Holiday, Mr. Rogers, Harry Houdini, Princess Diana, Atticus Finch, Ronald Reagan—all are among the celebrities, writers, poets, politicians, musicians, artists, scholars, and fictional characters who have gathered here this evening.

My martini arrives with the dish of olives. I thank the bartender with a Jackson, spear an olive with a toothpick, and drop it into my glass, then return my attention to the room.

In the far corner, a yellow and blue macaw sits in a cage hanging from the ceiling. The macaw's round, black eyes follow

Jake La Motta and Judy Garland as they walk past the cage and approach the bar. La Motta, the De Niro version from Raging Bull, is dressed in a black suit with no tie while Judy is wearing a white, low-cut satin dress with thigh-high slits that make me wonder if she's wearing any underwear.

While La Motta orders a beer and a gin-and-tonic, Judy looks me up and down and smiles and asks if I'm the Wizard of Oz.

I tell her I can be anything she wants me to be.

La Motta steps up to me and gets in my face. "You got a problem, big shot?"

I shake my head and tell him my only problem is that I'm alone while he's with the most beautiful woman at the party.

"You got that right, tough guy," he says, then he takes his date by the elbow and leads her away. Judy gives me several coy looks when La Motta isn't watching and I know that in less than five minutes I could have her for breakfast, lunch, and dinner. I've always wanted to have sex with Judy Garland. But tonight, sexual pleasure is not on my agenda.

At least not until I find what I came here for.

A few more guests arrive—Mozart and Carrie Bradshaw, Jackie Robinson and Snow White—but as far as I can tell, all of them are upstanding citizens. But that doesn't mean one of them can't be a double agent.

For the next forty-five minutes I sip my martini, engage in brief conversations with more than half the guests while observing the others, order a second martini, and begin to wonder if I'm going to have any reason to use the vial in my pocket. Then I hear the doorbell, followed immediately by three rapid knocks. The door opens and I can hear the shih tzu yapping, followed by

Morticia Addams greeting the late arrival. After a brief flurry of apologies and laughter, the new guest joins the party.

When the woman walks into the room, forty-nine pair of eyes follows her—fifty-one if you count the shih tzu and the macaw. The woman staggers across the floor on three-inch heels, her unencumbered breasts bouncing around inside her low-cut blue satin blouse like a pair of overfilled water balloons. She brushes her hair out of her face with an abrupt wave of her hand, then smiles and grabs a glass of champagne from a passing tray. She has lipstick on her teeth. Her upper lip is twitching.

I watch her as she moves through the other guests like a shopping cart with a bad wheel, stumbling into Barney Stinson, who helps her to her feet and himself to a handful of her left breast. She laughs and continues toward the tables of food.

I finish my second martini and order two more. After tipping the bartender another Jackson, I ask him if he would mind finding me a cigar. As soon as he's gone, I spear a single olive with the toothpick from my mouth and drop the olive into one of the martinis, then I reach inside my jacket pocket and remove the small vial with the white powder, which I empty into the other martini while everyone else is distracted by the new arrival. I spear two more olives with a toothpick and stir them into the glass before I take both glasses and make my way across the room toward the woman who appears to be a flawed rendition of Marilyn Monroe. Or possibly Jayne Mansfield. It's hard to tell. But with the way her breasts are balancing in the confines of her dress and teetering on the precipice of a nipple slip, I'm guessing Jayne Mansfield.

Jayne attempts to scoop some of the smoked salmon onto

a cracker but the salmon keeps falling to the floor. Charlie Chaplin approaches and offers to hold her champagne while she gives the salmon another try. She downs the champagne, hands Chaplin her empty glass, and tells him she's still thirsty. He leaves in search of a refill, his hopes of an easy conquest evident in his brisk walk.

The instant Chaplin steps away I take his place. Jayne looks at me and snorts laughter. "Who are you? Gumby?"

I smile and shake my head, though I tell her some of my female acquaintances have affectionately called me Pokey.

She laughs again, this time without the snort, and notices the two martinis I'm holding.

"You planning on drinking both of those?" she asks.

Not without some help, I tell her.

She smiles. It's a nice smile, even with the twitching upper lip and the lipstick on her teeth. I hand her the glass in my right hand, the martini with the two olives, and take a sip of my own martini while she removes the olives, slides them off the toothpick with her teeth, then slugs down the martini and the olives in one gulp. She hands the glass back to me with the toothpick in it and asks if I would mind getting her another drink.

I tell her it would be my pleasure.

The moment I leave, Chaplin is back with two glasses of champagne, talking the woman up and shifting his gaze from her face to the constant motion of her breasts. They're nice breasts. You can tell they're real. But I'm a betting man and I'm betting Chaplin won't get the chance to discover what they look like inside her blue satin blouse.

I set Jayne's empty martini glass on the bar, where the bartender hands me a Monte Cristo. I finish my martini, thank the bartender for his company and tip him another Jackson, then I give my regards to Morticia Addams on my way out the front door. I consider going back and liberating Judy Garland from La Motta, but I don't want to make a scene. Besides, I have plenty of women I can call for a late-night rendezvous.

As the gondola glides slowly along the cables toward the automobile courtyard, I light up my cigar and wonder if Honey Ryder would like to saddle up. If Pussy Galore has any to spare. Whether Holly Goodhead needs some practice.

I wonder how much it would take to get Miss Moneypenny out of her clothes.

CHAPTER 21

"I'd like to get her out of her clothes," says Nat.

"Who?" I say.

"The bartender," he says, taking a drink of his beer and pointing to the bleached blond Asian woman serving drinks to the other members of the Bruin Democrats—the UCLA chapter of the College Democrats of America.

"Yeah," I say. "Good luck with that."

Where we are is the bar at Palomino in Westwood in late September 2016, celebrating our recent canvassing of the UCLA campus to register voters for the upcoming presidential election. We're all feeling good about our candidate's chances. Not to mention that we kicked the Bruin Republicans' asses in our annual co-ed ultimate Frisbee game.

That's what they get for trying to regulate and oversee morality.

I became a member of the Bruin Democrats at the end of my freshman year, when it became clear to me that a career as a professional soccer player didn't offer enough in the way of personal fulfillment. I needed to find a different role. Something that gave my life more meaning.

So when I came across a voter registration table at the South Campus Student Center two and a half years ago, I found myself drawn to the cute redhead with a ponytail and an alluring smile sitting behind the table.

We talked for more than half an hour about life and politics and the next thing I knew, I was joining the Bruin Democrats and dating the cute redhead, whose name was Monica Kaplan. Our relationship didn't last long. We broke up after a few weeks when I realized she was fiscally conservative and didn't believe in global warming.

Nat, who doesn't really have any political aspirations and only joined the Bruin Democrats because I did, takes another drink of his beer, then puts his arm around me and says, "I think I'm in love."

"We've gone over this," I say. "I'm hetero."

"Not with you, bro." Nat points to a pair of women standing near the other end of the bar wearing UCLA garb. They're not part of our group, but they're apparently from school. "With one of them."

The tall brunette with endless legs looks like a young Anne Hathaway, while the cute little blonde standing five feet and change reminds me of a shorter version of Taylor Swift.

They're both what you would call major-league gorgeous. We're talking all-star material. And both of them are well out of Nat's league. If this is baseball, the blonde and the brunette are starting for the New York Yankees while Nat's batting .200 in Single A.

"Which one?" I ask.

"Both of them. But the blonde keeps checking me out."

He's right. She does keep looking our way, but I'm getting the distinct impression that she's looking at me and not Nat.

"She's into me," says Nat, nodding and taking a drink of his beer. "I can tell."

Nat has bad vision at the plate. He also gets thrown out a lot trying to stretch an infield single into a double. A triple is a rarity. And he strikes out more often than he gets a hit.

"She's totally hot," he says. "I bet she's even hotter naked."

"Yeah. And I bet you'd get off before your pants did."

Problems with control and consistency are the most common reasons players like Nat get sent back down to Single A ball.

"You're not exactly helping," he says.

"Well, you're not exactly Casanova, you know."

Nat takes a drink of his beer. "Okay then, Romeo. Tell me what I should do."

I look over at the blonde, who is most definitely checking *me* out, and I give Nat the same advice my father always gave to me.

"Just be who she wants you to be."

"How do I know who she wants me to be?"

"I don't know. But most women want a guy with confidence. Someone who knows what he wants and who isn't afraid to go get it. So start with that."

"Okay. So I just need to walk up to her and let her know that I want her."

"You might want to go with a little more subtlety than that," I say. "Women like to be nuanced."

"I'm a guy. I don't understand subtlety and nuance."

Like that's news.

"And it helps if you can make them laugh," I say.

Nat takes a drink. "I think I've got that covered."

More than once over the years I've seen a girl or a woman laugh at Nat's advances, sometimes right in his face. Which doesn't help with his self-esteem.

"It's all about playing the part," I say. "Adopting a persona. Pretending to be the right man for the right time."

"Like Captain Kirk?"

Nat has always had a man-crush on William Shatner.

"Not exactly," I say. "But if that's what works for you, sure. Just don't pull out your cell phone and ask Scotty to beam you up."

Nat takes another drink, then wipes his mouth. "All right. Let's do this. Let's be the men we're supposed to be."

Spoken like a true romantic.

"But just to be clear," he says. "I get the blonde and you get the brunette."

"Sure thing."

Though I'm guessing he won't end up with either. And with Nat, when it comes to women, nothing is ever a sure thing.

"Hello, ladies," he says, coming across as both desperate and drunk at the same time. It's a rare talent but one Nat has managed to cultivate over the years.

The brunette gives a forced smile and turns to the blonde. "I have to go to the bathroom."

Which is woman-speak for *I'm not interested in these losers.*

As the brunette walks off, the blonde smiles at me. "So are you two boys part of the Young Liberals?"

Her voice comes out smooth and lyrical, with a soft southern lilt.

I love a southern accent on a woman.

"Bruin Democrats," I say.

"You interested in joining?" says Nat, looking at her like an excited dog. If he had a tail, it would be wagging.

She finishes off her drink and shakes her head. "I don't believe in political parties. They're like organized religion. Eventually, everyone just ends up believing they're right and everyone else is wrong. I don't really see the point."

"The point is to get involved in something that's bigger than you," I say. "Do something to try to make a difference. Focus on the present and do your part to change the world."

She smiles and opens her mouth to say something but before she can, Nat points at her empty glass. "Hey, you're low on fuel. Can I get you another?"

"Sure thing, sugar." She hands him her glass. "Screwdriver. Grey Goose."

"Coming up," he says. "Don't go anywhere. I'll be right back."

After Nat heads off to the bar, the blonde turns to me. "So do you really want to make a difference? Change the world? Or is that just a line you use to try to get laid?"

"Are you talking about now or in general?"

She tilts her head and smiles. "I guess that depends on how focused you are on the present."

I glance past her to where Nat stands at the bar and I wonder how he's going to react when he realizes he's been benched for a pinch hitter. Not like this is the first time that's happened, but it's always kind of awkward when I bring her home.

When I look back at the blonde she's looking up at me, waiting for my response.

"You must live in the present," I say. "Launch yourself on every wave, find your eternity in each moment."

"That's lovely," she says, her voice as intoxicating as any drug. "Did you just make that up?"

I shake my head. "I borrowed it from Thoreau."

"Is he an actor?"

I smile. "Close enough."

She smiles back at me and holds out her hand. "By the way, I'm Delilah."

CHAPTER **22**

I'm sitting at my desk in my office at work the day after Halloween, staring at the headline on my computer for an article on CNN.com:

Another Los Angeles–Area Death Connected
to Black Market Egos

I'm not sure how long I've been gazing at my computer, but it's noon already and I have no idea what happened to the last hour. All I know is that I'm having trouble focusing on the text, which is giving me a headache. The words keep blending together, so I hit the video report and listen to the news anchorman explain what happened.

"According to a friend, the deceased had recently purchased a black market Ego in the Los Feliz area and had bought Egos from the same dealer several times before without incident. Police have taken the suspected dealer into custody. His name has not been released."

On the video over the anchor's left shoulder is a photo of a blond woman who looks vaguely like someone I've met. But then, in Hollywood, a lot of blond women look familiar.

"The woman, Abigail Parsons, died after suffering what appears to have been a massive brain aneurysm after attending an Ego party in the Hollywood Hills. She was found this morning dead in her car, a tragic irony considering that she'd attended the party as Jayne Mansfield."

The news anchor keeps talking but all I can see is me dressed in my dark green suit while holding two martinis, one of which I give to a woman who looks like . . .

Who are you? Gumby?

Part of me wants to believe it was just a dream and that this is just some bizarre coincidence—that my memory didn't really happen. But another part of me knows I was at that party with her.

The anchor goes on to say that this is one of more than three dozen confirmed Ego-related deaths to occur in the Los Angeles area in the last few months, fueling rising concerns about the safety of black market Egos. Bill Summers, a spokesman for EGOS, is quoted as saying: "This senseless tragedy is another indication that amateurs should not be meddling with science and selling inferior merchandise that hasn't been produced under controlled conditions and undergone the rigorous standards and testing that ensures a safe and reliable product."

He goes on to say that EGOS stands by its product and

invites anyone with questions or concerns to contact the company and speak with an authorized agent.

Then someone's talking about the cost and popularity of Big Egos and how the recent deaths associated with the black market versions could have a positive impact on sales of authorized Egos. The report ends with the news anchor mentioning that the police are continuing to crack down on the sale of black market Egos in the Los Angeles area.

I sit and stare at the computer monitor, thinking about the three dozen deaths the reporter mentioned, then I close my eyes. I see Jayne Mansfield and David Cassidy and Ace Ventura and more than a dozen other celebrities and fictional characters I've met over the past several months. I'm hoping all of them are okay and that Jayne Mansfield just died from a defective black market Ego and that I didn't have anything to do with it—except I'm not doing a very good job of convincing myself.

Could there be something wrong with the antidote? Could I have killed her? Or any of the others? Are they all dead? Is it possible I've been poisoning people all this time?

". . . something's wrong."

When I open my eyes, Vincent is standing in my doorway. At first I think I was talking out loud and he knows about Jayne Mansfield and the antidote and my fears that I might have killed a dozen or more people, but from the concerned expression on his face I get the feeling there's something else going on and that I missed the first part of what he said.

"What?" I say.

"Chloe," he says. "I think there's something wrong with her."

"Wrong?"

Vincent's look of concern is now directed at me. "Are you okay?"

I look back at the news story about Jayne Mansfield and I wonder if Applied Research knows anything about this.

"Yeah," I say.

I'm aware that I'm giving single-word, monosyllabic responses and struggling to form a sentence that contains a predicate and a verb. I close my eyes and shake my head, which I realize probably looks incongruous to the answer I just gave to Vincent. When I open my eyes, he's still standing in my doorway wearing his concerned expression. And I'm suddenly aware that his expression is contagious.

"Chloe?" I say, standing up. "What's wrong with her?"

I'm still more than a little freaked out about the news story, but at least I'm speaking in complete sentences.

"It's hard to say," says Vincent.

"What's she doing?"

"Nothing. She's just sitting there, staring at her desk, making these weird sounds."

I walk past Vincent and out of my office. "What kind of sounds?"

"Kind of like a pigeon or a dove," he says, right on my heels. "Or maybe an owl. Except that's not exactly it, either. It's more like . . ."

Even before I reach Chloe I can hear her cooing, soft and low. Then she stops for several seconds before starting up again. *Coo, coo, coo.* It's almost rhythmic. Except the closer

I get, the less it sounds like cooing and the more it sounds like . . .

"Whooping," says Vincent. "She's whooping."

Other than Chloe the office is quiet. Emily and Angela went out for lunch, Neil called in sick, and I don't know where Kurt is.

"Where's Kurt?" I ask.

"He's in Hawaii," says Vincent. "On vacation."

Vacation? When did Kurt go on vacation?

"Right," I say, figuring this is something I should probably remember, considering I'm the one who would have approved his time off.

Just add it to my growing list of What the Fuck.

When we reach Chloe's workstation she's sitting there with her back to us, staring at her desk, not moving, slightly slouched in her chair, head angled down, hands limp in her lap. I don't have to see her face to know something's wrong. Before I have a chance to say anything, her body moves ever so slightly, her shoulders shifting forward as she makes her strange call.

"Whoop, whoop, whoop."

"Chloe?" I walk up behind her. "Chloe, are you all right?"

No response. She doesn't turn around or acknowledge my presence. Not even when I reach out to touch her. It's like I'm not even there.

"Chloe?"

I wave my hand in front of her face, poke her in the shoulder. For a moment I think she's lost consciousness. And then:

"Whoop, whoop, whoop."

"Spotted hyenas sound like that, too," says Vincent.

I turn to look at him.

"And Bigfoot," he says. "I heard an audio clip on the Internet. They make the same sound."

"Whoop, whoop, whoop."

I kneel down next to Chloe, who remains focused on her desk. Her eyes are open and unresponsive, her hair hanging down across her face. Spit dribbles out of the corner of her mouth and pools in a wet spot on her shirt just above her right breast.

Somehow I don't think we'll be discussing Thoreau or Chaucer or Dante today.

"Chloe," I say. "Hey Chloe, can you hear me?"

Nothing. Just a blank stare, drool, and that same, incessant cry.

"Whoop, whoop, whoop."

I brush the hair back from her face and wipe the drool from her mouth, looking in her eyes for any sign that she's in there somewhere. I think about that night at the Blue Goose a couple of weeks ago, how she sat there with her chin propped in her hand and asked me if I wanted to have an affair. I remember the playful expression on her face, the wicked little smile, her eyes filled with mischief.

But there's nothing in her eyes now. Chloe is gone. Chloe is on vacation. Chloe doesn't live here anymore.

I stand up and walk over to Vincent. "How long . . ."

"Whoop, whoop, whoop."

". . . has she been like this?"

"I don't know. Maybe ten, fifteen minutes. At first I thought she was talking to herself or singing along to a song or something so I didn't really give it much thought. Then I noticed she kept saying the same thing over and over. So I stopped what I was doing and started listening. That's when I came over to look at her and found her like this."

I look back at Chloe, sitting there nearly catatonic, and I'm thinking about the anomaly Angela mentioned and wondering if this is somehow related.

"Call medical," I say. "Tell them to get down here now."

Vincent nods and picks up the phone. A moment later Chloe's nose starts bleeding, like someone flipped a switch and opened up a valve. But she doesn't notice.

"Whoop, whoop, whoop."

CHAPTER 23

Angela, Emily, Vincent, and I sit in the meeting room, the rest of the office empty except for Neil. I can hear him opening and closing his drawers, adjusting his chair, moving things around on his desk. He does this every night before he leaves. It's one of his compulsive routines. And I have to admit, it's got a nice beat. Kind of an OCD lullaby. The Obsessive-Compulsive Orchestra's Greatest Hits.

Open, close. Open, close. Shuffle, shuffle, slap.

Angela sits across from me, her hands on the table, twisting and grabbing each other, holding and clenching like a couple of wrestlers. I don't know if she's aware of what she's doing, but it's making me nervous just watching her. Next to her, Vincent flips through an old copy of *Wired* and appears much more relaxed, though I'm guessing it's just a front. At the far end of the table, Emily picks silently at her carcass of a Cinnabon.

Kurt, who is on vacation, is the only team member not in attendance. The rest of us are all waiting on Neil to finish his end-of-the-day ritual. Chloe, of course, is the reason we're all here.

"Do you know how she's doing?" asks Angela.

I shake my head. "The last I heard, she was being transferred to Metropolitan."

That would be the state mental hospital in Norwalk, about fifteen miles southeast of Los Angeles.

"Jesus," says Vincent.

Personally, I don't think Jesus had anything to do with what happened to Chloe. But then, my lack of faith in a higher power is part of the reason I'm sitting here. You can't do what we do and expect to sit in church on Sunday without feeling a little out of place. While we're not exactly cooking in God's kitchen, we're definitely making up some new recipes.

Angela takes a slow, quiet breath and starts chewing on her lower lip as her hands continue their wrestling match. Out in the office, Neil continues to serenade us with his obsessive-compulsive symphony.

Open, close. Open, close. Shuffle, shuffle, slap.

I'd yell for Neil to hurry up, but he has to go through his routine or he gets cranky. Plus I don't want to distract him and make him lose track and have him start all over.

"Did HR have anything more to say?" asks Angela.

Although a team from corporate came to discuss the incident and remind us about the availability of in-house counseling for anyone who wanted to talk to a therapist, they didn't shed any light on what actually happened to

Chloe other than to say we didn't have anything to worry about. So I met with Human Resources to see what they could tell me.

"Not much," I say. "They told me they couldn't release any personal information about Chloe because I wasn't family. But they assured me that whatever happened to her had nothing to do with her use of Big Egos."

"So they're saying she was using black market Egos?" says Vincent.

"That's the implication," I say.

"Do you believe them?" asks Angela.

"I don't know," I say. "Did anyone ever have any inclination that Chloe might have been buying off the black market?"

I'm answered with shrugs and shaking heads.

Chloe had been working with us for less than six months, so none of us knew her that well. Whatever secrets she had, she took them with her to Metropolitan. And what happened with her isn't leaving this building.

We're all under a legal gag order not to talk about what happened to Chloe outside of the company. Not to friends. Not to family. And definitely not to the press. It's part of the nondisclosure agreement we all signed when we started working here.

"What about the anomalies?" says Angela. "Did that come up in conversation?"

"No," I say, shaking my head.

"What anomalies?" says Vincent.

"We found them in the Icons," says Angela. "People who've injected certain fictional characters over a period of three years have shown a tendency toward a couple of repetitive behaviors."

"What kind of behaviors?" asks Emily.

"Seeing zeros or having them come up in conversation," says Angela. "And repeating some specific or unusual phrase."

"What? You mean like *super-duper* or *I like peanut butter*?" says Vincent.

"It varies from customer to customer," says Angela. "It's unique to each person, but it's there. The data confirms it."

Out in the office, I can still hear Neil doing his thing. I look at my watch and see that it's 5:05. Sure there's a zero with the other two numbers adding up to ten, a one and another zero, but it probably doesn't mean anything.

Truth is, it's just a number.

"Do you think what happened to Chloe is related to these anomalies?" asks Emily.

"I don't know," says Angela. "I suppose it's possible. Though Applied Research doesn't think there's anything to be concerned about."

"Well, that makes me feel better," says Vincent.

Sarcasm noted.

"Can we access Chloe's records to determine how often she used the Egos she took home?" asks Emily.

"Her records are confidential," I say. "But she didn't work here long enough to be exposed to as many Egos as the rest of us. And we're all fine."

I look around the table at everyone, but instead of looks of confidence, I see expressions of doubt. I can't blame them. I'm still trying to come to terms with the idea that I might be a serial killer.

"So maybe she did use black market Egos," says Vincent.

"Maybe," says Angela. Her head shakes once, not much more than a twitch. An involuntary movement. I watch her, looking for signs that it might be something more significant. But then she goes back to the wrestling match between her hands as she continues to chew her lower lip.

We sit there in silence for several moments, the last of the daylight having succumbed to an early November dusk as Neil continues his end-of-the-day ritual.

Open, close. Open, close. Shuffle, shuffle, slap.

Is it just me, or is he taking longer than usual?

"So what do we do now?" says Emily.

"About Chloe?" I say.

"Actually," says Emily, "I was thinking more about us."

I glance at Vincent, who nods in agreement. Next to him, Angela chews on her lower lip. Past her, I can see Chloe's workstation, which seems emptier than the others. Almost as if it's haunted.

I can still see Chloe's blank stare and the drool pooling on her shirt and hear her strange, incessant call.

Whoop, whoop, whoop.

"I think I'm going to stop using for a while," says Vincent.

The way he says it makes it sound like he's a drug addict and this is a Narcotics Anonymous meeting and we're all trying to get clean.

Maybe that's not so far from the truth.

"Me too," says Emily. "At least until I know what's going on."

I don't know about Vincent and Emily, but I don't think

giving up this lifestyle is going to be all that easy. Not when you've been doing it for the past three years. Not when sampling and testing Egos is part of your job description. Not when you've been going undercover two to three nights a week for the past few months to help eradicate black market Egos, only to discover you may have been killing people instead.

I tried to get a meeting with Bill Summers to share my concerns about the antidote, but he's out of town on business and won't be back until next week. So for now, I'm just going to try to think happy thoughts and avoid any more Ego parties until I've cleared this up with him.

The burgeoning autumn night presses against the windows, the air thick with doubt and concern and the weight of Chloe's absence as Neil's OCD allegro comes to an end. Moments later he emerges from his workstation and walks toward the meeting room, dressed all in navy blue, looking sharp and polished in a three-piece suit and tie. Maybe it's just my current state of mind, the way my thoughts keep coming back to all of these black market Ego deaths and the role I may have played in them, but he looks like a police officer.

CHAPTER **24**

There's a police officer at the front door.

He's talking to my mother, who's standing in her bathrobe, holding it closed with one hand, her other hand holding on to the door—her hair disheveled and her feet bare on the tiled floor. Red and blue lights flash in the darkness behind the open door and through the windows.

Nobody notices me.

I'm eight years old and standing down the hall where it makes an L shape, peeking around the corner outside of my bedroom, dressed in my favorite pajamas with the monkeys on them. The ones I received for Christmas the year I found out Santa Claus was a hoax.

Not that I'm bitter or anything.

I watch my mother with the policeman and I notice the way her head is shaking back and forth like she's disagreeing with whatever he's telling her and how she looks like at any moment she might fall down. I notice the officer's badge and his belt and his gun and how they all look so shiny and perfect and clean, like his uniform. He seems solid standing there, in control, projecting a sense of authority, a sense of order. Except when I look at the officer's face, he looks like Alex Trebek, only he's a lot shorter than he looks on television and this isn't a game show.

I'll take Confused Children for two hundred, Alex.

The police officer continues to talk to my mother, who looks at him with an expression of confusion and disbelief, like she doesn't believe he's real, either.

And then my mother starts to cry.

I'll take What the Hell Is Going On for six hundred, Alex.

I don't know why he's here. Or what he's saying. Or why my mother's crying. All I know is it's after one in the morning and I'm standing outside my bedroom wondering why it isn't my father at the front door talking to the police officer.

He was supposed to get home tonight from his business trip to Seattle, in time for my ninth birthday. He missed my last birthday. And the one before that. But he promised he'd be back in time this year. He also promised he'd bring me a gift from Seattle.

I walk down to the end of the hall and look into my parents' bedroom to see if my father is there. The bedside lamp is on, illuminating a corner of the room, and the covers are pulled back from my mother's side of the bed, the green digital numbers of the alarm clock on the night stand glowing 1:27. My father's side of the bed hasn't been slept in. The bathroom door stands open, the bathroom dark and empty.

I go into the bathroom and turn on the light. Behind the frosted glass of the shower door, I see a shape and I think it's my father hiding in the shower, playing some kind of game, maybe hide-and-seek. Except my father doesn't play games. When I open the shower, what I thought was my father is just a bath towel hanging on the shower caddy.

I walk out of my parents' room and glance back down the hallway at Alex Trebek consoling my mother, who is shaking her head and saying "No" over and over as if she's just learned a new word. A few moments later, she collapses to the floor, her bathrobe falling open, revealing the night-gown she's wearing beneath.

"Mom?"

She doesn't hear me, but Alex Trebek does. He looks up and sees me standing down the hallway. He doesn't say anything but just nods once, his expression serious, then he turns his attention back to my mother.

I want to go to her, to hug her and make her stop crying, to ask her where my father is and why Alex Trebek is at our house after one on a Tuesday morning. Instead, I just stand in the hallway and watch my mother as she continues to cry.

CHAPTER **25**

Delilah stands in front of me in a red thong and a red bra. I can see the little scar on her left hip and the mole just beneath her left breast. I can also see the outline of her nipples and her labia, but I'm not interested in exploring her anatomy at the moment.

Right now, I'm more interested in watching the news and searching the Internet, trying to determine if any black market Ego deaths have occurred since I stopped going to parties and giving out the antidote.

"Are we going out tonight?" says Delilah.

I'm on the leather couch trying to watch the TV through my 3-D glasses and Delilah's mostly naked figure. It's not easy to do, even considering that she's only a hundred and twenty pounds wearing chain mail.

And don't think we haven't played Sir Lancelot and Guinevere before.

"I have work to do." I shift to my right so I can see the television. On MSNBC is a news conference with the CEO and the executive vice president of EGOS.

"Work?" says Delilah.

"Work," I say, turning up the volume.

The CEO is saying that the recent tragedies involving black market Egos should be a reminder to everyone that you can't cut corners when it comes to personal safety. I tap my glasses and change the channel to CNN, where they're talking about how the recent deaths might have a positive impact on the holiday sales of legally manufactured Egos.

Delilah takes the 3-D glasses off my face and tosses them on the couch. "You've been coming home late a lot lately."

"I can't help it," I say.

"You can't help it?"

"It's part of the job."

"It's part of the job?"

Either Delilah has echolalia or she's beginning to lose her hearing.

I make a move to retrieve the 3-D glasses but Delilah pushes them farther away, out of my reach. I look up at her standing there in her red underwear, staring at me. If she's waiting for an answer, I already gave her one.

"You've been acting different lately," she says.

"I've been acting different?"

"Are you seeing someone?"

"Am I seeing someone?"

Great. Now I'm doing it.

She stares at me, her arms folded beneath her breasts, making them look fuller than normal.

While I've always appreciated the way Delilah looks, both in her underwear and out of it, even when she's au naturel, she's not really. In addition to her breast implants, she colors her hair, whitens her teeth, has had a nose job, and gets regular collagen injections to make her lips fuller. So there's nothing really naturel about her.

I've traded my mother's fake meals for my girlfriend's fake body.

"No," I say. "I'm not seeing anyone."

"So where is it you've been going at night?" she asks.

"I told you. It's work-related."

"Related how?"

"Related in that it has to do with work." I get up off the couch and walk into the kitchen to get myself a beer.

"Meaning what?"

"Meaning I can't tell you," I say, opening the refrigerator.

"You can't or you won't?"

"There's not really any difference."

"There is to me."

"It's classified," I say, pulling out a Guinness.

"Classified? You're not a secret agent, you know. Not in real life."

I look at the unopened beer in my hand and I'm suddenly getting a James Bond vibe. For a few seconds I feel him moving around inside my head, taking charge, filling me with a sense of invincibility. Then he's gone.

The Taoist philosopher Lao Tzu said to be content to simply be yourself. But sometimes I'm not sure who I am anymore. What I'm supposed to be. The role I was meant to play. And when you have unlimited access to a product that allows you to be a famous person or a fictional character and you're used to playing those roles as many as five nights a week, it becomes harder and harder to be yourself.

The problem with pretending to be someone else is that eventually you start to forget who you were in the first place.

I put the beer back in the refrigerator. "I think I'd rather have a martini."

"A martini?" says Delilah. "How can that be your response?"

"Response to what?" I grab the jar of olives and set it on the counter. "I didn't realize you'd asked a question."

"It's the same question I've been asking you for the past few minutes."

"Which is?" I set the bottles of Grey Goose vodka and Boissiere vermouth on the counter next to the olives.

"Why have you been spending so much extra time working?"

"I told you." I pull out a martini glass. "It's none of your business."

Delilah grabs the martini glass and throws it against the wall, where it explodes like a fireworks display. Then she stands there, staring at me, her fists clenched, her breasts rising up and down with her breathing, her nipples hard, her skin flushed, her eyes staring at me, full and unblinking, daring me to retaliate.

I walk up to her, grab her hair by the back of her head, and look into her eyes. At this point I've forgotten about my martini. But I'm definitely getting that James Bond vibe again.

I kiss her, my lips pressing roughly against hers, and she

kisses back, our mouths open and our tongues searching. I reach behind her with my other hand and unhook her bra in one fluid motion and then my hand is under her bra and cupping her breast, flicking her nipple and then pinching it. She gasps and kisses me harder and presses up against me, pulling at my pants, unbuttoning and unzipping them, her hand reaching inside my boxers and grabbing hold of me.

I let go of the back of her head and reach down to slide my hand inside the waistband of her thong. She beats me to it and peels off her underwear. At the same time, I drop my pants and boxers and then I'm grabbing her and lifting her up and her arms are wrapping around my neck, her legs wrapping around my waist. I slide inside of her and she lets out something that's between a gasp and a moan and I do the same. Then I'm walking out of the kitchen and into the living room, wearing Delilah like a redheaded bulletproof vest, my hands holding on to her ass, pulling her thighs farther apart as I sit down on the couch.

Next thing I know Delilah's beneath me, her legs and arms still wrapped around me and her lips brushing against my ear, her breath coming out in rapid exhalations and encouragements. I thrust harder, our tempo building, our bodies entwined and locked and moving together, grinding and rotating, slick with sweat.

"Who do you want me to be this time?" she whispers, biting my ear, her fingernails digging into my back.

While I've always enjoyed having sex with Delilah in all of her role-playing and her different Ego incarnations, right now I want her just the way she is.

But even when she's being herself, I'm not sure what role I'm going to get. Sometimes I get the quiet introvert. Sometimes I get the outspoken socialite. Sometimes I get the brooding teenager. But it's never the same from one night to the next. And more often than not, whoever she ends up pretending to be follows me into the bedroom.

I guess that's what I get for getting involved with an actress.

Sometimes I wonder how much of what I like about Delilah is her and how much is just an act. Sometimes I'm not sure where she ends and the fantasy begins.

When I look down at her, she's not Delilah but Ann-Margret. I blink and she's Scarlett O'Hara. I blink again and she's Jessica Rabbit.

I don't want her to be any of these other women. I just want her to be Delilah. But all I see when I look at her is someone else. So I close my eyes and I bury my head in the crook of her neck.

She smells like cinnamon.

CHAPTER **26**

The smell of cinnamon drifts down the hallway into my bedroom.

"Honey!" my mom calls. "Come and get it!"

"Be right there!"

I finish cleaning my room, putting away my toys and my dirty clothes, then I stop in front of the mirror and I look at myself. I'm ten years old. I can tell because I don't have the faint scar above my left eye from the time I rode into a ditch and flew over the handles of my bike and cut my forehead open, which happened in August before sixth grade, just a couple of days after I turned eleven. Nat was there. Panicked, of course. Screaming for help even though we were out in the middle of the Sepulveda Dam Recreation Area and the only ones listening were a pair of crows picking at the carcass of an unfortunate jackrabbit.

Some memories are more detailed than others.

I didn't panic. Not even with blood pouring from my forehead and turning my L.A. Dodgers T-shirt into an impromptu Rorschach test.

It looks like two Charlie Sheens high-fiving each other around a vagina.

But that's another memory for another time.

Right now, I'm a ten-year-old boy in my ten-year-old room with my ten-year-old thoughts, no Charlie Sheens or vaginas in sight.

"Come on out when you're done, honey," my mother calls from down the hall. "We've got a big day ahead of us."

I walk out of my room, a sense of excitement building inside me as I wonder what the big day is my mother has planned. But along with the anticipation is an underlying apprehension. I don't remember any big days with my mom, especially after my ninth birthday. But I'm hoping maybe I just forgot this memory. I'm hoping we're going to Disneyland or Magic Mountain or even the Santa Monica Pier.

Except I don't want to get my hopes up, in part because I don't want to be disappointed, but mostly because this memory feels wrong. Fake. No, not fake, exactly. More like forced. As if this is the way I wish things would have been between my mother and me rather than the way they really were—my subconscious filtering my memories through the proverbial rose-colored lens. But I'm willing to go along with it to see what happens.

My mother is in the kitchen humming a familiar tune, something by the Beach Boys or maybe the Four Seasons. I can almost make it out but then the melody changes, blending into another song, like "The Age of Aquarius" and "Let the Sunshine In," only my mom was never a big fan of the Fifth Dimension.

When I walk into the kitchen, I find my mother wearing a white sundress and a red apron, her hair pulled up in a bun as she uses a teaspoon to scoop cookie batter out of a mixing bowl and onto a plate, where she rolls the ball of dough in a mixture of cinnamon and sugar before placing the infant snickerdoodle on a cookie sheet with its siblings. Then she places the cookie sheet into the oven before she removes another cookie sheet covered with freshly baked snickerdoodles.

I see a bag of sugar and a carton of eggs and a bottle of cinnamon on the counter. When my mother turns to look at me, she smiles and I see a wisp of flour across her forehead and I know something's off.

My mother never baked cookies from scratch. She never made *anything* from scratch. Even her lemonade was made from frozen juice concentrate. And the only cookies she ever baked came from a Pillsbury slice-and-bake cookie dough roll.

So this most definitely is not my mother.

"Well there you are." She gives me a big smile before turning back to her cookies. "How's my little man?"

"I'm fine." I sit down at the kitchen table. Except I'm not fine. And I realize I'm not so little anymore.

I'm older. Maybe nineteen. And I'm naked. I don't know what happened to my clothes or how I've suddenly become a young man, but I'm more disconcerted about being naked in front of my mother than I am about the fact that I've aged nearly a decade. I look around for something to cover myself with, an apron or a place mat or a hand towel, but the only thing I can find handy is an oven mitt.

My mother stands in front of the oven, transferring the hot cookies onto a plate, her back to me, oblivious to my current condition. I'm about to get up and run out of the kitchen to find something to wear when my mother turns around with a plate of snickerdoodles in her hands.

Only she's not my mother. She's Ann-Margret. Not *Grumpy Old Men* Ann-Margret but *Carnal Knowledge* Ann-Margret. Thirty years young, seductive, in full, busty bloom, not-wearing-a-bra Ann-Margret.

"Would you like a cookie?" she says.

"Um . . ." I look from the tray of fresh-baked snickerdoodles to Ann-Margret's breasts as I sit trapped naked in my chair, holding the oven mitt over my penis—which fortunately remains disinterested. "Um . . ."

"Go ahead." She offers the plate of cookies to me, holding it right in front of her breasts. "Grab a handful."

She doesn't seem to notice that I'm nineteen. Or that I'm naked. Or maybe she does, which might explain the wry smile on her lips. It's all a little much for me to process.

My mother is Ann-Margret.

Ann-Margret is my mother.

The last thing I need is an Oedipal moment.

She stands there smiling, still bending toward me, her cleavage the backdrop to the plate of snickerdoodles, and I'm wondering if I'm really me or if I'm someone else.

"Go ahead," she says, as I look past the plate of cookies and down the top of her white sundress to her nipples. "They're delicious."

I reach out and grab a snickerdoodle and take a bite, chewing it slowly as Ann-Margret morphs back into my mother, who graces me with a smile. I'm ten years old again and fully clothed. And there's not an exposed nipple in sight.

My mother sets the plate of cookies on the table, gives me a kiss on my forehead that feels both alien and wonderful, then turns around and walks back to the oven as she starts humming Madonna's "Like a Virgin."

CHAPTER **27**

"Have a seat," says Bill Summers, closing the door to his office.

I sit down in the chair across from Bill's island of a desk, looking out through his window at Beverly Hills floating beneath the gray November sunset. Since being given my secret assignment nearly six months ago, I haven't seen Bill except in passing or from across the room on several occasions, but he still looks like a man who is used to getting what he wants.

"I heard about your crew member, Chloe Lee," he says, sitting down behind his desk, his suit jacket hanging on the back of his chair. "I'm sorry. I understand she was a talented investigator."

"Yes, she was. We miss her."

He gives an understanding nod. "How is everyone else on your team holding up?"

"They're good," I say. "Thank you."

Bill flashes a friendly, empathetic smile, then leans forward on his desk. "Now, how can I help you?"

I'm not exactly sure what I want to say or how I want to say it, so I decide to just start with the first question that comes into my head. "Is there anything going on I should know about?"

Not the most specific of questions, but at the moment I'm not being choosy.

"I'm not sure I understand," says Bill. "If you're referring to the incident with Miss Lee, rest assured you and your crew have nothing to worry about."

I shake my head, though in response to Bill or to rearrange my thoughts, I'm not sure. "Is this happening because of what I've been doing?"

I realize I'm being vague but right now vague seems to be the only language I can speak.

"Is what happening?" says Bill, looking at me with his manicured hair and his no-nonsense tie and his dimples. He hasn't offered me a drink, which I guess means he's not interested in any foreplay this time.

"You know," I say. "All of the stuff about black market Egos that's been in the news."

I'm like a shark, circling my prey, sizing it up, waiting for the right moment to strike. Only in this case, my prey is an intelligent question.

Over the past few days I've searched the Internet for stories about all of the black market Ego deaths that have occurred in Los Angeles since July. While I don't recognize the circumstances of every story, enough of them strike a familiar chord to convince me that I may have played a role in the deaths of more than two dozen people.

Not exactly the kind of thing you want to have as an epitaph.

"I'm sorry," says Bill, "but I don't know how to help you if you can't be more specific."

"Okay," I say, trying to get to the point. "Is there a problem with the antidote for the people who purchased black market Egos?"

Bill looks at me as if I just asked him why he has an alien head growing out of the side of his neck.

"Excuse me?" he says.

"The antidote you gave me," I say. "Is there something wrong with it? Has anyone reported back that it's producing unintended side effects?"

And by *producing unintended side effects,* I mean *killing people.*

That same bemused look remains on his face. "I have no idea what you're talking about. I never gave you any antidote."

I'm waiting for him to smile, to let me know he's just kidding, but his expression never changes. It's like the discussion I had with my father when he told me there's no such thing as Santa Claus.

A tight smile spreads across my face and I let out a nervous laugh, thinking he's just messing with me, but he continues to stare at me like he has no idea what I'm talking about.

"We sat right here almost six months ago," I say. "I drank water and you drank tequila and you asked me to help test an antidote that would counteract the retroviruses in black market Egos."

I look around as if to confirm this to myself. Everything is just as I remember, right down to the wet bar with the highballs and the rock glasses and the bottles of top-shelf liquor. The only difference is that an unopened bottle of tequila now sits next to its nearly empty twin.

"I think you're mistaken," he says.

I stare at him, still waiting for him to admit he's joking. I can feel perspiration forming on the back of my neck and at my temples. My pulse is racing and my stomach is filling up with acid that's starting to work its way toward my throat.

"We never had any meeting," he says. "And I never heard of this antidote you mentioned."

His voice sounds like it's coming from inside a well and the air around me starts to grow warm and thick. I'm having trouble breathing. Inside my head, someone is playing a shell game with my memories.

"But you promised me a six-figure bonus and stock options and a penthouse suite," I say.

"I have absolutely no idea what you're talking about," says Bill, who then looks at his watch and stands up, slipping into his suit jacket, signaling that our meeting is over. "Now . . . if there's nothing else you have to discuss, I have a full schedule today."

CHAPTER **28**

I'm alone in my office trying to rationalize my meeting with Bill Summers. I've been sitting here for the last couple of hours, running through everything I remember, over and over again, trying to convince myself my memories are real and that I'm not crazy.

I look up at the digital clock on the wall as it changes from 7:59 to 8:00.

When he escorted me from his office, I expected Bill to finally admit it was all an elaborate joke. He was just kidding around, ha-ha, wasn't that funny? Even now I'm still waiting for someone to give me the punch line.

An Ego Investigator walks into a bar . . .

Either I imagined the entire conversation I had with Bill Summers back in May or else he's pretending it never happened. Except I *know* I didn't imagine it. I couldn't possibly have imagined it. Could I?

As I'm sitting there struggling to come up with an answer, I become aware of the sound of someone crying.

Not sobbing. Not whimpering. Not stoic weeping. Not where they're bawling so hard they have to take big, gasping sucks of air.

It's more like the type of crying where it could be laughter.

Either someone's in distress or else they're making their own fun. Except as far as I know, I'm the only one here. Everyone else went home for the night.

I get up from my desk and step out of my office, trying to pinpoint the direction of the crying. It sounds amplified, echoing through the room like someone's on speakerphone, except the only lights in the office are the low ambient lighting. None of the light sensors for the individual workstations are activated. I'm about to go search the office anyway but before I can take another step, the crying stops. I stand and listen, waiting, hearing nothing but the whispers of doubt in my head.

After a few moments I walk around the office and check everyone's workstation, but all I find is Emily's partially eaten Cinnabon, which she forgot to throw away.

I'm standing by Emily's workstation, the sky outside dark and the low ambient light illuminating the office, thinking I must have imagined the whole thing, when the crying starts again. This time it sounds less like laughter and more like someone sniffling, the way a child might if she's left all alone, frightened and lonely in a strange place. Of course, it could be a *he*. But this doesn't sound like Neil or Vincent or Kurt. I check anyway, just to be sure, and discover the crying is coming from Kurt's workstation.

At first I think Kurt has somehow managed to leave his voice mail playing and it's a message from one of his numerous conquests. I half expect to hear her lament how much she misses his throbbing cock. Then I notice the intercom light glowing on his phone and realize someone in the office has called his extension. I check the digital readout and recognize the extension calling him belongs to Angela.

When I go back for a second look, the motion sensors turn on the lights in her workstation and I notice Angela's phone isn't in its cradle. I'm wondering where her phone could be when I hear the crying again, only this time both on the intercom and coming from beneath Angela's desk. When I crouch down, I find Angela curled up in a ball in the shadows of her desk, lying on her side with one hand under her head and the other one holding the phone cradled to her ear, crying softly, her face wet with tears. Her eyes are closed, so she doesn't see me just a few feet away. Then I say her name.

"Angela."

I say it with a sense of tenderness, soft and gentle, the way you'd call out to someone who was sleeping and you wanted to wake them up without alarming them. But Angela reacts as if I'd shouted in her ear.

Her eyes open wide and she yanks the phone away from her ear, holding the phone out at me like a weapon. Her hand is shaking. I notice that her left nostril is bleeding.

"Hey Angela, it's me," I say, trying not to frighten her while doing my best to remain calm. "What's the matter?"

Her expression suddenly changes from fear to mirth and she relaxes, pulling the phone up against her chest and cradling it like a cherished memento. Before I can say anything else, she bursts out in a fit of laughter.

"Angela . . . ?"

She continues to laugh, almost to the point of not being able to breathe. Then her laughter turns to tears and she's sobbing, her face pinched and red, her mouth open in anguish, saliva dribbling out, the blood from her nose mixing with tears and saliva and dripping down her chin.

I call her name again. When she doesn't respond, I reach out with my left hand and touch her on the arm. Before I can react, she drops the phone and grabs my hand and pulls it against her chest, holding on to me as if she were drowning and my hand was the only thing keeping her head above water.

We stay like this for several minutes until Angela's sobs start to subside. I can feel her heart pounding beneath my left hand, like she's been running for her life. I reach out with my other hand and stroke her hair, brushing it out of her face, hoping that eventually she'll be able to tell me what's wrong. Then she opens her eyes and looks at me.

"Who am I?" she says.

"Angela," I say in my most reassuring voice. "Your name is Angela."

She smiles and closes her eyes, as if the question was for me to answer and she knew it all along. Then her eyes open and grow wide with doubt and she looks at me again.

"Who are you?"

CHAPTER **29**

"Who are you?" says the female Buddhist monk at the front of the room.

Where I am is the Kadampa Meditation Center in Silver Lake three years ago at their Wednesday-night meditation, seeking the spiritual path to enlightenment with more than a dozen other men and women. This is just a few weeks before Big Egos first hit the shelves.

No one is strung out on false identities.

No one is Cleopatra or Humphrey Bogart or Wonder Woman.

Everyone here is just trying to get in touch with their inner Buddha.

We're all sitting on pillows, our legs crossed in lotus or half lotus, our shoes off, our backs straight. The instructor, a female Buddhist monk named Chookie, is talking to us about ego and self as illusion.

"Are you your thoughts?" she asks.

I look around. Most of the men and women I recognize from coming here every Wednesday night for the past six months. Some of them are in my Tuesday-night Bikram yoga class. A few attend seminars with me at the Zen Center of Los Angeles. Others I've seen at the New Bodhi Tree Bookstore in West Hollywood or the Mystic Journey Bookstore in Venice. And one woman is in my Sunday-morning tai chi class in Pan Pacific Park.

While it's taken me nearly twenty-four years to discover Buddhism, I think I've finally found the role I'm supposed to play.

Chookie walks up to a young man I've never seen before who has a full head of hair and a five o'clock shadow. "Are you your thoughts?" she asks.

"Sure," says the newbie.

Chookie just smiles and walks away. "Does anyone else believe that you are your thoughts?"

A few nodding heads, but no one else says anything.

"Most people have an identity based upon their mind." Chookie walks back over to her own pillow and sits down next to a miniature gong. "This means that you believe you are the thoughts in your head. Everyone thinks in his or her own unique way and believes they are what they think."

Makes sense to me. Descartes said: *I think, therefore I am.* If I'm not what I think, then what am I? How do I exist if my thoughts aren't my own?

"What are some of these thoughts?" asks Chookie, though it's a rhetorical question because she keeps on talking. "I am fat. I am ugly. I am successful. I am lazy. I am a waiter. I am a lawyer. I am a failure. I am unhappy. These thoughts are not you."

I look around to see if anyone else is as confused as I am, but if they are, they're hiding it. Or pretending to understand. Typical L.A. crowd. Wanting to fit in for the sake of fitting in, without really knowing why.

"These thoughts originate in your mind due to external stimuli in your world," says Chookie. "They depend on how your mind has interpreted the world around you."

I glance at the other people in the room, at the walls and the floor and the altar, and try to interpret the world around me. As far as I can tell, it's pretty self-explanatory.

"That is the Western way of thinking." Chookie looks out at us from her pillow at the front of the room. "Interpreting the world and defining yourself by your reactions to them. Defining yourself by your thoughts."

Freud said the ego separates what is real and helps us to organize our thoughts and make sense of them and the world around us. He said the ego is the part of our unconscious personality that has been modified by the direct influence of the external world.

Right now, I'm thinking Freud makes more sense.

The newbie raises his hand.

"Yes?" says Chookie.

"Is there going to be a test on this?"

She laughs. "Not in the traditional sense of the word, no. The test is how you work on yourself and develop an understanding of the separation of your ego from who you truly are. That is what meditation is all about: finding your own path to enlightenment and happiness and the true nature of your own existence."

I like the sound of that. After all, finding the true nature of my existence is why I'm here.

"Our thoughts are not us," she says. "When you meditate, you are attempting to separate your thoughts, and thus your identity, from yourself."

Maybe it's just me, but separating my identity from myself sounds like a good way to end up with schizophrenia.

In addition to my meditation practice and spiritual seminars and yoga classes, I also have a Zen garden and have taken up calligraphy and flower arranging. I even convinced Delilah to get in on the act by signing up for some Tantric sex classes. I haven't converted to vegetarianism yet because bacon tastes so damn good.

Apparently I'm not alone. I hear some vegetarians are lobbying to have bacon reclassified as a vegetable.

"You want to get rid of all of your thoughts so that you arrive at a state of emptiness," says Chookie. "That is what we're striving for in meditation. To make yourself empty and filled with nothing, though even nothing possesses an essential, enduring identity."

In Taoism and Buddhism, nothing or emptiness is represented by zero, while in Latin the number zero is derived from the expression *nulla figura,* which when translated means *not a real figure.* For some reason, this seems important but the reason escapes me.

"Are there any other questions?" Chookie looks around. "Okay then. Everyone take a deep breath and relax. Backs straight but not rigid, head tilted slightly forward, eyes closed or looking along the line of your nose, hands folded in front of you or on your knees."

I close my eyes and imagine a zero floating in the darkness in front of me, growing larger and larger as I drift closer to it. I can almost feel myself falling into the middle of it, tumbling into the darkness and emptiness, into the nothingness, and I sense an answer to a question about my own identity that has always eluded me, hovering just at the edge of my awareness. Then Chookie rings her miniature gong and the answer slips away.

CHAPTER **30**

"We need to talk," I say.

"About what?" says Nat.

I almost tell Nat that I think I'm a mass murderer and that two of my coworkers have been shipped off to Metropolitan State Hospital for mental evaluation, but I don't think this is the place.

We're standing in line for lunch at Pink's on La Brea a week before Thanksgiving with about three dozen other men and women, most of them in a normal state of existence—though I see Michael Jackson and Whitney Houston at the front getting ready to place their order, so not everyone's themselves.

"We need to talk about what you're doing," I say.

"Can you be more specific, bro?"

"It has to do with your recent lifestyle change."

I haven't seen much of Nat over the past month, not

since I told him I thought he had a problem with Egos. The few times I have seen him, he's been someone else.

Robin Hood. Mickey Mantle. The Dude.

All of them are part of the EGOS product line, but Nat hasn't been getting them from me. I tried to make peace with him by offering him some Egos I knew he'd enjoy, but he told me he didn't want to be my charity case. And since Nat can't afford to legally alter his identity on what he makes, that means he's been buying his Egos on the streets of Hollywood and Los Feliz. That worries me. And not just because of the dangers of black market Egos.

While Bill Summers insists that we never had a meeting back in May, I know we did. I remember it as clearly as I remember my father's funeral and when I met Delilah and the day I found out there was no such thing as Santa Claus. I also remember what Bill said about other EGOS employees testing the antidote on unsuspecting black market users, so I can't take the chance that someone might target Nat. The last thing I want is for my best friend to end up on the news as another casualty.

"I'm worried about you," I say.

"Worried? About what? I'm better than I've ever been."

"I know. That's what worries me."

"There's nothing to be worried about, bro." Nat looks up at the menu. "Although I am having trouble deciding between a chili cheeseburger and a chili cheese dog."

"I'm serious," I say.

"So am I," he says. "I can't make up my mind. What are you getting?"

On the menu is an assortment of burgers, fries, and more

than two dozen types of hot dogs and specials to choose from, including the Lord of the Rings Dog, the Mulholland Drive Dog, the Chicago Polish Dog, and the Bacon Chili Cheese Dog.

I can barely focus on the menu. I don't know if it's because I can't stop thinking about the way Angela looked at me with her haunted eyes and asked me who she was or because it's been more than two weeks since I've injected an Ego and I'm going through withdrawals, but I seem to have trouble making even the smallest of decisions. Like ordering lunch.

Nat looks away from the menu, then nudges me and nods toward the back of the line. "Hey, I'd like to give her a chili cheese dog."

Nat really needs to work on his sexual metaphors.

I look behind us and see a tall brunette with olive-colored skin standing by herself and studying the menu, her arms crossed. The international sign for Leave Me Alone, I'm Not Interested.

With her exotic complexion, shoulder-length hair, full pouty lips, and supermodel figure, she's not only out of Nat's league, she's out of his galaxy. We're talking supernova gorgeous. Even the men standing near her don't know whether to look at her in awe or look away for fear of going blind. Or getting slapped by their girlfriends.

"I'm sure a lot of guys would like to give her a chili cheese dog," I say. "But most of them would . . ."

And I can't think of an analogy that doesn't make me want to throw up in my mouth.

"Hold that thought," says Nat.

He steps out of line and walks toward the back, right up to the brunette, and starts chatting her up. I'm not sure who's more shocked by this—the brunette, me, or everyone else in line. I watch as she nods hesitantly and seems a little put off by Nat's aggressive entry into her atmosphere, but then she smiles and unfolds her arms and, after another thirty seconds or so, offers up a small laugh. They chat for a bit longer, then she extends her right hand and Nat takes it, holds it briefly while shaking it, then he gives her hand back along with his card and returns to me.

"What was that all about?" I ask.

"What do you mean?"

I nod toward the supernova brunette. "The way you handled her was not the Nat I know."

"You're thinking of the old Nat," he says. "This is the new and improved Nat, with more Nat in every serving."

Whatever that means.

I glance back at the brunette, who is looking our way. And she's most definitely not looking at me.

"Did you get her number?" I ask.

"I don't need her number."

"Why not?"

"Because she'll call me."

"What makes you think she'll call?"

He looks up at the menu. "I just know."

I stare at Nat and realize just how much he's changed. Although he's not under the influence right now, it's apparent that using Egos has given Nat a newfound confidence. And not only with women.

"I'm thinking about changing jobs," he says as we approach the front of the line.

"To what?"

Nat has never thought about changing his hairstyle, let alone how he earns a living, so I have a hard time believing it's anything more than just a thought.

"I was thinking of applying for an administrative job at one of the local universities."

"A university?" I say. "Are you qualified?"

"No. But I know I can do the job."

Just like he knows he can do the brunette.

"I don't think you can just apply for a job at a university," I say. "I'm pretty sure you need a master's degree."

"What are you? Donnie Downer?"

"I'm just being practical."

"Screw practical. No one ever got anywhere in life by being practical."

While I'm pretty sure I can prove Nat wrong, right now I can't think of any examples.

"Besides, you always told me to be the person I always wanted to be," he says. "Play the role I was meant to play."

My father's words coming back to haunt me.

"So now that I'm ready to play that role, you're telling me I should just keep doing what I've been doing?" he says.

"No. That's not what I'm saying."

"Then what *are* you saying?"

We move closer to the order counter as the other customers in line pretend to ignore us. I can't tell Nat about the antidote or about my concerns for his physical safety, so I keep playing the vague card.

"I just think you need to consider the consequences before you jump into anything."

"That's easy for you to say," he says. "You're earning a six-figure salary with stock options and a five-figure annual bonus. So don't talk to me about considering my options."

And that's the end of *that* conversation.

When we finally get up to the window, Nat orders two chili cheese dogs and a Coke while I finally decide on the Chicago Polish Dog with an order of chili fries and an Orange Crush. In line behind us, I keep catching the brunette glancing our way.

Once we get our food, we sit down at one of the tables out back. "So where are you getting your Egos?" I ask.

"What does it matter?" he says, around a mouthful of chili cheese dog.

"Because if you're getting them off the street, they're not safe."

"According to who?"

"According to whom," I say.

"What are you? My copy editor? Come on, bro. No one talks that way in real life."

"It doesn't matter," I say. "The point is they're not safe. In more ways than one."

"Who says?"

To be honest, most of the questions about the safety of black market Egos have come from studies backed by experts and scientists on the EGOS payroll. While the studies are based on sound data, they're not exactly unbiased.

"Trust me," I say. "If you're getting them off the street, then you don't know what you're getting."

"My connection guarantees the quality is good," says Nat. "He assures me they come from the factory."

"Of course he says that. What else is he going to tell you? That they're made in an apartment in Compton that doubles as a meth lab?"

And that's not too far from the truth. Although unauthorized Egos aren't made with ingredients like propane, paint thinner, chloroform, and Freon, long-term users of Egos sold on the black market can develop symptoms similar to crystal meth addicts that include psychosis, paranoia, hallucinations, obsessive-compulsive behavior, memory loss, and delusions.

Or worse.

"I'm not an idiot." Nat finishes his first chili cheese dog and starts in on the second. "I know what I'm doing."

"Not this time," I say.

"What does that mean?"

"I can't explain it to you," I say.

"Why not? Do you think I'm too stupid to figure it out?"

The people at the nearby tables look over at us. Not that I mind being the center of attention, but this isn't exactly a conversation I want to have in public.

"It's not that," I say, lowering my voice. "It's just . . . never mind."

"Come on," he says. "I want to hear you say it."

"Say what?"

"That you don't think I can make my own decisions," he says. "That I can't solve my own problems. That without you I couldn't think my way out of a fucking nursery rhyme."

"That's not what I was going to say."

"But you were thinking it."

"Well, not word for word," I say, trying to lighten the mood.

"Fuck you, bro."

The people who were looking over at us are now trying to pretend that we don't exist.

"You know, the only reason I tried Egos in the first place was because I thought it was the only way we could stay friends," says Nat. "But now, I don't even know if I want to be your friend anymore."

"Nat, come on . . ."

"And in spite of what you might think, you're not any smarter than me. And you sure as hell don't know what I want or what I need. This is *my* life, not yours. I can make my own decisions."

"You have to trust me," I say. "It's not safe for you to buy black market Egos. You have no idea what might happen to you if you keep using them."

"Thanks for the concern," he says. "But I'll take my chances."

Then he gets up and storms away from the table, leaving my concerns and his half-eaten chili cheese dog behind.

CHAPTER **31**

*M*y . . . *crew* . . . *is* . . . *nowhere to be found.*

Captain's Log, stardate 2021. I have entered a . . . gathering of some sort . . . a party . . . in a three-story Spanish-style home on Roxbury Road, just off the Sunset Strip in West Hollywood. There's . . . no sign of Spock or Bones . . . or the rest of my crew. I don't know where . . . they are but . . . I don't have the time . . . to wait for them.

I turn off the recorder on my communicator and walk through an arched doorway from the formal dining room into the breakfast room, then through another archway and into the den and bar area, which contains a number of men and women engaged in various acts of frivolity.

Drinking. Smoking. Flirting. Laughing.

Clark Kent and Peter Parker are putting the moves on a barely clothed Nova from Planet of the Apes, *who is flashing a lot of skin in her furry bikini and not saying much of anything. Quiet. Thoughtful. The kind of woman I can appreciate.*

I find her . . . most uncommon.

Nearby, looking somewhat put out, Lois Lane and Mary Jane Watson watch their dates, drinking Manhattans and giving Nova the stink eye.

"It's a madhouse!" screams a drunken Taylor, who comes streaking through the room being chased by some guy in a gorilla suit. "A madhouse!"

While I appreciate his passion, that guy is such an overactor.

At the bar, Doc Brown and Doctor Who are discussing time travel over a bottle of scotch while Ellen Ripley and Sarah Connor arm wrestle to see which one of them gets to make out with Mad Max. Princess Leia relaxes on a chaise longue in her slave outfit, sipping a cocktail.

Space may be the final frontier, but I'd rather explore her strange new worlds.

"Make it so," says a familiar voice from over in the corner, followed by a chorus of feminine laughter. I look over and see Picard entertaining a harem of women that includes Dana Scully, Buffy Summers, and Xena the Warrior Princess.

Picard sees me and gives me a nod. I nod back. But I'm just being cordial. I can't stand Picard, the Shakespeare-quoting French prick.

I look around and see Buck Rogers, Malcolm Reynolds, Flash Gordon, and Lando Calrissian, among others. None of them is the object of this rescue mission, so I head down to check out the basement. At the top of the stairs, I pass Rick Deckard and Han Solo having a heated argument. The Blade Runner has his finger in the smuggler's face.

"I wouldn't do that if I were you," says Solo.

Down in the basement, a converted home movie theater with soundproof walls and oversized chairs, Trinity and Morpheus are grinding against one another in their black leather coats, their tongues giant slugs trying to escape into each other's mouths as Neo battles Agent Smith on the 120-inch projection screen.

No one else is down here, so I head back upstairs, where Deckard and Solo are now in a shoving match. I've always enjoyed a good fight and I'm tempted to join in. Or else walk over and show Picard what I really think of him. I kicked his ass once and I can do it again. Instead, I ascend the circular staircase to the top floor, hoping I don't run into Khan or a couple of Klingons or maybe even that pesky Gorn.

The first bedroom I come to is locked. I put my ear up to the door and listen, but all I hear is someone saying "Klaatu barada nikto" over and over while something that sounds like a headboard bangs repeatedly against the wall.

In the hallway I pass Wonder Woman, who is asking Luke Skywalker if he'd like to show her his light saber, and I nearly run into Neo, who is wearing his sunglasses and a foam I'm-Number-One finger on his left hand.

"Have you seen Trinity?" he asks.

"Try the basement," I say.

"Thanks, dude."

I consider following him down to see what happens, but I still haven't completed my mission. And I'm concerned that if I don't find who I'm looking for soon, there might be trouble. So I keep looking.

In the second bedroom, I find a character who appears somewhat out of place in this universe, dressed in his blue crushed-velvet suit with a frilly lace cravat and black horn-rimmed glasses. He's in the middle of putting the moves on Barbarella, who's wearing a sleeveless pleather leotard and black thigh-high boots.

"Are you horny, baby?" he says. "Do I turn you on?"

Not very subtle, though.

"Not really," says Barbarella.

"Oh come on," he says, looking her up and down. "You're incredibly hot. I bet you shag like a minx."

His existence here, in this universe, to quote my dear friend Mr. Spock, is illogical. It would make more sense if this was a planet of parody characters or a galaxy of superspies, but it's apparent he doesn't belong here. And while the Prime Directive dictates that there can be no interference in the natural course of a society, even if well-intentioned, I have an obligation to remove him before he gets into trouble.

"Mr. Powers," I say. "May I have a word?"

When he turns to look at me, Barbarella slides past him and walks out of the room, giving me a meaningful glance on her way out.

There's something about me that women can't deny. I call it the Kirk Phenomenon. Maybe it's because I once made a gun out of bamboo that shot diamonds.

Let's see Picard top that.

"Where are you going, baby?" Austin Powers follows Barbarella to the doorway, then he turns to me and smiles. "She was very shagadelic, wouldn't you agree?"

I look at him for any signs of a nervous tic or a twitchy eye.

Burst blood vessels or dilated pupils. Those are the first symptoms. If you catch it early enough, then you still might have a chance, but brain damage caused by prolonged use of black market Egos isn't reversible.

I just hope I've caught it in time.

"Hey, what's your bag?" he says to me. "I like your look, man."

"Come on." I take him by the arm and lead him out of the bedroom and down the stairs. "We're getting out of here."

"But why? I'm having a smashing time."

"Because it isn't safe."

He stops when we reach the bottom of the stairs and looks around. "Is Dr. Evil here?"

"No. Dr. Evil is not here."

"Random Task?"

"No."

"Goldmember? Fat Bastard? Mini-Me?"

"No." I continue with him toward the front door. "None of them are here."

"Then why are we leaving, man? Let's stay and have some shits and giggles."

I stop and look around, checking out the other inhabitants of this planet, wondering if any of them are watching us with hostile intent. Other than Fox Mulder, who is studying everyone with an emotionless expression, I don't see anyone who looks like they mean us any harm. Still, I can't take that chance.

"Are you okay, man?" asks Austin.

I turn to look at him and notice that his left eye is twitching. I smile and act like nothing's wrong.

"I'm sound as a pound, my friend," I say, putting an arm around him and leading him out of the house. "Now let's go have some of those shits and giggles you were talking about."

He gives me a big smile and says, "Groovy, baby."

CHAPTER **32**

I wake up to the sound of bees sending me a message in Morse code.

Bzzzzzzzzzzzzzzz...Bzzzzzzzzzzzzzzz...Bzzzzzzzzzzzzzzz...

Maybe I'm wrong, but it seems like they're sending the same letter over and over. Since I don't speak bee, I can't tell for sure. For all I know bees only have one letter in their alphabet and it has different meanings, kind of like *Aloha*.

Maybe they're Hawaiian bees.

I open my eyes hoping to find myself on a white sand beach beneath a palm tree with the Pacific Ocean lapping at the shore. Instead I'm on my hardwood floor beneath a ceiling fan with a headache thumping at my temple.

The insistent bees are still trying to get their message across. When I look over I see my cell phone on the floor and realize it's on vibrate. Someone's calling me.

I'm not really up to talking right now. My lips are dry and my tongue is sticking to the roof of my mouth. It feels like someone opened a glue factory in my gums.

The phone stops vibrating, so at least I don't have to deal with that decision. Right now all I have the energy to focus on are my basic bodily needs, like hydration and urination, maybe something to get rid of this headache. So I get to my feet and walk into the kitchen and fill up a glass with cold water.

My phone starts vibrating again, the bees sending out their indecipherable message. Whoever it is must really want to talk to me, so I grab the phone without looking and answer it on speaker.

"Yeah?"

"Where are they?" says Nat's voice.

"Where are what?"

"You know damn well *what*."

I take a long drink of water, washing away the glue factory, and try to make some sense of Nat's question. With my pounding headache and Ego withdrawals, I don't have any idea what he's talking about.

"I don't know what you're talking about," I say.

"Don't play games with me, bro. What did you do with them?"

"What did I do with what?"

"My Egos," he says. "You took them."

"When did I take your Egos?"

"Last night. This morning. It doesn't matter. I know it was you. Just give them back."

For a moment I think Nat is imagining things, and then it comes back to me in flashes and snippets.

Last night, after I found Nat and his Austin Powers alter ego, I took him out, got him drunk, drove him home, and tucked the passed-out secret agent into his bed. Then I searched his apartment until I found his stash of black market Egos.

In addition to The Austin Powers, he has knockoff versions of The Captain Kirk, The James Dean, The Al Pacino, The Dirty Harry, The Sundance Kid, The Han Solo, The Jim Morrison, and The Ryan Reynolds.

Even at their discounted prices, his collection of Egos had to set him back at least four or five thousand dollars. Not a lot of money in the grand scheme of things, but I know Nat doesn't have that kind of money to burn.

"I want them back," he says. "And I want them back *now.*"

Delilah walks into the kitchen in her underwear and one of my T-shirts. She doesn't say anything but just stands there and stares at me like she's mad about something.

She needs to take a number and get in line.

I pick up my phone and turn off the speaker. "I know you want them back," I say to Nat, "but I'm keeping them."

"You can't do that. *They're not yours!*"

I hold the phone away from my ear but I can still hear him screaming.

"*They're mine! You don't have any right to take them from me!*"

"Who are you talking to?" says Delilah.

I signal her with an index finger to hold off for a moment, then I walk into the living room to continue my conversation.

"It's for your own good," I say to Nat.

"No. It's for *your* own good," he says. "You have all those stock options that are worth more money if people buy your Egos instead of getting them on the street."

"That's not true," I say.

"Then what *is* true?"

I can't explain my additional concerns about Nat's safety without implicating myself in the deaths of at least two dozen people, but I have to try to find some way to convince him.

"It's not safe for you to use them," I say. "They're dangerous."

"What's dangerous is me coming over to kick your ass if you don't give me back my property."

While he sounds convincing on the phone, I'm not worried about Nat carrying through with his threat. He's all bluster.

"Nat, listen . . ."

"No. *You* listen. You either give me back my Egos or else you can consider this the end of our friendship."

"You don't understand . . ."

"*You* don't understand. I mean it. Make your choice. Me or my Egos."

I don't want to lose Nat. He's the one person who has always been on my side, the only constant in my life that's been real. But in order to keep him that way, I can't give him what he wants.

"I'm sorry, Nat."

He hangs up. I consider calling him back but decide it would be pointless and instead I toss the phone aside, sit down on the couch, close my eyes, and run my hands through my hair. When I open my eyes, Delilah is standing in the dining room with her arms folded, staring at me, still looking pissed off.

"So what did you do last night?" she asks.

"I can't tell you," I say.

Delilah nods and gives me a tight-lipped stare, then turns and walks back into the bedroom.

CHAPTER **33**

"I'm sorry, but I'm not at liberty to discuss that information with you," says David Cook, the executive vice president at EGOS.

I wanted to talk to the president or the CEO, but they wouldn't see me, so here I am, two days before Thanksgiving, sitting in a chair across the desk from the EVP.

"What do you mean you're not at liberty?" I say. "This is my team we're talking about. I think I have a right to know what happened to them."

I can still see Angela. Not the way she was for the five years we worked together, the way she kidded and giggled and shared her tales of horrible dates, but the way she was at the end, curled up beneath her desk, her eyes wide and filled with fear.

Who am I?

Who are you?

"I'm sorry," says David. "But these are personal matters pertaining to the individuals involved, and company protocol doesn't allow me to discuss them with you or with anyone else who is not an immediate family member."

"Not even if the information might be relevant to the safety of the other members of my team?"

While Chloe's possible use of illegal Egos is up for debate, I know Angela never shopped on the black market. So it seems reasonable that what happened to her could happen to the rest of us. Or to anyone else who has been using Egos for more than three years.

David Cook flashes me a practiced smile that looks exactly like the one I got from Bill Summers. They must buy their smiles at the same store.

"There's nothing to be concerned about," he says. "You can rest assured there's no danger to the other members of your team."

While Emily, Vincent, Kurt, and Neil all seem perfectly fine, I can't help but think about the anomaly that Angela found in regular consumers of certain fictional Egos.

"So you're saying Big Egos didn't play a role in the fact that both of them had mental breakdowns?"

"Big Egos are perfectly safe when used properly," he says, regurgitating the company line. "Whatever happened to Angela Bennett and Chloe Lee, while unfortunate and tragic, was most likely due to external mitigating factors, such as recreational drug use, preexisting medical conditions, or the use of black market Egos."

I stare at the executive vice president of EGOS, sitting there at his desk in his Armani suit with his manicured hands and his perfect hair, acting like he has a reporter's microphone shoved in his face, and I wonder what he knows that he's not telling me.

"Can you tell me if this is happening in other departments?" I say. "Have there been other cases? Or is this just happening in Investigations?"

Any information coming out of the other departments is being filtered through corporate and no one's talking for fear of losing their jobs along with their stock options, which is all part of the nondisclosure agreement we all had to sign in order to work here.

I had no idea how much freedom I was giving up when I signed that damned thing.

"It's my understanding that the episodes with your team members are isolated cases," he says. "That's all I can tell you. If you want additional information, I'd suggest talking to HR."

"I've already been to HR," I say. "They told me to talk to R&D, who told me to talk to Operations, who told me to talk to HR."

I've gone around in so many circles I'm beginning to feel like I'm chasing my own tail.

"I'm sorry," he says. "But I've told you everything I can. Now if you'll excuse me . . ."

And then I'm shown the door.

I stand out in the waiting room, trying to think about what I should do next. Even if I could get a meeting with the CEO or the president or anyone with a corporate title, I'd just be wasting my time. All they'd give me is the same old song and dance. And anyone in any of the other departments who might be able to give me a straight answer isn't going to talk straight. Instead they're just going to send me around in more circles.

Someone's keeping the truth from me. From all of us. I need to find someone who's willing to talk. Someone who knows what's going on. The problem is, other than the remaining members of my team, I don't know who I can trust.

CHAPTER **34**

"Are you spying on me?" I say.

Delilah's reflection regards me with an expression that's part indifference and part irritation. It's one of her trademark looks and one she's been giving me more and more lately, with an emphasis on the irritation.

"Why in the world would I be spying on you?" she says.

I watch Delilah in the bathroom mirror, applying a coat of lipstick, and I wonder if she's telling me the truth or if she's just putting on an act. I'm beginning to think she's always performing and that the person I think is Delilah is another act. A role she's playing just for me.

Before I met Delilah in my last year of college, she hung out with friends who got her into Irish dancing. Before that she dated a Beat poet and that became her passion. Before that she got involved with a crowd that was into poly-paganism.

She's like a chameleon, taking on the identity of her peers, adopting their likes and passions in order to blend in and belong. The perfect type of person to be a spy.

Or maybe I'm just paranoid.

"You haven't denied it," I say, talking to her reflection.

We have entire conversations like this. Delilah at the sink, flossing her teeth or applying makeup or plucking her eyebrows and me off camera somewhere—on the toilet seat, toweling after a shower, watching her from the doorway. Our eyes only meet in the reflection of the bathroom mirror. She never turns to look at me.

"I haven't denied it because it's ridiculous," she says.

She seems annoyed about something, what I don't know. But that's twice she hasn't denied that she's a spy. If she doesn't deny it a third time, I'll know it's true.

Somewhere that logic makes perfect sense.

I think Schopenhauer said that every truth passes through three stages before it's recognized. In the first it's ridiculed. In the second it's opposed. And in the third it's regarded as self-evident.

Which means Delilah's guilt by nondenial is almost self-evident.

Part of me realizes there's something flawed in my thinking and that relying on a nineteenth-century German philosopher to guide my thought process is a little suspect. Maybe it wasn't even Schopenhauer who said it. And even if it was, what the hell does he know?

Still, there's something about threes I can't seem to let go of. Maybe it's that good things come in threes. Or the third time's the charm. Or three on a match is bad luck.

"Why are you counting on your fingers?" asks Delilah, her tone matching her irritated expression.

I look down and notice I have three fingers held up. "That doesn't matter. What matters is why you won't answer the question."

"Which was . . . ?" Delilah raises one plucked eyebrow in the mirror.

Which was? Which was? What *was* the question?

I have a moment of panic when I realize I have no idea what we were talking about. Then I look down and see I'm still holding up three fingers. With an effort, I try to figure out why, which takes me back to Schopenhauer and then to Germany, which makes me think of Nazis and Indiana Jones. And then it comes back to me.

"Are you spying on me?"

Delilah finally turns around to look at me. "Is there a reason I should be spying on you?"

I think back to Schopenhauer, to what this means, since Delilah didn't deny the truth a third time. Does that mean she's not spying on me? Or is she just trying to confuse me?

"I don't know what is wrong with you but I don't have time to play around." She turns back to the mirror. "I have to finish getting ready. Are you going to get dressed?"

I look in the mirror at my reflection, which is wearing a T-shirt and a pair of boxer shorts with little shamrocks all over them. Delilah gave them to me last St. Patrick's Day, called me her little good luck charm. Which gets me to thinking about Elvis and Deborah Harry and deep-fried Twinkies and I realize I've forgotten what we were talking about.

"Dressed for what?" I ask.

"We're going to an Ego dinner party in Santa Monica for Thanksgiving," she says. "You promised we could go."

I vaguely remember making a promise about a Thanksgiving dinner, but it feels like a memory that belongs to someone else.

"Who are you going as?" I ask.

"Jackie Kennedy Onassis," she says, exasperated. "We went over this already."

That means I'm probably going as JFK, so I'm thinking I should probably put on something more appropriate.

I turn around to get dressed, trying to get a grasp on my train of thought, when I notice a bouquet of red roses sitting in a vase on the table near the bedroom window.

"Where did those come from?" I ask.

"Where did what come from?"

"The roses."

There's a long pause before she answers. "I got them for my birthday."

Delilah's birthday is November 20. That was this past Saturday. I don't remember getting her roses for her birthday. I don't even remember celebrating her birthday. Which I realize might be a problem.

"Did I give them to you?" I ask.

She lets out a single, humorless "Ha!"

I'm afraid to ask, but at this point I'm too lost to do anything else. "What does that mean?"

"It means I bought them for myself," she says.

Uh-oh. This can't be good. "Why did you buy them for yourself?"

Delilah marches over and shoves me once, hard, in the chest. "Because you forgot my birthday, you fucking asshole!"

That would explain why she's been so irritated with me.

"I've been ignoring you all week and dropping little hints," she says, "waiting for you to figure it out and apologize, but you haven't even noticed. You've hardly even spoken to me. It's like you don't even know I'm here!"

"I'm sorry," I say.

I know it sounds flimsy and hollow but at the moment, I don't know what else to say.

"What were you doing Saturday night?" she says, folding her arms beneath her breasts and staring at me. "Where were you that was so important you missed my birthday? More work-related bullshit?"

It takes me a moment to answer her because I'm not sure where I was. Then I remember Captain Kirk and Austin Powers and my rescue mission.

"I was with Nat," I say.

Delilah stares at me, not saying anything, then she grabs the vase of flowers and throws it at me. I duck and the vase shatters against the wall, scattering glass and water and roses everywhere.

CHAPTER 35

There are flowers everywhere.

Roses, carnations, and daisies. Gladiolas, chrysanthe-
mums, and snapdragons. Lilies, hydrangeas, and asters.
In reds and whites and yellows. In sprays and wreaths and
hearts. Mixed with lemon leaves and baby's breath and dag-
ger ferns.

The flowers are scattered all over the floor, near the closed
casket, while I stand at the front row of folding chairs, looking
around with my hands behind my back. I'm the only kid in
attendance. The grown-ups stand around, some crying, some
shaking their heads, some consoling others. A few chairs are
knocked over. The sun pours in through the windows on one
side of the room. Behind me, someone whispers my name
and something about my father, but I miss the rest of it.

When I look back to see who it is, no one's talking.
No one's looking at me. No one's owning up to anything.

They're all just standing there wearing dark suits and black dresses and solemn faces.

So I turn back to look at the flowers.

Where I am is Emerson's Funeral Home the week after my ninth birthday. The week after Alex Trebek came for a midnight visit. The week after my mother found out the truth about my father.

The flowers all used to be in nice arrangements, displayed around my father's coffin, free-standing on easels, laid across the top of the casket. But now they're broken and crushed and strewn around the viewing room, petals and stems and leaves all over the place like some kind of floral massacre, while my uncle and my grandfather hold my mother to one side of the casket as she strains to get free, her feet kicking at what used to be a wreath of white carnations and red roses.

"You bitch!" my mother half yells, half sobs at another woman who stands by herself. "You fucking whore!"

It's the first time I've ever heard my mother swear, or even raise her voice. She's never been the type to try to get her point across with shouting and violence. At least not for the first nine years of my existence. Apparently, my mother's decided to reinvent herself.

Inventing realities seems to run in my family.

"How could you do this to me?" my mother shouts before she collapses to her knees in what used to be a spray of snapdragons and daisies. My grandmother rushes in and puts her arms around my mother, whether to offer comfort or hold her down I can't tell.

I look around at the other mourners watching the show and wonder if this is the kind of service my father would have wanted. At least it tops the charts in entertainment value.

"I didn't know," says the woman standing ten feet away on the opposite side of my father's casket. Her black dress is torn, exposing a bare shoulder and a black bra strap and a trio of fresh scratches that are starting to bead with blood. "I didn't know!"

I'm standing alone in the front row, watching all of this, looking at my mother and the flowers and my father's coffin, trying to figure out what kind of lesson my father is trying to teach me this time.

It turns out that for the past six years, my father had been living a double life.

Those business trips he took? Those two and three and four days of each week he was gone someplace like Des Moines and Phoenix and Reno? Those phone calls to my mother from the road? He never took any business trips. He never went to any of those places. Or at least if he did, he never went alone.

He was married. To someone else besides my mother. To the woman with the torn black dress and the scratch marks on her shoulder and the mascara running down her cheeks. The woman my mother now wants to kill.

My father had taken on another identity. He had another name and another job and he lived in another house in another town with another wife. I don't know if he had a dog or a cat or a fish tank, but he didn't have any other children. Just me.

No one told me any of this. I learned it all by listening to the conversations of my relatives and to my mother's one-sided phone calls and to the whispers of my parents' friends.

I don't understand why my father would want to be married to two different women. It seems like a lot of work to me. But I'm sure he had his reasons.

Maybe after I was born he decided he didn't really want children. Maybe he wanted one family with children and one without. Maybe he just wanted another life.

I glance down at my mother, surrounded by scattered lilies and lemon leafs, kneeling on crushed gladiolas and asters, sobbing and shaking, saliva and mucus dripping from her mouth and nose, and I wonder if she did something to drive my father away or if I did.

I look over at my father's other wife, her face in her hands, her shoulder bare and bleeding, and I wonder if this is as hard for her as it is for my mother. I wonder if she ever went anywhere with my father. I wonder if he was the same man with her that he was with us.

Cold. Distant. Instructive.

The last thing my father said to me was to tell me how to properly chew my food.

I don't know how he managed to live two separate lives. Or what made him think he could get away with it. He didn't leave any note. He didn't offer any explanation. He didn't make any apologies. Whatever reasons he had went with him when he fell asleep while driving back home late at night, drifted onto the shoulder of the freeway, and slammed into the concrete support column of a highway overpass.

I look up from my father's two wives to his casket at the front of the room and I think about all of the lessons my father taught me. How he told me life wasn't a game. How he taught me about choices and sacrifices and commitments. How he said that everyone had a role to play.

As it turns out, my father's role was pretending to be my father.

I think about how he told me not to believe in anything or anyone but myself. Not Santa Claus. Not the Easter Bunny. Not the Tooth Fairy. Not God. But considering that my father was lying about who he was all of this time, I don't know what to believe anymore.

So I just watch my mother and the woman who was my father's secret wife as they both cry on either side of the coffin while I pretend that I'm a normal, happy kid.

CHAPTER 36

"I'm wet just thinking about you. I'm like a dripping faucet."

I'm sitting in my office the Tuesday after Thanksgiving, the last day of November, listening to Kurt play his voice mail on speakerphone and trying to stay on top of things after everything that's happened to my team and what's happening to me, when there's a loud crash followed by someone shouting, *"Fuck! Fuck! Fuck!"*

I'm not sure if that's Neil's voice or if Kurt's phone calls have taken a turn for the homoerotic, but before I can get up to find out which one it is, Emily appears in my doorway. "You better come quickly."

I follow Emily to the break room, where Neil is pacing back and forth from wall to wall, his lips moving in a silent mantra, his arms folded around his chest, hugging himself. Then his hands go up to his head, one on either side as if he's trying to hold it in place or keep something from getting out. The entire time his eyes are clamped shut.

Today he's dressed all in green, which strikes an uneasy chord. It also reminds me that we're behind on the reports for The Kermit.

Kurt shows up a moment later, with Vincent trailing behind him.

"What happened?" asks Kurt.

Emily shrugs. "I have no idea. He opened up the refrigerator and started screaming."

The refrigerator door stands open, one of the shelves on the floor, half the contents of the refrigerator spread out across the tile, bottles broken and containers leaking. It looks like an appliance terrorist bombing, with condiments and soda cans and Subway sandwiches among the collateral damage.

"Hey Neil," I say. "What's going on?"

His lips continue to move in a constant whisper, like he's saying a prayer. I can't hear what it is, so I step farther into the room.

"What did you say?" I ask.

Neil stops pacing and turns to look at me, his face red, his lips twisted in fury. "They're gone!"

"Uh oh," says Vincent. "Here we go again."

"You're not helping," I snap. But he's right. This doesn't seem like just an OCD freak-out.

I turn back to Neil. "What's gone?"

He walks over to the refrigerator and points an accusatory finger at it, his hand shaking and his lips quivering. "They were in there this morning, same as always. And now they're *gone*. There's nothing left. Nothing!"

"Okay, what was in there?" I ask in a soft, soothing voice, trying to calm him down. But I'm pretty sure I know the answer before he gives it.

"My juice boxes!" He walks away, his hands alternating between hugging himself and trying to hold his head on while he repeats "fuck" in triplicate.

When he resumes his pacing, I walk over to the refrigerator and bend down to look inside. Neil did a pretty thorough job of emptying the contents, so I don't know what I expect to find. Maybe Mrs. Butterworth and the Pillsbury Doughboy looking out at me from one of the shelves, shrugging their shoulders, their forefingers circling the sides of their heads.

Yeah, tell me something I don't know.

I stand up and turn around. "Are you sure you didn't—"

Neil is in my face before I can finish my sentence.

"I didn't *do* anything!" Spit flies from his lips, hitting me in the face. Not just a couple of strays but a full deployment of spit. It's like I'm the USS *Enterprise* being bombarded with saliva photons.

And just like that, the attack is over and Neil is pacing back and forth again, hugging himself and whispering some secret phrase over and over.

I walk over to Emily, Vincent, and Kurt as I wipe the spit off my face with one sleeve. "Does anyone know what happened to his juice boxes?" I keep my voice low and my eyes on Neil, who is now standing in the corner like Little Jack Horner with his back to us, his hands holding on to his head instead of his Christmas pie.

Kurt shrugs.

"I didn't take them," says Vincent.

"Me either," says Emily. "But I swear I heard him slurping this morning when I got in to work."

Neil always drinks one of his juice boxes at the exact same time every morning. Never a minute early. Never a minute late. He's as inevitable as a Hollywood sequel.

"Should I call someone?" asks Vincent.

"Not yet," I say. "Stay here and keep an eye on him. I'll be right back."

I walk through the office to Neil's workstation, where I pull out his garbage can. Inside are five empty juice boxes. I'm not sure what I find more troubling: the fact that he's finished all five juice boxes and doesn't remember doing it, or that he's finished them all and it's only Tuesday.

I walk back to the break room carrying the garbage can, which I show to the others. Kurt looks in and raises both eyebrows and gives a whistle. Emily and Vincent say nothing.

I walk over to Neil, who is still standing in the corner. "Neil?"

He turns around so fast I nearly stumble back. That's when I notice his left nostril is bleeding. Just like Emily and Chloe.

"I . . . found your juice boxes." I say it soft and easy, hoping to engender a sense of calm.

"Where are they?!" he screams. *"Where are my fucking juice boxes?!"*

So much for calm.

"They're in here." I nod toward the garbage can in my hands, which I hold out for him to see.

Neil looks in the garbage can, then up at me, then back down in the garbage can. "Who put those there?"

"I think you did."

He looks into the garbage can one more time, then back up at me, his face turning red, his mouth opening in a scream.

"WHO?! DRANK?! MY?! FUCKING?! JUICE BOXES?!"

An explosion of spit flies from Neil's lips, so I back away to avoid the barrage and step in something spilled on the floor. Ketchup or yogurt or a ham sandwich. Whatever it is, my foot slips on the tile and I lose my balance and start to fall—my arms flailing, both feet coming out from under me, the garbage can flying from my hands and the empty juice boxes tumbling out like dice. I hear Emily calling out and Neil shouting a string of profanities that turns into an unintelligible scream.

Then I hit the floor and my head snaps back and everything goes dark.

CHAPTER **37**

It's dark and quiet and I can't see a thing. My eyes are blindfolded as Chloe leads me by the hand, telling me we're almost there. When she finally stops and lets go of my hand, the blindfold comes off and everyone shouts:

"Surprise!"

Where I am is the meeting room at our EGOS office three months ago in August for my birthday party. The members of my team are all shaking my hand or giving me a hug or patting me on the back. Someone brought a cake, a store-bought monstrosity covered with white frosting and candles and HAPPY BIRTHDAY spelled out in blue letters. On the table next to the cake sit half a dozen gifts wrapped in paper and bows and ribbons. Helium-filled balloons in assorted colors float in the air. Everyone's wearing party hats. On the overhead speakers, the Beatles are singing "Birthday."

You say it's your birthday. It's my birthday, too, yeah.

Chloe gives me a big hug and a kiss on the cheek. Kurt shakes my hand and grins and says something about being ready for another year. Neil raises a plastic cup of punch in my direction, avoiding any physical contact but offering a smile and a nod. Angela cuts up pieces of cake and puts them on plates as Vincent sucks helium out of a balloon and pretends to be a Munchkin from the Lollipop Guild. Emily stands next to him, laughing.

I look down and there's a glass of punch in my hand, so I drink half of it. It's just sugar and water and artificial flavoring and a little rum, but it tastes like a tropical drink on a beach in the Caribbean.

Then the glass of punch is empty and someone takes it from me for a refill and someone puts something else into my hands. When I look down I see it's a small box about the size of a paperback book, wrapped in bright, festive birthday paper. When I look up, I see Chloe standing in front of me, wearing a smile as big as Texas and saying, "It's from all of us," and then asking me to open it. So I do. At least my hands do. It seems like they're operating independently of my brain. And they're taking a long time.

I'm suddenly aware that no one is talking and everyone is watching me, smiling and waiting in anticipation for my reaction. I don't know what's in the box, but I suddenly feel a pressure to love whatever it is.

When I finally get the paper removed, I'm holding a white box. I open it to find a smooth silver case with the words THE CATCHER IN THE RYE engraved on the front.

My favorite book is *The Catcher in the Rye*.

I take the silver case out and open it. Inside, the case is lined with blue velvet that surrounds a small Plexiglas bottle labeled HOLDEN CAULFIELD.

"We all chipped in and placed a special order," says Chloe. "We knew how much you wanted it."

I look up and see Chloe and Vincent and Emily, all of them watching me. Somehow I manage to say, "Thank you."

I look back down at the Plexiglas bottle in its cushion of blue velvet, then I close the case and run my fingers over the engraved title. Nobody's ever given me a gift like this before. Not Nat. Not Delilah. Not my parents.

My throat is tight and I'm having trouble talking.

My face is an ear-to-ear smile to fight off the tears.

On the overhead speakers, the Beatles are singing "In My Life."

Emily puts a plate with a piece of cake into my hands and asks me if I'm surprised. I manage to say "Yes" and "Thank you," then I set the plate down and excuse myself to use the bathroom. As soon as the door shuts and locks behind me, I start to cry.

I don't remember the last time I cried. My father always told me crying was a sign of weakness and that to show weakness was to show that you'd given up, that you were no longer in charge. No matter whether you feel pain or grief or joy or madness, the trick is to maintain the appearance of equanimity.

I'm nothing if not my father's son.

I take a few deep breaths and splash some cold water

on my face, then I look in the mirror, at the water dripping from my chin and glistening on my cheeks, and for a moment I get the impression that my face is melting and I no longer recognize who I am. Then the moment passes and I dry my face and head back out to join the party.

CHAPTER **38**

It's all become clear to me. Or at least as clear as it can, considering I'm still having moments and days when I'm not able to think straight. The mild concussion I received from hitting my head on the break room floor isn't helping matters.

I've never had a concussion before so I don't know how it's supposed to feel, but my thoughts are getting mixed up, like they're being copied and not collated. Other times I see something on television or read something in the paper or have a conversation and twenty minutes later, whatever I saw or read or heard plays back in my head as if I'm experiencing it for the first time.

It's like having my life on tape delay.

Because I'm struggling with my focus and concentration, and because I suffered a head injury on the job, I've been given a medical leave of absence from work for the entire month of December. Actually it's more like I've been forced to take some personal time. Company policy, according to HR. Standard procedure. But I know the real reason they've sent me home.

They don't want me to learn the truth about what they're doing. About what's going on and what they're covering up.

I don't know what the company told Neil's family about what happened to him, but I know it wasn't related to his OCD—just like I know Angela's anti-anxiety medication had nothing to do with her breakdown and Chloe wasn't using black market Egos.

This is what the company is claiming, the stories that have been leaked to the other departments. And that's exactly what they are. Stories. Fabrications.

I know the truth. The FDA was right. Egos *are* dangerous. And not just the ones being sold on the black market.

Truth is, the company is trying to cover up the truth.

Not only regarding the safety of Big Egos and what happened to Chloe and Angela and Neil, but the company's role in the deaths of dozens of black market Ego users.

I don't have any documentation of my meeting with Bill Summers, and the bonus and stock shares and penthouse suite he promised never materialized, but that only confirms my belief that the company is trying to hide the truth about what I was asked to do. At first I thought that would be impossible, considering there were other EGOS employees like me out testing the antidote. But since I wasn't told the truth about what I was doing, I have no reason to believe that there was anyone else going to Ego parties and giving the antidote to unsuspecting black market Ego users. I was the only one.

Truth is, I'm pretty sure I was set up.

I haven't shared this with anyone because I don't know who I can trust. I'm not even sure I can trust Emily, Kurt, or Vincent, who are all going through mandatory counseling while continuing their work, apparently under the supervision of Bill Summers—which only raises my suspicions further.

For all I know, Emily, Kurt, and Vincent are part of the cover-up. All three of them were already working here when I started, so maybe they've been involved all along. Maybe they're spies.

Even if they aren't, I can't take the chance that they might talk to someone else or tell the wrong person. This isn't something they can help me with. This is something I'm going to have to handle on my own.

I know I'm taking a risk continuing to inject Egos, but this is the only way I can think of to do what needs to be done, to make things right. Besides, I've spent so much time over the past three years pretending to be someone else that I've grown accustomed to not being me. It's my comfort zone. It's when I feel the most in control. It's when I feel the most myself.

I pick up the smooth silver case and run my fingers along the engraved letters, then I undo the latch and remove the small Plexiglas bottle from its bed of blue velvet and insert the syringe into the bottle. Once the syringe is filled with two milliliters of amber fluid, I reach around to the back of my neck, inject the needle into the base of my brain stem, and depress the plunger. Almost immediately my appearance starts to shift and my conscience starts to drift, the part that is me retreating into a corner as the DNA-laced cocktail calibrates my brain and readjusts my face, turning me into someone new.

Truth is, reality is overrated.

CHAPTER **39**

Romeo stands behind the DJ table, spinning "I'm Your Boogie Man" by KC and the Sunshine Band, while Juliet and Holly Golightly dirty dance with Harry Potter—rubbing up against him from the front and the back, making a wizard sandwich. They motion for me to come join them but I don't know what to do with women. The trouble with me is, once we get started, I never know if they want me to stop or keep going. Most guys don't stop. I can't help it. I keep stopping. Either that or I fall in love with them. Women can drive you crazy. They really can.

Instead I just wave and pretend like I don't know what they want and I stroll through the party and look around. I don't see any crooks yet but you ask me, every place has them. Someone is always being a goddamn crook. That's why I wore my favorite hat. My red hunting hat. My people-hunting hat. And I'm hunting for a specific person.

Over in the corner, Sam Spade and Philip Marlowe are drinking and laughing, their mouths open as big as goddamn manholes. The way they're laughing you'd think one of them was a regular comedian. I mean, no one can be that happy. I bet they're just a couple of phonies. If there's one thing I hate, it's phonies. They make me sick.

More laughter comes from the couch, where Tyler Durden is chatting up Madame Bovary and Jane Eyre, charming as hell, trying to get them to buy some of his homemade soap. I don't know if they believe any of his crap but if you ask me, he just wants to take them both into a room and give them the time. That's all most of these phonies want to do with women. Give them the time. They don't have any respect. He probably doesn't even know their first names.

That's what's wrong with the world. It's full of goddamn phonies.

Nearby, Hester Prynne sits on a chair, wearing this red dress that's sexy as hell as she flirts with Patrick Bateman, Atticus Finch, and Jake Barnes. I don't know what the hell Barnes is thinking. Even if he does get Prynne alone, he won't be able to give her the time. What a lousy moron.

Over by the bar, Elizabeth Bennet and Elinor Dashwood are both hitting on Sherlock Holmes, who's wearing this corny deerstalker hat, while Dr. Henry Jekyll mixes up drinks for everyone. I walk over and order a scotch-and-soda and Holmes looks at my own hat and tells me it's grand. If there's one word I hate, it's grand. It's so phony.

As I'm waiting for my drink, I notice Willy Wonka handing out candy to Lolita and Alice. Humbert Humbert sits a few feet away, checking them out, sipping his cocktail, nervous as hell and sweating. When he catches me looking at him, he gives me a phony smile.

Jekyll finally gets me my drink and as I'm walking away, Captain Ahab limps past, bumping into me and knocking my drink out of my hand and muttering "To hell with the white whale" as he heads over to join the growing suitors gathered around Hester Prynne. Behind me, Holmes and Jekyll are laughing at me, the bastards, while Ebenezer Scrooge plunders the dessert table, shoving cookies and cupcakes into his pockets. Blanche DuBois and Stanley Kowalski stand a few feet away, arguing.

"To be or not to be, that is the question . . ."

Hamlet stands on a chair, a cocktail glass in one hand, and spouts out the rest of his famous goddamn soliloquy. He's always doing things like that, boring as hell. I can't stand bores. I'm not kidding.

I look over at Romeo and motion for him to turn up the music. He looks at me and nods, cranking up "Play That Funky Music" by Wild Cherry and drowning out the rest of Hamlet's speech.

While I'm looking around and thinking about ordering another scotch-and-soda from that bastard Jekyll, Kilgore Trout walks up and starts talking to me, acting like he's some terrific friend of mine, clapping me on the back and shaking my hand, telling me his life story like we haven't seen each other in years.

People like that annoy the hell out of me.

I tell him I have to go to the bathroom, which I don't, then I grab a bottle of Patrón Silver tequila from the bar and walk down the hallway toward the kitchen. On my way, I pass a room filled with books, some kind of library, and I see Guy

Montag standing in the middle of the room, turning slowly around in circles.

When I ask him what he's doing, he gets this corny expression on his face and says, "Just thinking."

I shrug and head into the kitchen, one of those big custom-design jobs with an island and a breakfast nook and about half a million cabinets. It's the kind of kitchen that's so goddamn big you could just about live in it.

Tarzan and Jane Porter are in the kitchen, half naked in front of the refrigerator with the doors open. I mean, Tarzan and Jane are always half naked, but Jane isn't usually hanging on to the top of the refrigerator doors with her legs wrapped around Tarzan's hips. They don't seem to mind me, so I sit down at the breakfast nook and wait for them to finish. Peter Pan comes into the kitchen, stands next to me, and watches with his goddamn mouth and eyes wide open.

"I've changed my mind," he says. "I want to grow up."

What really knocks me out is that they know we're watching them but they don't stop until they're finished.

When they're done, Jane smooths out her leopard skin skirt, gives us a smile and a wink, then grabs a tray of puff cheese pastries and walks out of the kitchen with Peter Pan following close behind.

I smile at Tarzan and say, "You're just who I've been looking for."

Tarzan looks at me like he's trying to figure out who the hell I am. Then he points to himself. "Me Tarzan."

"No kidding," I say. "And that was Jane."

He smiles. "Tarzan like Jane."

Who wouldn't like Jane? I'd give her the time, but like I

said, I'd probably end up stopping on account of the type of guy I am. Which makes me feel lousy as hell.

Tarzan follows up his declaration of love for Jane with a rapid beating of his chest.

What a goddamned phony. I mean, anyone who read their Edgar Rice Burroughs knows that the Tarzan in the novels is educated and intelligent, not the syllable-challenged film version. It just goes to show that this phony has no appreciation for literature.

I set the bottle of tequila on the table. Tarzan's eyebrows raise and he gets this big, goofy smile on his face. "Tarzan like tequila. Tarzan get shot glasses."

He grabs a couple of tall shot glasses out of one of his half a million cabinets and sits down at the table with me.

I pour each of us a shot, then I raise my glass to him and drink mine. He does the same, then wipes his mouth with a grimace and a grunt. I pour us each another shot and we drink those down fast as hell. The thing is, I can't stand tequila, but I knew Tarzan wouldn't be able to resist. The goddamn phony.

Before I'm halfway done with my second shot, Tarzan slams his shot glass down on the table and pounds his chest and lets out one of his goddamn yells.

That's something else that gives me a royal pain. Show-offs. I can't stand show-offs. They're even worse than bores and phonies.

I pour us each another shot but before we drink them, I ask Tarzan if he has any limes. Tarzan beats once on his chest, then gets up and moves like an ape over to the refrigerator. When he does, I reach into my shirt pocket, pull out a capsule, and crack it open, dumping the powdered contents into Tarzan's shot glass.

"And some salt," I say. "We need some salt for Christ's sake."

When Tarzan returns with the shaker of salt and slices of lime, the contents of the capsule have dissolved in his tequila.

"Limes," says Tarzan. "And salt."

He's a regular goddamn genius.

I lick my hand between my thumb and index finger and pour some salt on it, then I grab my shot glass. After two shots of tequila I'm feeling pretty lousy, but I don't have much of a choice. Tarzan dumps salt all over his hand, then licks it up, makes a face, and slams down his shot as I choke down mine.

Tarzan pounds his chest again, then jumps up on top of the table and lets out another one of his head-splitting yells. I don't wait around to watch what happens to him but get up and walk out of the kitchen and stagger down the hall and end up outside throwing up in the bushes while Rhett Butler and Jay Gatsby laugh at me over their martinis.

The lousy goddamn bastards.

CHAPTER **40**

I wake up on my side on a couch facing a giant plasma television, half hearing the news playing on CNN, wondering where I am and what day it is. Spittle has pooled on the pillow beneath my mouth, which feels like it could use some disinfecting.

On the television, the news anchor is telling a familiar story.

"This is another of the growing number of deaths over the past several months linked to the illegally manufactured products."

My head is pounding. When I sit up, I feel like I might vomit. But from the taste in my mouth, I'm guessing that wouldn't be anything new.

On the floor next to a pair of brown dress loafers is a red hunting hat with earflaps.

I pick up the hat and look around and realize I'm in my living room. I still don't know what day it is, but from the soft, filtered light coming in through the windows I'm guessing it's pushing sunset. I glance at the clock and see that it's 4:33 in the afternoon. I hate December. It's dark before five o'clock.

I toss the hat on the couch, then get up and go into the kitchen and fill a glass with cold water as the news anchor continues to talk about the deaths related to the use of black market Egos. When the anchor says the victim is someone with ties to Engineering Genetics Organization and Systems, I nearly drop my glass of water.

"We go to reporter Rachel Harrison for details on the latest victim."

I sit back down on the couch next to the hat and put on the 3-D glasses as the video feed switches to an attractive woman standing out in front of a black iron gate between two brick walls, behind which sits a rather large and expensive-looking home.

I turn up the volume.

"Over the past several months here in Los Angeles, California, there has been a startling rise in the fatalities of people who have purchased Egos on the black market, but none more startling than the death that occurred at this Bel Air residence last night."

The house looks familiar. But then, when you've seen one Bel Air mansion, you've seen them all.

"Bill Summers, an executive with Engineering Genetics Organization and Systems, the developer and manufacturer of Big Egos based here in Los Angeles, collapsed and died early this morning at a party he was hosting, apparently after injecting a black market Ego."

Rachel Harrison continues to talk, but I'm just staring at the television, watching her lips move and not really hearing what she's saying.

Bill Summers? Did she say Bill Summers? That might explain why the house looks familiar. And I'm suddenly wondering where I was last night.

I hear the sound of a key rattling in a lock. Moments later, the front door opens and Delilah walks in carrying a Prada shopping bag. When she sees me, she stands there wearing red leather pants, a black leather jacket, and a look of disappointment.

"Well, look who finally woke up," she says.

I have this vague recollection of a dream where I was at a party with a bunch of famous literary characters. At least I think it was a dream. Some of the details are so vivid that I have the feeling it wasn't a dream at all. And I remember something about tequila shots, which would explain the headache and the taste of vomit in my mouth.

For some reason, the thought occurs to me that Bill Summers was a tequila drinker.

"While no official word has been released by the company, the death of one of their own has come as a shock to EGOS," says Rachel Harrison. "Further complicating matters is the question as to why a company executive who has led the charge against illegally manufactured Egos would risk using a product he publicly decried as dangerous."

"What are you wearing?" asks Delilah as she sets her Prada shopping bag on the dining room table. "I've never seen that outfit before."

I look down at my clothes and notice that I'm wearing a blue V-neck sweater, a white collared shirt, and gray sharkskin slim-fit pants. When I look at the red hunting hat with earflaps lying on the floor, a thought goes through my head.

This is my people-hunting hat. I hunt people in this hat.

Delilah walks over and stands next to the couch, looking down at me. "So where were you last night?"

I look up at the TV. Bill Summers's house sits dark and quiet in the approaching twilight behind Rachel Harrison as she wraps up her story.

"When asked about the possibility that Bill Summers's death was caused by one of the company's own Egos and not one of those available at a discount on the black market, a spokesman for EGOS refused to comment."

"Hello?" says Delilah. "Are you listening to me?"

CHAPTER **41**

"**A**re you listening to me?" says Martin Scorsese. "Did you hear what I said?"

Scorsese is standing in the middle of my parents' kitchen, which is more like a Hollywood movie set. I see boom mics and stage lights and a film crew standing off in the shadows behind him. Although I can't make out all of their faces, I recognize Chloe and Vincent and the rest of my team. I even see Delilah standing near the camera, looking annoyed.

Big surprise.

Where we are is . . . I don't know when.

It takes me a moment to realize Scorsese is my father. And that he's talking to me.

"Yes," I say from my seat at the kitchen table. "I'm listening."

"Good, because I'd really like to get this scene wrapped before lunch." Scorsese goes to sit back down in his chair.

"Let's take it from the top, only this time, with a little more feeling. Let's show some emotion."

My mother stands over by the sink, leaning against the counter, smoking a cigarette, which is weird because my mother never smoked. And she's my mother now, not from twenty years ago, or at least what she probably looks like now. I haven't seen her since I graduated from high school so I have no idea if she's taken up smoking or skydiving or has a hundred cats.

We never exactly stayed in touch.

I'm sitting at the kitchen table. I'm me as an adult but I feel like I'm a little kid. Eight years old and trying to please my father, but knowing that's not likely to happen. Not unless someone has written a new script.

"You all set?" Scorsese says to me.

My mother lets out a laugh, then takes another drag on her cigarette while I remain seated at the table, wondering why she's laughing, and I realize I have no idea what my lines are.

"What's the scene again?" I ask.

"For Christ's sake!" My mother taps her ashes into the sink. "Do I really have to work with him? Can't we get someone more professional?"

One of the members of the film crew, an intern or some kind of assistant, comes over with an ashtray for my mother, which he holds out for her while she taps her ashes into it. It takes me a second before I realize the assistant is Nat.

Scorsese stands up and walks over to the kitchen table and leans on it, resting his weight on both hands as he stares down at me. "What are you doing?"

I look up at my father, at Martin Scorsese, and I wonder if he's still pissed-off that he lost the 1990 Best Picture Oscar to *Dances with Wolves*. "I think I've forgotten my lines."

He looks at me and shakes his head and lets out the smallest of sighs. The look of disappointment on his face is as familiar as my own reflection.

"What have I told you about playing the part?" he says. "We've gone over this time and time again. Always know your role."

"I know. I'm sorry."

"And never apologize. It's a sign of weakness."

I look past him to the rest of the crew, where Delilah stands next to the director's chair with a script in her hand. She's either the script supervisor or the assistant director, I don't know, but she doesn't look happy. Next to her, Neil sits behind the film camera while Chloe holds the boom mic and Angela and Emily stand off to the side, gaffers or grips or some other film job you read on the closing credits but you have no idea who the people are or what they actually do. Vincent sits in the background wearing headphones. I don't see Kurt.

"Line!" yells my father, not looking away from me.

Delilah rolls her eyes and reads from the script. "When is Dad coming home?"

Well, that narrows it down. This could be one of any number of times I asked my mother that question.

"What's the next line?" I ask.

My father continues to stare at me.

"Then your mother says, 'Soon, honey. He'll be home

soon.'" Delilah looks up from the script. "Do you need your next line?"

"Please."

"How soon is soon?"

I never realized how many times my mother and I had the same conversation about my father.

My father stands up. "You got all that?"

Behind him, the film crew waits for my response. None of them look happy.

"Sure," I say.

"You're going to have to do better than that to convince me," he says.

"Do you mean now or once we start filming?"

"As far as I'm concerned, there's not a difference." My father turns and walks back to the camera and sits down in the director's chair.

I'm beginning to think I'm not cut out to be an actor.

"Okay," says my father. "Let's try this again."

"First positions!" shouts Delilah. "Everyone quiet. Going for picture."

My mother turns her back to me. At first I think she's doing it because she's fed up with my lack of professionalism, until I realize she's just getting into position.

"Sound?" says Delilah.

"Sound's clear," says Vincent, who is apparently the sound engineer.

"All right," says Delilah. "Roll sound."

"Speed," says Vincent.

Delilah gives me one final look. "And roll camera."

"Rolling."

Emily walks out in front of the kitchen table with a clapperboard and turns toward the camera. "Where's Dad? Scene thirteen. Take twenty."

Apparently we've been at this for a while.

Then Emily slaps the clapsticks together and moves out of the way.

My father looks us over and then raises his right hand in the air, his index finger extended and moving in small circles. "And . . . action."

"When's Dad coming home?" I say.

"Soon, honey." My mother says her line with her back to me as she washes something in the sink. "He'll be home soon."

"How soon is soon?"

"As soon as he can, dear."

I don't remember my mother sounding this exasperated when I was a kid, but at least the lines are starting to come back to me.

"Tomorrow?"

"Maybe," she says.

"Do you think he'll bring back something for me this time?"

"Maybe. But I wouldn't get your hopes up."

That's an understatement. In order for me to get my hopes up about my father bringing me a present, I would have to climb down into a cellar.

I look away from my mother and down at the table, where a piece of Sara Lee apple pie sits on a plate in front of me, so I take a bite.

"Can I have some ice cream?"

"Cut," says my father.

"Jesus Christ!" My mother takes off her apron and throws it on the floor before storming off the set with Nat trailing after her.

"What?" I say. "What did I do?"

"That's a cut," says Delilah. "Everyone take five."

The crew gets up and heads over to grab some coffee and snacks as my father gets up from his chair and walks over to me.

"Did I miss my lines?" I ask.

"It's not the lines." He sits down at the table across from me. "It's just that I'm not feeling it from you."

"Feeling what?"

"Sincerity, son. You have to surrender yourself to the role. Make me believe it's you."

But I am me, I think. How can I not know how to play me?

My father leans forward on his elbows. "You need to put a little more passion into it. Give it some emotion. Make it more *real*."

He gives me a long, disappointed look, then stands up and turns around and walks away. Delilah approaches me a moment later and throws a copy of the script down on the table in front of me.

"Try not to screw up your lines again," she says.

CHAPTER **42**

My cell phone rings. When I open my eyes, the bedroom is bathed in darkness and shadows. Delilah lies beneath the covers with her back to me and as far to the other side of the bed as possible. She doesn't stir. Either she's in a post-Ego coma or she's ignoring me.

I pick up the phone and press ANSWER. Before I can say anything, Nat's already talking.

". . . don't know what to do! You gotta help me!"

He sounds out of breath and frantic. On the bedside table, the green digital numbers of the calendar alarm clock tell me it's 2:08 in the morning on Tuesday, December 7. "Do you know what time it is?"

"I'm in trouble, bro!"

More than once over the past couple of weeks I've thought about calling Nat to try to reconcile, extend the proverbial olive branch, but I figured he would just slap it away or set it on fire. So my first thought is that Nat's changed his mind about not wanting my friendship and is falling into old habits, calling me to come to his rescue in order to break the ice. I don't think there's anything really wrong.

"What kind of trouble?" I say as I get out of bed and walk out of the bedroom, not wanting to wake up Delilah and invite her wrath.

"You gotta come get me!" he says.

I let out a sigh. "Where are you?"

No response but I can hear faint sounds, feet running and someone breathing hard, followed by something that sounds like glass breaking, then Nat shouting out either in pain or surprise.

"Nat?"

No response. And I'm suddenly beginning to think he might actually be in some kind of trouble.

"Nat, what's going on?"

"I went down to Hollywood to get some Egos," he says, his words coming out rushed between breaths. "This guy who sells them off Wilcox. I couldn't help myself."

I should have known he'd do something like this, which makes me feel bad about the way I took his Egos away.

"But then something happened," he says. "And I just took all of them and ran."

"Wait . . . you took them?" I say.

I hear street noises in the background. Traffic. Voices. Someone shouting. The sound of a siren.

"It was just . . . I always wanted to be like you, you know?" he says. "Popular and confident. I couldn't stand who I was but I couldn't seem to do anything about it, no matter what I did. But then I started injecting Egos and everything changed and I didn't want to go back to the way I was."

This is the first time Nat has ever shared any of this with me. I open my mouth to tell him I'm sorry, but that sounds so trite and I don't know what else to say.

"I fucked up, bro." There's a pause and all I hear is the sound of Nat breathing, followed by a single choked sob. "I'm sorry I didn't listen to you."

I can hear him crying now, his breath coming out in hitched sobs. Someone in the background is laughing.

"Nat, where are you?"

"I'm on Hollywood Boulevard," he says, sniffling. "Near the Hollywood/Vine station. Can you come get me?"

"I'll be right there," I say. "Just stay put."

There's another pause, only this time I don't hear Nat breathing. For a second I think I've lost the connection and I'm about to hang up and call him back, then I hear his voice again, but it doesn't sound like he's talking to me.

"Oh fuck."

"Nat. What's wrong?"

I hear voices and more shouting, mixed in with Nat's panicked breathing. It sounds like he's running.

"Nat?"

A car horn blares and I hear the sound of tires screeching. Somebody shouts out something unintelligible.

"Nat?"

I hear the voices getting closer, followed by Nat's voice, calling for help. Someone shouts, *You motherfucker!*

"Nat!"

CHAPTER 43

Wires run from Nat to the EKG monitor next to his bed at the Los Angeles Medical Center on Sunset Boulevard. He's hooked up to a ventilator and a feeding tube and some other contraption I can't identify. There are so many machines plugged into him that he looks like a science experiment.

Are you still you if machines are keeping you alive?

In the bed next to him, behind the dividing curtain, an older woman with a raspy voice keeps coughing and spitting up phlegm and calling out for help.

"Nurse?" she says.

It's after 10 p.m. on Tuesday night, twenty hours after Nat called me and a little over two weeks before Christmas. I've been sitting here for the past three hours talking to him, looking for some kind of response, anything to let me know that he hears me. That he knows I'm here. But he remains motionless except for his chest moving up and down from the ventilator inflating his lungs. The only noises he's making are coming from the machines keeping him on life support. The only one doing any talking other than me is the elderly woman next door.

"Nurse?"

"Nat? Can you hear me, buddy?" I say. "If you can hear me, I just want you to know that I'm sorry for . . ."

For what? For not being there when he needed me? For taking his Egos? For getting him hooked on Egos in the first place?

"I'm sorry for everything," I say.

I look at him lying there, not saying anything, so I keep talking. I've been talking so much that I've started to grow tired of the sound of my own voice. But I have to keep trying, just in case Nat can hear me. And not talking seems to make the guilt that much harder to bear.

On the other side of the curtain, the old woman continues to call out for help.

"Nurse?"

"Hey," I say. "Remember that time we were playing Emergency and you set your garbage can on fire and nearly burned down your bedroom and we convinced your mom you just burned a couple of pizzas?"

Nat just lies there, unresponsive.

"Or that time you got trapped in the trunk of your mom's car while playing Hostage?"

Not a nod or a twitch.

"Or when we played the Seven Plagues of Egypt and that

gopher snake got down your pants and bit your left testicle and wouldn't let go?"

My laughter floats through the room alone.

All of this reminiscing about the two of us getting into trouble, all of these memories that we shared over the course of our childhood, and I'm the only one who gets to enjoy it.

"Is anybody there?" asks the old woman.

I look at Nat, at the bruises and the abrasions and the broken nose, at the cast on his right shoulder and the bandage wrapped around his shaved head, my anger mixing in with my guilt. Someone should have to answer for what happened to Nat. Someone other than me.

I take hold of his hand. "Hey pal, you still in there?"

He answers with more silence.

"If you can hear me, just give a squeeze."

His hand is dead weight in mine.

"Wiggle a finger. Raise an eyebrow. Flip me off. Anything."

Nothing. Not a hint of a wiggle or a smile.

Next door, the woman coughs and spits up more phlegm.

"Can someone raise my bed?" she says.

I don't want to leave Nat, so I press the call button for the nurse. Then, still holding Nat's hand, I close my eyes and do something I've never done before because my father taught me not to believe in anything but myself. Not Santa Claus. Not the Easter Bunny. Not God.

Truth is, I don't know what I believe in anymore.

But I figure it couldn't hurt to try. So I ask whoever or

whatever might be out there to help Nat. To make him better. To show me how I can help him. To show me what to do. Then I sit and listen to the respirator and the EKG machine, waiting for an answer. But the only response to my prayer is the sound of the woman next to us coughing and hacking and calling out for help.

"Someone help me," says the woman. "I can't breathe."

I'm about to get up to go over to help her when the door opens and the nurse walks in.

I'm probably imagining things, but she looks like Nurse Ratched from *One Flew Over the Cuckoo's Nest*. For a moment I wonder if she's on an Ego trip or if it's just a natural resemblance. I also wonder if I'm at the Los Angeles Medical Center or the Metropolitan State Hospital. Then I glance down and see I'm wearing black pants and loafers instead of white scrubs and slippers, which is a relief. I just hope Jack Nicholson and Danny DeVito don't come walking through the door.

"Is everything okay?" asks Nurse Ratched.

I nod. "I think the woman in the other bed needs some help."

The nurse disappears behind the curtain and I sit and stare at my comatose best friend, at his chest artificially rising and falling, at his broken body and the wires and tubes and machines feeding him and keeping him alive. Tears threaten to fill up my eyes and spill down my cheeks, but I can't give in to my grief. Not now. Not when Nat needs me the most.

I sit and stare at him and think about how we used to

play Emergency and how Nat would get into trouble and I would have to figure out how to solve the problem. This is a lot like that, only this time, it's real.

"I'm going to fix this," I tell him. "I'm sorry I wasn't there for you before, but I'm going to find a way to make it right."

Next door, the woman starts coughing and gagging and retching.

CHAPTER **44**

The Easter Bunny is throwing up in the bushes.

He's heaving, his entire body working to cleanse his insides of the alcohol that has poisoned him, his deep, anguished cries following the beer and bile out of his mouth.

"*Waaaaaaaaaaaaaggh!*"

He sounds like a tuba having an orgasm.

"You think we should call a doctor?" says Nat, who is dressed up like a satyr, with faux fur chaps and a real goatee he grew all by himself. Even his horns look almost real. Either that or I've smoked way too much pot.

"No," I say as a cute little brunette wearing a pink satin corset and a pink chiffon skirt with matching wings walks up to the Easter Bunny and taps him on the back with her wand. "It looks like the Tooth Fairy is coming to his rescue."

Where we are is the front porch for the annual Mythical Creatures party at Alpha Kappa Phi during November of our junior year at UCLA. I'm sitting on the porch wall in my red Santa suit with my white wig and synthetic beard while Nat stands nearby, checking out the action. In addition to the Easter Bunny and the Tooth Fairy, the other party guests includes gargoyles, leprechauns, vampires, werewolves, zombies, the bogeyman, a mermaid, Poseidon, Lady Luck, Satan, a guy in a diaper dressed up as Baby New Year, and some blond joker wearing a neoprene particle mask and heavy-duty blue mortician's gloves who claims he's Death.

It's the party of the year. Everyone is here pretending to be someone else. And most of them are really drunk. Like Peter Cottontail over there.

The Easter Bunny continues to heave into the bushes, coughing and spitting, as the Tooth Fairy finishes off her bottle of beer and sets it on the ground. When she bends over, I notice that she's wearing a thong. She comforts the Easter Bunny as he finishes throwing up, then gives him some Chiclets and leads him back inside the fraternity.

A petite redheaded elf with pointy ears and dressed in a green micro-miniskirt, green leggings, and a low-cut green V-neck T-shirt skips past, looks over at me, and smiles and waves and says, "Hey Santa!" before she skips off into the night.

"Bro. Did you see that? She's totally into you."

"Yeah," I say, trying to drink my beer but my beard keeps getting in the way. "That's why she ran away."

I reach up and scratch at my face, then unhook the synthetic white beard from around my ears and shove the beard into my sack of toys, which is really a sack filled with blocks of Styrofoam. Then I take a drink and I wonder if I should lose the wig and the fake plastic belly.

"Why are you taking off the beard?" asks Nat.

"Because it itches."

"But it's part of the costume. And chicks love sitting on Santa's lap."

"Yeah, well, they don't love synthetic beards." I take off the wig, then reach under my coat and unhook the fake plastic belly. "Or beer bellies."

"Maybe you can be a young Santa," says Nat. "I mean, even though he's always portrayed in the white beard and all, he had to be twenty-one at some point, right?"

"Hypothetically," I say. "But we are talking about someone who's just a mythological amalgam of a nineteenth-century Dutch figure, Father Christmas, a Norse god, and a fourth-century gift-giving saint. So to say that he would have been a young man is kind of a pointless justification."

"Hey, don't channel your father's practical, dream-crushing bullshit to me," says Nat.

"He just prepared me so I wouldn't be disappointed."

"Whatever." Nat takes a drink of his own beer. "No offense, bro, but your dad should go down in history as the world's biggest douche bag."

"No offense taken."

"I just appreciate that you didn't ruin Santa for me," says Nat.

"Yeah, well, that wasn't easy, considering you believed in him until you were eleven."

"I can't help it if I'm a believer."

A couple of drunk leprechauns stumble past us and into the fraternity while Bigfoot and Mothman walk out onto the porch and start talking about how they both want to kick the shit out of the Jersey Devil.

"In all honesty, bro," Nat sits down on the wall next to me. "Me to you, no bullshit . . . I think you'd make a *great* Santa Claus."

"You're so fucking stoned."

"I know. But you'd still make a great Santa."

"Thanks."

Nat and I sit there on the porch wall, drinking our beers, listening to the music thumping inside and watching the menagerie of mythical creatures, when three women wearing identical long white robes step outside to share a clove cigarette.

"Who are they supposed to be?" says Nat.

"I think they're supposed to be the Moirai."

"The more-eye?" he says. "You mean like spiders? Spiders have eight eyes, you know."

"Jesus. Do they look like spiders?"

"No," says Nat. "But I wouldn't mind getting caught in their web."

"The Moirai," I say. "The Fates. It's from Greek mythology. One of them spins the thread of life, one of them measures it, and the other one cuts it."

Nat checks them out. "I think I'll stay away from the one with the scissors. But I've got something the other one can measure."

He puts his hand up in the air for a high-five. I just shake my head and drink my beer, so Nat takes his unreciprocated celebratory hand gesture and fingers one of his horns instead.

"I think I'm getting a little horny," he says.

"You keep saying that."

"I know. And it never gets old."

The Moirai finish their clove cigarette, then turn and head back to the dance floor. One of them glances back at Nat and smiles, then follows her friends inside.

"Did you see that?" says Nat.

"I saw it."

"She digs me. She just doesn't know it yet."

"Why don't you go enlighten her? Educate her on all that is the glory of Nat?"

Nat nods in agreement but he doesn't move. "You think I should?"

"You're a satyr. You're subversive and dangerous. A lover of wine and women. Ready for every physical pleasure. Of course you should."

Nat rubs his horns again, as if to verify what I'm saying. Or else to give himself some courage. If there's another reason he keeps playing with his horns, I don't want to know.

"You think so?" he says.

"Isn't that why you chose the costume?"

"You're right." Nat drains the rest of his beer. "It's time I find me a nymph, bro."

Nat jumps off the porch wall and heads off after the brunette, strutting along, trying to play the role of a sexually appealing and evocative creature. If I were taking odds on his chances of finding a nymph, the smart money would be ten to one that he comes back out alone. But maybe he'll get lucky. Maybe his costume will help him to overcome his social ineptitude.

That's the beauty of the Mythological Creatures party. Or any party where the guests can get dressed up in costumes and shed their inhibitions. It's amazing what kind of transformation takes place when you put on a mask or a corset or a pair of horns and allow yourself to become someone or something else. To let go of your preconceived notions of who you are.

The shy, awkward kid who sits by himself at lunch and gets picked on in gym class puts on a pirate costume and becomes the life of the party.

The soft-spoken blonde who sits in the back row and wears sensible clothes with long sleeves and no revealing cleavage dresses up in a Playboy Bunny costume and turns into an instant seductress.

The dignified teacher and father of two who listens to classical music and never stays up past eleven dons his disco suit and boogies like John Travolta.

Oscar Wilde once said: *Man is least himself when he talks in his own person. Give him a mask, and he will tell you the truth.*

Truth is, we're all just looking for the right mask.

CHAPTER **45**

"You wanna be someone else?" says the Ego hustler, looking up and down the sidewalk in the dim glow of the streetlights, talking to me fast and low, his hands shoved into his pockets. "I can get you what you're looking for."

I'm at the corner of Hollywood and Wilcox just past midnight, two weeks before Santa comes calling, wearing my hunter green Italian suit and standing in front of Lady Studio Exotic Shoes near three graffiti-covered newspaper dispensers. The stores are all closed for the night, their metal security gates pulled shut and covered with black and white paintings of movie stars like Bob Hope, Alfred Hitchcock, and Ann-Margret.

For some reason, this makes me think of my mother.

Just down Wilcox on the other side of the street, a prostitute who looks like Doris Day propositions two men in a

Volvo who decide they're not interested in what she has to offer and drive off.

"Where does the product come from?" I ask.

"A reliable source," says the hustler. "My guy guarantees top quality. None of these other losers out here selling can compete."

On Hollywood Boulevard, Chevy Chase approaches us pushing a shopping cart filled with aluminum cans, talking to himself. He stops at a garbage can and starts digging through it.

"How do I know it's not one of those black market Egos I've read about that kills people?" I ask.

"Hey pal, if I sell something that kills my customers, then I got no customers and I'm out of business. And that ain't good business."

A black BMW drives down Wilcox, another potential client for Doris Day, but it passes her by without any interest as she yells and gives the driver both middle fingers.

"How do I know you're not giving *me* the business?" I ask.

"Look pal, if you don't want to buy nothin', don't waste my time. I've got plenty of customers lining up to get what I've got."

I look around at the other people sharing the street with us, mostly homeless people and addicts looking for their next fix, and I wonder where the line starts.

Across Wilcox, next to an exotic women's lingerie store, is the *You Are the Star* mural of a movie theater filled with Hollywood legends and characters from the silent films to the 1980s, all of them sitting in their seats and looking out at the street as if we were the film being projected onto the movie screen.

We are the stars.

Bogart and Bacall sit in the front row with Marilyn Monroe and Charlie Chaplin, while W. C. Fields babysits Shirley Temple and James Dean points to Antony and Cleopatra. In the remaining rows sit another five dozen, two-dimensional movie stars and fictional characters from James Cagney to Superman, all painted in color on the side of a building.

Woody Allen, Laurence of Arabia, and John Wayne.

Rhett Butler, Katharine Hepburn, and Robin Hood.

The Marx Brothers and Butch Cassidy and the Sundance Kid.

It's like seeing my life flash before my eyes, only without the near-death experience.

All of these famous and fictional Hollywood icons are looking out at me in my fitted green suit with my matching tie and the street hustler in his baggy jeans and sweatshirt with his hands shoved in his pockets and his shoulders hunched up to his ears.

"Suppose I'm interested," I say. "What do you have?"

"Ain't no supposin'. You're either interested or you're not."

A siren wails out on Hollywood Boulevard and the hustler looks ready to split. Seconds later, a fire engine blows through the intersection heading east toward Vine, red lights flashing across the buildings. Then it's gone.

"Okay," I say. "Then I'm interested."

"Now we're talkin'." He takes his hands out of his pockets and pulls out his cell phone. "Give me a couple of minutes."

The hustler walks to the other side of the street and stands by the mural, right in front of Bogart and Bacall, blocking their view. If I were Bogart, I'd get up and kick his ass.

A half block down on Wilcox, across from Doris Day, Paul Newman and Audrey Hepburn walk out of Cabana, a new Cuban restaurant, and head my way. Newman is dressed up like he just walked off the set of *The Sting* while Hepburn is in full Eliza Doolittle mode, complete with black and white touring hat. They're the second 1930s Newman and *My Fair Lady* Hepburn I've seen tonight. Not to mention the two Butch Cassidys and the Holly Golightly I saw earlier out in front of Grauman's Chinese Theatre.

That's what you get when you come down to Hollywood Boulevard: a bunch of overexposed Egos and superfluous personas out trying to be fashionable. Everyone picking the same personality, the hottest Big Egos fashion, the latest trendy pick on *Entertainment Tonight*'s Top Egos segment.

On the most recent episode, the picks of the week were Newman and Hepburn. The week before that it was Marlon Brando and Elizabeth Taylor, so you saw a bunch of Vito Corleones and General Kurtzes on the golf course. And every time you walked into a Starbucks you were standing in line behind Cleopatra.

But that's the thing about people. Everybody wants to have the latest fad so they can feel like they belong. So they can feel like they're hip. No one wants to be original, an individual, make a statement. They'd rather let someone dictate their fashion trend and follow the masses.

These wannabe stars.

These part-time celebrities.

These walking clichés.

If you're going to jump on the Brando bandwagon, at least pick a character like Sky Masterson or Terry Malloy. Or better yet, just be Brando. He was cool enough on his own.

But the Godfather? That's about as original as a major network television sitcom.

As Paul and Audrey walk past, Newman gives me a subtle brush of his index finger across his nose, while Audrey offers a demure smile and a nod of her head. Once they pass, Newman whispers something and Audrey glances back at me and bursts out laughing.

I think Eliza Doolittle needs a good spanking.

The Ego hustler walks back over and motions with his head for me to follow. From across the street, Doris Day makes him an offer but he ignores her sexual advances, so she turns her attention to me.

"How about you, honey?!" she shouts, flashing a leg covered with fishnets and varicose veins. "Feel like having some fun?"

"Maybe another time," I say.

"Come on," she says. "What does a girl have to do to turn an honest trick?"

CHAPTER **46**

"The trick," says my father, "is to always take advantage of your opportunities. That's how you build a successful life."

I nod with enthusiasm. Or at least with as much of it as I can muster, considering the circumstances.

Where we are is the Los Angeles National Cemetery on South Sepulveda Boulevard near the 405 freeway on a Saturday morning in July 2003, about a month before my ninth birthday. When my father told me he wanted to take me someplace, I was thinking Venice Beach or Hollywood Boulevard or Universal Studios. Maybe even Magic Mountain. Instead, my father takes me to the cemetery.

"*Carpe diem*," says my father. "It means to seize the day. To take life's moments and act upon them while you have the chance."

Why my father brought me to a cemetery to teach me about life, I have no idea.

I glance up and watch the Saturday-morning traffic driving north and south on the 405 and wonder how many of them are going to the beach or to an amusement park or someplace else that's fun. I'd even settle for catching a movie at the Cinerama Dome. Instead, I get to spend half of my weekend hanging out in a graveyard.

I guess I shouldn't complain. I usually only see my father for an hour or so at night during the week when he comes home from work and sits down to eat dinner, and most of that time he spends reading the news or talking to my mother, so we don't get a lot of quality father-son time. And seldom do we hang out together on the weekends. At least two weekends each month my father's on a business trip and on the weekends when he is home, he and my mother spend a lot of time together in their bedroom with the door closed.

"What do they do in there?" Nat asked me one time.

I told him I didn't know, so I put my ear up to their bedroom door one Sunday afternoon when my father was home to see if I could hear what he and my mother were doing. I could hear them whispering, almost as if they knew I was right outside the door, sometimes making sounds of exertion like they were wrestling or building a fort. When Nat asked me what I heard, I told him I couldn't understand what my father was saying but whatever it was, my mother kept agreeing with him.

"You need to embrace the opportunities that are given to you if you want to get what you want out of life," says my father, here in the cemetery. "You need to remember that, son. It's an important lesson."

My father is always teaching me important life lessons.

Like radical self-reliance, how to tie a tourniquet, and which direction to head in case of an EMP strike.

"South, son. Always head south."

Somehow, after the collapse of society, I have a hard time believing things would be any better in Mexico.

But right now, we're talking about the secret of success.

He sweeps his hand toward the tombstones. "How many of these people do you think got what they wanted out of life? How many do you think grasped their moments and made the most of them?"

I stand and look at the hundreds of identical tombstones stretching away from us and wonder if my father would be willing to make this a multiple-choice question.

"Maybe all of them, maybe none of them," he says, saving me from having to answer. "But my guess is most of them didn't finish on top of the podium."

I just nod. It seems to work more often than not, especially when I'm not really sure what my father's trying to teach me.

"Remember, son, being the runner-up isn't anything to celebrate. It just means you're the first one to lose the race."

"Yes, sir."

I almost always call my father "Sir." Sometimes I call him "Dad" or "Father." When I was younger I used to call him "Daddy," but he told me I needed to grow out of that. My father rarely calls me by my name. Sometimes he calls me "son" or "kid." Most of the time he just points his face and talks.

"And another thing you need to remember, son. To succeed in life, you have to pretend to be the person the situation calls for rather than the person you are."

I nod, but not because I can conceptualize what my father's talking about. It's a little out of my range of personal experience. Mostly I nod because I don't want my father to think I'm not paying attention.

"Do you understand what I'm telling you?" he says, as if he can read my thoughts.

I nod again. My father nods back, seemingly satisfied. That's about the extent of the fun we're having today.

The traffic flows past on the 405 and I wish I were in one of the cars going anywhere but here.

"But win or lose, success or failure," says my father, picking up where he left off and gesturing once more toward the acres of tombstones, "eventually, everyone ends up here."

That's a cheerful thought. I wonder if the other kids are having this much fun at Disneyland or Universal Studios.

I look around at all of the graves and markers, not because I want to, but because I know it's what my father expects me to do. He wants me to think about his words. To equate what he's told me with the reality of our surroundings. So I act like I'm concentrating and hope he doesn't quiz me on anything.

"Seize the moment, son," says my father. "Don't let it pass you by, because chances are it won't come your way again. So do what needs to be done and do it now."

Chapter **47**

My father's words echo in my head and for a moment I think I see him standing in front of me, surrounded by headstones, then he vanishes and instead there's Doris Day trying to flag down another potential client with a squeeze of a breast and a flash of a pale, fishnet-clad thigh. Just up the street, Chevy Chase pushes his shopping cart up to a garbage can to dig for more treasures.

I follow the hustler down an alley between Cabana and a fenced parking lot, past the back entrance for Wilcox Tattoo, to an open space out behind Hollywood Hookah and the old Fox Theater, which is now a nightclub called the Playhouse.

A car horn blares on Hollywood Boulevard, followed by someone shouting, *"Fuck off!"* From out on Wilcox Avenue, I hear Doris Day offering her services to any paying customer who will have her, though it doesn't sound like she's having any luck.

Que sera, sera.

"Here's the guy," says the hustler when we reach the back of the open lot, his hands still shoved down into the pockets of his baggy pants. Whether he's talking to me or to the tall guy smoking a cigarette near a Dumpster by the back door to the Playhouse, I don't know. But I figure I'll make the first move.

"Bond," I say, extending my right hand. "James Bond."

The dealer looks at me without shaking my hand and lets out a single bark of laughter, then he looks over at the hustler. "Where the fuck did you get this guy, Eddie?"

Eddie shrugs and wipes his nose, then shoves his hand back into his pocket and gives me a sideways glance like he's pissed-off at me or something.

"You look more like the Wizard of Oz in that suit," says the dealer.

"Funny," I say. "Judy Garland told me the same thing."

The dealer sizes me up, probably trying to figure out how much money he can squeeze out of me.

"So, you looking to be a secret agent?" he says. "I've got plenty to choose from. James Bond. Austin Powers. Jason Bourne."

"I'm actually looking for something else."

He nods. "Did you have anything in mind?"

"I'm not sure," I say. "Surprise me."

He takes another drag on his cigarette. "First thing's first. Eddie, make sure he's clean."

Eddie walks up from behind and asks me to raise my hands, then starts patting me down.

"What's this for?" I ask.

"Just precautions," says the dealer.

"A few nights ago some fucking loser pulled a toy gun on us and tried to run off with half our stock," says Eddie from behind me.

"Did he get away?" I ask.

"Let's just say I don't think he'll be in any condition to try it again anytime soon," the dealer says, then flicks away his cigarette. "So don't get any ideas."

"I wouldn't think of it," I say with a smile.

"He's clean," says Eddie, stepping away.

The dealer claps his hands and rubs them together. "Okay, Mr. Bond, now let's see what we've got that might surprise you."

From behind the Dumpster he produces a metal brief-case, which he sets down on top of an upside-down oil drum, then he unlatches the case and flips it open. Inside the case is lined with custom foam compartments containing more than four dozen plastic vials, all filled with ten milliliters of clear, amber fluid.

"Are these the real deal?" I lean in for a closer look, playing the role of the eager buyer.

"Straight from the factory," says the dealer. "Nothing but top-quality, manufacturer-tested product."

While your average Jane or Joe buying a black market Ego might be inclined to believe the claim of authenticity, I know it's bullshit. First of all, with the control measures in place, it's virtually impossible for any Egos to go missing from the factory without raising an alarm. But the obvious giveaway is his merchandise. We don't offer The Rush Limbaugh, The Kim Kardashian, or The O. J. Simpson.

"So what do you think?" He points to the vials as he names them off. "Elvis? James Dean? Superman? Newman and Brando are popular picks right now."

I shake my head. "I'm not interested in the latest trend. I don't want to be who everyone else is. I want something fresh and bold. Something that makes a statement."

He gives me an appraising smile, no doubt meant to make me feel as though he understands me. "Are you looking for reality or fiction?"

"Is there a difference?"

He looks me over a second, then nods. "Yeah. I think I've got what you're looking for."

He reaches into the suitcase and brings out a vial labeled DR. STRANGELOVE. "Perfect for the man who has everything. Or who wants more."

"Strangelove's still a little too vanilla," I say. "What else have you got?"

He puts the vial back and looks over his selection. "If you're interested in going with something a little darker, I just got in a new shipment that includes The Jack the Ripper, The Al Capone, and The Genghis Khan."

"A little too dark," I say. "I was hoping for something a little more creative or artistic."

"A fan of the arts," he says. "I think I have just what you're looking for. If you're musically inclined, I've got The Kurt Cobain, The Jim Morrison, and The Bon Scott. Or if your tastes run more to the literary world, I have an exclusive on The Kurt Vonnegut and The Philip K. Dick."

"Do you have a quantity discount?" I say.

"That depends," he says. "How many are you interested in buying?"

"As many as ten grand will buy me," I say.

He stares at me a moment, probably trying to decide if I'm serious. "You have the cash?"

I pull a wad of hundreds from inside my coat and hold the cash up with my left hand. He stares at the money, then offers up a smile.

"Well, I think we can work something out," he says.

"Great," I say. "So now that you know I'm here to do business and not to steal your stock, how about doing me the courtesy of making this transaction without someone looking over my shoulder."

"Eddie," he says, "why don't you go wait at the entrance to the alley."

"You sure?" says Eddie.

"Yeah," says the dealer, eyeing my wad of Franklins. "We're good."

Eddie gives me a parting glance before he walks away and heads back down the alley. As soon as he's gone, I turn back to the dealer, my right hand palming the syringe that I had up my sleeve.

"Okay," I say with a smile. "Let's make a deal."

CHAPTER **48**

Delilah stands over me, her sunglasses on top of her head, a garment bag over one shoulder and a duffel bag in her hands. She's wearing skintight jeans, mid-calf boots, and her long black leather coat. She looks angry. I'm not sure why. I don't remember doing anything to piss her off, but I don't remember what I was doing before this or how I ended up on my back on the floor. So I figure anything's possible.

"Did you hear what I said?" she says.

"No." I shake my head to drive home the point. "I must have missed it."

"I said I'm leaving."

"You're leaving?" I stare up at her. From this perspective, she seems a lot taller. "When will you be back?"

"I'm not coming back."

"You're not coming back?"

"No."

I blink my eyes but I can't seem to muster the energy to sit up. It's just so comfortable here on the floor. Either that or I'm paralyzed.

"Why not?" I ask.

"Because I can't deal with this anymore," she says. "You go out on your own and you don't tell me where you've been or what you've been doing. I hardly see you anymore. And when I do see you, you're asking me if I'm a spy or telling me to mind my own business or ignoring me. That's not my idea of a healthy relationship."

"So where are you going?" I ask, calm and easy. Like she's getting a manicure. Like she's meeting a friend for lunch.

"I'm staying with Tami until I get my own place."

Tami. I don't know any Tami. At least I don't think I do. Maybe I should know her. Or at least act like I do.

"Tell her I said hi."

Delilah just stares at me. Actually, it's more like a strong glare. I'm thinking about asking if I can borrow her sunglasses.

"Is that all you have to say?" she asks.

I know there's probably more I should say but right now, I can't think of anything. To be honest, I'm not even sure this is really happening.

I seem to be getting a lot of that lately.

"When will you be back?" I say.

Delilah stares at me without saying a word, then she pulls down her sunglasses, turns around, and walks out of my view—which, admittedly, is somewhat limited.

I listen as her footsteps echo away across the hardwood floor. Then the front door opens and closes and I'm alone in the house on the floor on my back, staring up at the ceiling fan and the crown moldings and the decorative plaster ceiling, thinking about the day I moved into this place with Delilah. I notice how the crown molding looks like birthday cakes, which gets me thinking about the surprise party my team threw for me, which leads to thoughts of Chloe and Angela and Holden Caulfield blended with memories of Tarzan and Nat and my father.

My thoughts mix and mingle, like guests at a party—except people at parties tend to cluster together in comfortable groups rather than moving about. And my thoughts aren't exactly clustering. Instead I see them as square dancers, allemanding to the left and do-si-doing, circling and promenading one another. Though in square dancing you usually end up back where you started, and I'm not sure where one thought ends and another begins. So I'm thinking my thoughts are more like shadows on a busy city street, blending into each other as they pass until I can no longer keep track of them.

I try to focus on my thoughts and memories, to hold them in place so I can get a good look at them and keep them from slipping away, but they're not cooperating. They won't sit still, no matter how hard I try. But even if I could get one of my memories to cooperate, there's no guarantee it would be an accurate depiction of what actually happened.

The problem with memories is that they're not objective.

One person's memory is another person's fiction. Everything is a matter of perception, defined by individual feelings, beliefs, and desires. A single, objective reality doesn't exist. All of the input and stimuli we encounter gets filtered through personal experience and interpretation and mood. Nothing is definite. There are no rules for how something looks or tastes or smells from moment to moment or from one person to another.

The color of a sunset.

The taste of a peach.

The scent of a rose.

Truth is, subjectivity is the only truth.

And right now, my truth is in need of some transformation.

CHAPTER **49**

I glide through the room like an ancient shaman, revelers and worshippers reaching out to touch me, to feel the magic of my existence. I embrace their adulation as I float along, riding the waves of desire.

A rider on the storm of love.

Donna Summer stops me and gives me a kiss and tells me I light her fire. Patsy Cline rubs up against me and says that we could be so good together. Dusty Springfield grabs my ass and whispers in my ear that she'd like to love me two times.

I think I could get used to this.

I continue through the room, the center of attention, but I'm not concerned about who sees me or who knows I'm here. Everyone is high on something, stoned immaculate, and I'm their vision. Their dream. When they awake from their slumber, I'll be nothing more than a fleeting glimpse of a shadow, a ghost who slipped out of their consciousness like a last breath slipping from the lips of a dying man.

When you're strange, no one remembers your name.

I step over John Bonham and Bon Scott, who are both passed out on the floor in their own vomit. George Harrison and John Lennon laugh at them and take pictures, which they post on Facebook as Freddie Mercury moves through the room in a black-and-white-checkerboard leotard and tights, clapping his hands together above his head and singing "Fat Bottomed Girls." Mama Cass Elliot and Karen Carpenter linger around the dining room table, eyeing the selection of appetizers like two tortured souls battling their inner demons.

Mick Jagger walks up and greets me with faraway eyes and an intoxicated smile. "Hey Jim, it's good to see you, man. How've you been?"

When he talks I almost feel as though I could fall inside his cavernous mouth.

I give him an answer about strange days and roadhouse blues and he starts telling me about how he can't get no satisfaction. I listen and nod and wonder what he's doing here since he hasn't broken on through to the other side yet, but I don't really care about Mick. He's not who I came to find, so I look around the room to see who else is here.

Buddy Holly, Richie Valens, and the Big Bopper sit around a coffee table covered with empty and half-empty beer bottles, passing around a bong with Steve Gaines and Ronnie Van Zant, all of them talking about taking a road trip to New Orleans. Holly suggests they charter a plane and I know nothing good can come of that.

Off in a corner, Jimi Hendrix, Janis Joplin, Kurt Cobain, Brian Jones, and Amy Winehouse are all doing shots of tequila and lines of coke. Joplin calls out for me to come over and hang out with them, but something tells me I don't want to join their little club.

Bob Marley and Jerry Garcia are sharing a laugh and a joint over by the fireplace while Johnny Cash and Roy Orbison, both dressed all in black, are hitting on Etta James. Marvin Gaye grooves all by himself in the middle of the room, singing "Got to Give It Up."

Mick is still talking, going on and on about how you can't always get what you want. I'm ready for a different scene, so I tell him I'll be right back and make my way to the kitchen, where I run into Joey Ramone and Sid Vicious doing shots of whiskey. For some reason I'm filled with a sense of déjà vu, like we've all been here before.

My brain seems bruised with numb surprise.

I do a couple of shots with Joey and Sid and we talk for a while about whiskey, mystics, and women before they wander off to rejoin the party. I'm about to follow them when I notice a set of sliding glass doors leading outside, standing open to the night, so I take the bottle of whiskey and walk out to a deck overlooking the Pacific Ocean. The water is black beneath the midnight sky, stretching away from the Malibu shore and blending seamlessly with the infinite night, the world dark and endless and full of mystery, the water reflecting the quarter moon like an alien world.

Out here on the perimeter, there are no stars.

Sitting on one of the deck chairs, eating what appears to be a fried peanut butter and banana sandwich and drinking from a can of Pepsi, is just who I've been looking for.

"Mind if I hang out?" I ask.

"Be my guest," says Elvis in his trademark drawl, his mouth full of peanut butter and banana and white bread.

I sit down and look at him, feeling unsettled for some reason I can't quite grasp. A recognition born from some mysterious source.

This is the strangest life I've ever known.

"Would you like some grub?" says Elvis. "All the fixings are in the kitchen, so feel free to help yourself."

"Thanks," I say. "But I'm more into tacos or a good, thick steak."

"Don't have any tacos or steaks." Elvis takes another bite of his sandwich. "How about a cupcake or an Eskimo Pie?"

"Maybe another time."

We sit there in silence for a minute or two, looking out at the ocean, the December sky clear and the quarter moon reflecting off the water's surface, shimmering like a mirage.

"It's not Graceland," says Elvis, washing down a mouthful of his sandwich with some Pepsi and motioning out toward the moon over the Pacific. "But it sure is pretty."

I nod. "There's something about the winter air that makes it crisp and clear."

"And bright," he says. "The moon's never bright like this in Memphis."

And that's my cue.

"How would you like something to make it a little brighter?"

I reach into my shirt pocket and remove a single liquid-filled capsule, which I drop into the palm of Elvis's hand. He takes the capsule, pops it into his mouth, clinks his Pepsi can against my whiskey bottle, then takes a long swallow.

"*Thank you,*" he says. "*Thank you very much.*"

"*Don't mention it.*"

"*How long will it take to kick in?*"

"*Not long,*" I say with a smile.

He looks at me with his own smile, like we're sharing a joke or like he's remembering something from another life. Another reality. Then he takes another bite of his sandwich, chases it with more Pepsi, and follows that up with a hearty belch.

"*Hey,*" he says. "*I think I'm starting to feel something.*"

My work done, I give my regards to Elvis and head back into the house. No one's in the kitchen when I walk inside and close the sliding glass doors behind me, so I decide to rejoin the party for a little while.

Bonham and Scott are still passed out in their own vomit, while Marvin and Freddie are attempting to break up a cat-fight between Mama Cass and Karen Carpenter. Orbison has won the Etta James sweepstakes, leaving Cash brooding on the fireplace singing "Oh Lonesome Me."

Lennon stops me and asks if I'd like to come with him and George on a little acid trip. I'm more of a peyote guy myself, so I decline, then make my way over to Marley and Garcia, who are sharing another joint. I enjoy their company for as long as I can until Jagger comes strutting over and insinuates himself into the conversation. Somehow, Marley and Garcia manage to get away, leaving me with Mick and his Grand Canyon of a mouth. Fortunately, Patsy Cline and Donna Summer rescue me and take me into a dark corner where we do our best to set the night on fire.

Sometime later, Janis Joplin starts walking around the room and asking the guests if anyone has seen Elvis.

Well, I guess I'd better go now.

I tell Patsy and Donna I'll be right back, then I walk down the hallway toward the back of the house. No one notices when I slip away through the service entrance, a backdoor man, a spy in the house of love.

I know the dream that you're dreaming of.

I know your deepest, secret fear.

Once I'm outside, I look up at the quarter moon hovering in the blackness like a half-open portal, offering a glimpse into another world. The longer I stare at it, the more it feels like I'm falling into it, as though my consciousness is rising from me, being drawn into the heavens, sucked into the moon's glow, and I realize my ride on the crystal ship is about to come to an end.

Before it does, I climb into my '59 T-Bird, then I turn the ignition and pull away, heading south toward Los Angeles on a moonlight drive.

CHAPTER **50**

The Pixies' "Where Is My Mind?" plays on the radio as I drive south along the Pacific Coast Highway toward Santa Monica, the quarter moon reflecting off the ocean as Malibu recedes in the rearview mirror. After one in the morning in mid-December, there's not much traffic heading in either direction, so I have the four-lane highway nearly all to myself.

On the radio, Black Francis yowls through the song's lyrics, which don't make any sense to me but I sing along with them anyway, the effects of my Ego gradually fading—though I still feel the Lizard King lurking just below the surface.

I'm singing that I have my feet in the air and my head on the ground.

Although I've been Morrison before on a couple of occasions, there was definitely something about this time that felt different. I don't know if it had anything to do with the fact that it was a black market Ego, but the experience was more intense than I remember. Like a rock concert in my head, complete with drugs and amplifiers and a bass guitar beat that thrummed throughout my body. At a party full of rock stars, I was legendary. An icon among icons.

I'm not sure why I've never been interested in spending much time as Morrison and reveling in his air of subdued menace—embracing his ability to be surly, sexy, and mysterious all at the same time. For some reason, I've always been drawn more to the likes of John Lennon or Elvis Presley.

Speaking of The King, it was surreal talking to one of my favorite Egos. While I run into one every now and then, I don't generally interact with them, but just seeing them is always a little unsettling. It's like looking into a mirror and seeing a reflection of yourself, only it's not you.

I'm singing that my head will collapse but there's nothing in it.

Up ahead of me, near the entrance to the Pepperdine University campus, a police car is headed my way, its siren silent but its lights flashing across the asphalt, lighting up the otherwise nearly empty highway in a strobe of blues and reds. It races past in the opposite direction without slowing down.

I watch the police car in my rearview mirror as I continue south on the PCH, singing along to the Pixies, belting out a couple of lines in my best Morrison, though I can't quite capture his tone. It comes out sounding more like Elvis. And a little bit of Lennon. The weird thing is, I can sense all three of them swimming around just below the surface of my consciousness.

I'm singing that I'm going to try this trick and spin it.

When the song ends, I turn my Sirius satellite radio to a local news station and catch the weather forecast, which is for clear and sunny skies with a high of seventy degrees. Following the weather is a report of a Beverly Hills couple who died last night apparently as a result of injecting black market Egos. According to eyewitness testimony, Dean and Gabrielle Gordon started to experience seizures at a private Ego party they were hosting before they both went into cardiac arrest.

A second police car appears on the highway and flies past, heading in the same direction as the first.

The news report goes on to say that both Dean and Gabrielle Gordon served on the Board of Directors for the Los Angeles–based Engineering Genetics Organizations and Systems, with Dean Gordon serving as the board's chairman. The death of the Gordons, along with the recent death of the company's head of Applied Research, Bill Summers, is a significant blow for the multimillion-dollar bioengineering giant, which had seen its stock price and profits take a hit in recent months—ironically from the proliferation of black market Egos.

The report wraps up with a statement from Paul Lawson, the president of EGOS, expressing his sadness for the deaths of the Gordons and his shock at learning that black market Egos had claimed the lives of two more members of the EGOS family. Then the sports update comes on and someone is talking about the Lakers and Clippers game.

I turn off the radio and roll down my window, continuing my ride in silence, enjoying the feel of the fresh ocean air blowing into the car, caressing my face and ruffling my hair. I notice something tickling my upper lip and think a wayward bug has landed on my face. But when I reach up and wipe it off with my hand, my left index finger and thumb come away red. So I pull over to the shoulder, put on my emergency blinkers, and turn on the interior light.

When I look at my reflection in the rearview mirror, it's not me staring back. It's Morrison. And his nose is bleeding.

I've never had a bloody nose in my life. Not as a kid. Not that I can remember. But there's no denying the blood trickling from my left nostril and onto my upper lip.

An ambulance comes racing north along the PCH following the police car. It passes and continues toward Malibu in my rearview mirror, lights flashing and siren wailing.

CHAPTER **51**

An ambulance races past, its siren obeying the Doppler effect, but I only hear the ambulance, I can't see it. All I see in the rearview mirror and out the windshield is white.

I'm sitting in the driver's seat of my Aston Martin, staring through the windshield at what appears to be a complete whiteout. Not like a dust storm or a snowstorm, but more like a blank, white page. A universe of white.

It's as though nothing exists outside of the car.

Nat sits in the passenger seat next to me, not saying a word, just looking around with a puzzled expression on his face.

"Where are we?" he says.

I stare at the emptiness around us. "I don't know. I think this is supposed to be a memory."

"Mine or yours?"

"I'm pretty sure it's mine," I say.

"How do you know?"

"Because this entire conversation is taking place in my head."

Nat looks at me, then down at himself like he's thinking about what I just said. "So I'm not really here?"

"I don't think so."

He nods again and looks around, then starts to open the passenger door.

"What are you doing?" I say.

"This place sucks," he says. "If I'm not really here, then I don't see any reason why I have to stick around."

He pulls up on the handle and swings the door open.

"I don't think that's a good idea," I say.

"Why not?"

I stare out at the endless, white nothingness. "Because I think if you leave this car, you'll cease to exist in the real world."

"But if I'm not real, then how can I cease to exist?"

"It's hard to explain," I say. "But you're just going to have to trust me."

Nat scowls in concentration and purses his lips, then he finally closes the door. "Can we drive out of here?"

I turn the key in the ignition but there's nothing. Not a click or the whine of the starter. The engine's completely dead. "Looks like we're stuck here for a while."

We sit in silence for a few beats. It's a comfortable silence, born from years of friendship. Still, it seems like there's something important one of us has to say. But I don't know which one of us is supposed to say it.

"What time is it?" asks Nat.

I look down at my watch to give Nat an answer, but my watch isn't there. There's not even a tan line to indicate that I've ever worn a watch. When I look up, the readout on the dashboard clock is a bunch of blue, digital zeros.

As an empty circle, zero represents both the nothingness of death and the totality of life. Kind of a poor man's yin and yang. As an ellipse, the two sides of the zero represent ascent and descent, evolution and involution—which, in philosophy, is the turning in on one's self.

I don't know if I'm turning in on myself, but this sure doesn't feel like a step in the right direction.

"Do you know how we got here?" I say, looking around.

Nat shrugs and scratches his head. "This is your memory, bro. I was kind of figuring you had that information."

Yes, I should have that information. Something should be familiar and grounding this memory in reality, but it's as if this part of my memory is blank. I'm thinking maybe all this nothingness represents part of my mind that has been wiped clean and lost forever, kind of like a reformatted hard drive.

"What time is it?" asks Nat.

"You just asked me that."

"And what was your answer?"

"I don't know."

"You don't know what your answer was?"

"No. I don't know what time it is. My watch is gone." I show him my naked wrist for emphasis.

That's when I notice that my wrist is thicker and hairier

than normal and that my hand isn't my hand. It should be mine because it's attached to my arm, which is attached to the rest of me, but I don't recognize it. It's too big, the fingers too long, the hair too coarse.

It's like I'm Dr. Jekyll turning into Mr. Hyde.

CHAPTER **52**

I stand with my back to the hospital room, looking out the window at the December sunset. Christmas is just ten days away, but I'm not exactly thinking about chestnuts roasting on an open fire or Jack Frost nipping at my nose. And no amount of turkey or mistletoe is going to make the season bright.

"Hey bro," says Nat, in a cheerful voice behind me. "You should see some of the nurses they have here. We're talking hot hot hot. You know, like the Buster Poindexter song, not the song by the Cure."

I continue to look out the window, unable to face Nat, though I can see his reflection in the glass. The bed next to him is empty. The older woman who was here the last time I visited is gone. I don't know what happened to her. The way things have been lately, I wouldn't be surprised if she never existed in the first place.

"I keep asking the nurses to give me a private fashion show, but they claim it's against hospital policy," says Nat.

I don't want to turn around because if I do, then I'll have to admit to the truth of the situation and as long as I continue to watch the sunset I can pretend everything's okay. But I know I can't keep pretending forever, even though pretending has become a running habit.

"They dig me," says Nat. "They just don't know it yet."

I stare out the window a few more moments before I turn around.

Nat lies in his bed, his eyes closed and his lips slightly parted around the ventilation tube, his chest rising and falling as the ventilator pumps oxygen into his lungs and the feeding tube delivers fluids and nutrients and medicine to his stomach.

While the doctor and the nurses have all told me that it's likely Nat can hear everything I say to him, no one expects him to talk anytime soon. They say the chances of him coming out of his coma are about one in a thousand. But it makes me feel better to imagine I can hear his voice.

"Bro, tell me the truth," says Nat. "Is this a good look for me?"

I walk up to him and give him my most convincing smile. "Absolutely. Women dig the whole comatose-feeding-tube-in-the-stomach look. Brings out their nurturing side."

"I was kind of hoping it would bring out their human-vegetable-fetish side."

"That might work if you were a cucumber rather than a baby carrot," I say.

Nat smiles. Not really, but the fantasy is preferable to

the reality—which is how I got into this mess in the first place.

I sit down next to his bed. "If it makes you feel any better, you're the second-most attractive guy in the room."

"What would make me feel better is a hand job."

"Hey, I know we're best friends," I say, "but I think we need to keep some boundaries."

"Not from you. I was thinking about the hot redhead who works the graveyard shift."

"I'll see what I can do," I say.

"Speaking of redheads, how's Dee?"

"I think she left me."

"What happened?"

"Long story."

"I'm not exactly going anywhere."

"I'll tell you next time," I lie.

For a moment, Jim Morrison glides through my head in his concho belt and black leather pants, his baritone voice like an epitaph.

This is the end, my only friend, the end.

"You know, you two wouldn't have even met if it wasn't for me," Nat says.

I give him a faint smile. "I know."

We sit there for several moments, neither one of us saying anything.

"Well, if you're not going to tell me about *your* redhead," says Nat, "then how about being my wingman and finding me one of my own?"

Morrison slips away just as the nurse comes in to check on Nat. It's not the redhead Nat was looking for, but a blonde who looks like Hot Lips Houlihan from *M*A*S*H*. The Sally Kellerman version, not Loretta Swit. I don't know if she actually looks like Sally Kellerman or if I'm just imagining it, but the instrumental version of "Suicide Is Painless" plays in my head. I glance out the window to make sure we're still in Los Angeles and not South Korea.

Hot Lips asks how I'm doing and how Nat's doing and I lie to her on both counts. Then I help her to move Nat into a new position to help prevent bedsores. It feels good to be able to do something for Nat, even if it's not what he had in mind. But as we're shifting him to one side, I notice that Hot Lips has one of her hands on Nat's left thigh, just inches from his crotch, and I can't help but honor his request.

"Excuse me," I say. "But would you mind giving my friend a hand job?"

CHAPTER **53**

Gandhi hands me my triple espresso, places the palms of his hands in front of his green apron, gives me a slight bow of his head, then smiles and tells me to have a nice day. When I thank him, I realize it's not Gandhi but just someone who looks a lot like him, sans Ego. Or maybe I'm just imagining things. It wouldn't be the first time.

I'm at the Starbucks in West Hollywood across from Hamburger Haven. Outside, white holiday lights adorn the trees on Santa Monica Boulevard while inside, Harry Connick Jr. is wishing everyone a merry little Christmas while the Starbucks elves hand out espresso treats in red postconsumer recycled cups, making the yuletide gay.

I take my infusion of caffeine and sit down at one of the tables. At the table nearest me, the Queen of Hearts and Marie Antoinette drink peppermint mochas and gingerbread lattes and discuss the challenges of being a female monarch. I'm not interested in either of them, so I pull up today's edition of the *Los Angeles Times* on my smartphone and come across an article about the death of David Cook, the executive vice president of EGOS, who died at his Malibu home while hosting an Ego holiday party. It's believed he died from complications after injecting a black market Elvis Presley Ego.

The second death of an EGOS executive in less than two weeks, along with the deaths of two members of the Board of Directors, has prompted opponents of the company to call for an investigation into the safety of Big Egos. Protesters have doubled their efforts at Big Egos stores nationwide, picketing in cities and towns across the country, and setting up a twenty-four-hour camp outside the EGOS factory in Los Feliz. In Washington, D.C., protest organizers are calling for a march on Capitol Hill.

I have my doubts that these increased protests will solve anything or save anyone, let alone something as esoteric as the ego, which could refer to any number of things. Self-esteem, an inflated sense of self-worth, or, in pure philosophical terms, one's self.

Freud said the ego is based in reality, governing the id, and that the id has no organization and produces no collective will, but only focuses on innate desires and the observance of pleasure.

If that's the case, then a lot of people in the world today are all id.

I continue reading the *Times* and come across a human interest story about a married couple in Santa Barbara who purchased Big Egos for The John Steed and The Emma Peel two months ago and who now walk around full-time dressed up like The Avengers and speaking with English accents. Their neighbors and friends are worried about them, but the couple claims they've never been happier.

Maybe they just really enjoy 1960s English fashion.

Maybe they're like Method actors, staying in character even when they're not on camera.

Or maybe they discovered that their lives are boring in comparison and that they'd rather be British government agents.

And who can blame them? Most people lead lives of quiet desperation and spend their days and nights wishing they could be something else while failing to live the lives they'd imagined. Thoreau said that. Or something like that. Or maybe it was this guy I met at an Ego party in the Hollywood Hills who was channeling Thoreau and it just sounded good. Or maybe it was my dad. I seem to recall he said something about taking advantage of opportunities and to act upon them when you have the chance.

I'm having trouble keeping my thoughts straight.

The point is, if the opportunity to realize your wildest dreams presented itself, if you had the chance to actually live the life you'd imagined, wouldn't you jump in headfirst? Or would you just stand aside and watch as the opportunity passed you by?

Not everyone has their life all figured out.

Not everyone knows what they were born to do.

Sometimes you don't realize who you're supposed to be until the moment comes.

But when the lines between reality and fantasy begin to

blur and you lose yourself in an identity that's just a mirage, what happens when the mirage becomes reality? What happens when the dream becomes something from which you can't wake up?

It's only a matter of time before everyone gets lost in a reality that isn't theirs.

At the table next to me, the Queen of Hearts clinks her coffee mug with Marie Antoinette and says, "Off with their heads."

There's another story in the *Times* about two black market Ego dealers who were found dead in an alley just off Hollywood Boulevard last Saturday morning. According to authorities, the dealers appear to have been the victims of a robbery or a deal gone wrong. Police are interviewing witnesses who were in the area at the time, but so far they don't have any suspects other than a homeless man and a prostitute who both claim to have seen a man in a green suit who looked like James Bond.

CHAPTER 54

I wake up in an alley and I don't know who I am.

For an instant there's nothing. Not a hint of identity. There's just an empty room in my head where I should be and a VACANCY sign lit up out front in bright, flickering, neon red letters. Not the kind of sign you'd see outside a luxury bed-and-breakfast in Beverly Hills, but more like the type you'd see outside a cheap motel in downtown Los Angeles. Someplace with a name like the Oasis or the Ambassador that comes with free 24/7 porno flicks and residential crack whores.

At least that's the kind of mood I'm in.

Then the VACANCY sign flickers off and my identity returns. Only it's not me unpacking my bags, it's Elvis.

I sit up and look around and wonder what I'm doing in an alley rather than in my California king at Graceland. There are empty parking places next to a faded white, one-story building on one side of me and on the other side, the muted brown stucco wall of a two-story building. The sky is dark but there's just a hint of light, which means it's either dusk or dawn, I don't know which. I notice that I'm wearing a suit. And not my white jumpsuit, either.

The coat and slacks are charcoal gray. The shirt ivory white. The tie royal blue. The shoes midnight black. Definitely not Elvis attire. More like something James Bond or JFK would wear. Only I'm not feeling the secret agent or presidential vibe. And I'm hankering for some ham bone dumplings and sour milk cornbread.

The thought of food gets me to my feet and I'm wondering if there's a doughnut shop nearby. Or maybe Roscoe's. I could go for some chicken and waffles. And a big side of bacon. But before I can get out of the alley and figure out where the nearest source of food is, The King is gone and I'm Captain Kirk, looking around, wondering what planet I'm on and where my away team is and why I'm not wearing my uniform.

What . . . happened to me? Where . . . am I?

I pull out my communicator and try to raise the *Enterprise,* though my communicator has a touchscreen that doesn't look familiar. I start pressing buttons but all I get is a digital clock on the screen with today's date. At least I know what month it is. Eventually I manage to bring up another screen filled with several rows and columns of thumb-sized icons. I hit the one that looks like a microphone and is labeled VOICE RECORDER.

"Scotty," I speak into the screen. "Can you read me?"

Nothing happens. Not even the hint of an image or a

signal. So I walk out of the alley, hoping I don't run into Khan or a gang of Romulans.

And where the fuck is Spock? That emotionless Vulcan bastard is never around when you need him.

A moment later, Kirk is gone and Philip Marlowe has taken his place.

Once out on the street I discover I'm on Santa Monica Boulevard, across from the Formosa Cafe, its neon green sign glowing like a bug light. Only it's meant to attract humans, not bugs. And it's doing the trick. I could use a drink. The faint light in the sky is coming from the west, which means it's evening, cocktail hour, so at least I'm in the right place.

I step off the curb to cross the street and find my way to the bottom of a glass full of bourbon when a car drives past, blasting its horn. I jump back onto the sidewalk and I'm Indiana Jones.

There's enough of me inside my head to realize I'm in trouble. And not in a stolen-historical-artifact-how-to-deal-with-Nazis-trying-to-kill-me kind of trouble. This goes beyond the imagined world of my alternate personas.

It's as if the gears of my mind are slipping, like a car with a clutch that's going out, shifting from third to fifth to second, the teeth of the gears worn-out from overuse. Only instead of a bad clutch, I've got a bad Ego that keeps slipping from one identity to another.

Slip.

I'm Jim Morrison.

Slip.

I'm Holden Caulfield.

Slip.

I'm back to Indiana Jones.

I'm beginning to wonder if I'm ever going to slip back to myself. Or how much of me exists anymore.

But for the moment I'm Indiana Jones: full-time professor of archaeology, part-time retriever of valuable historical artifacts, and occasional Nazi ass-kicker. I don't know what I'm supposed to be looking for, or if there's someone's ass I should be kicking, but I seem to have lost my fedora.

Traffic drives past on Santa Monica Boulevard. Across the street, a couple, a man and a woman, walk out the front doors of the Formosa beneath the black-and-white-striped awning. The man glances my way, then leads the woman around the corner. I don't know if he's suspicious or if it's just my imagination, but before I realize it, I've slipped from Indiana Jones to James Bond.

I look down at the phone in my hand and check the time and date, which tells me it's 4:51 p.m. on December 19.

I have no idea how long I was unconscious in the alley, but I'm wondering if I was drugged. Or ambushed. If somebody put me there or if I ended up there on my own. I don't feel like I've been hit. No sore spots on my head. No visible wounds. When I put my phone away and check my jacket pockets to make sure I wasn't mugged, one of my hands comes out with my wallet and the other hand comes out holding a business card.

On one side of the card is the name Joey Balsama, professionally printed, with a phone number and nothing else. The name seems familiar. A hint of a memory. An itch at the back of my brain that I can't manage to scratch. I flip the card over and on the other side is a handwritten address on North Rockingham Avenue, near where O. J. Simpson once lived. Which also seems oddly familiar. Not in a I-used-to-be-a-celebrated-athlete-who-was-accused-of-killing-his-wife-and-her-friend-and-ended-up-doing-time-for-stealing-a-bunch-of-sports-memorabilia-at-gunpoint kind of familiar, but more like I know the address. The question is: Did I already go there? Or is that the next item on my agenda? My plans for the evening?

This would be so much easier to figure out if my identities would cooperate.

I study the address on the card for several moments, hoping to coerce some information from my memory, waiting for an epiphany that never comes. It's a mystery that I'll have to resolve later. Right now, James Bond needs his signature drink.

As the fading light of the setting sun slips behind the roofs of West Hollywood, I put the card into my wallet and return the wallet to my coat pocket, look both ways along Santa Monica Boulevard, wait for the traffic signal to change, then walk across the street and into the Formosa Cafe.

CHAPTER 55

Genghis Khan walks into a bar.

I'm waiting for the rest of the joke, but apparently the joke's on me because Genghis looks like he's in a bad mood and he's headed my way.

Where I am is Barney's Beanery in West Hollywood, which for much of its hundred years has been a hangout for movie legends, rock stars, and writers.

Clark Gable and Errol Flynn.

Jim Morrison and Janis Joplin.

Charles Bukowski and F. Scott Fitzgerald.

While the bar is rich in Hollywood history and used to have a bit of an overused charm to go along with its world-class beer menu, today it's more of an overdone sports bar and restaurant with enough items on its food menu to serve a small nation without anyone ordering the same thing. The food is just above average and the service likewise.

But even so, you're still likely to see the occasional film or television celebrity in a booth chowing down on a Dagwood Burger and some hot wings or sitting at the bar drinking a Cosmopolitan or one of the numerous beers on tap.

But Genghis Khan isn't a regular.

He walks in, sits down at the bar next to me, and orders a Tsingtao.

"We don't have Tsingtao," says the bartender. "How about a Stella?"

I can tell Genghis isn't happy about this development by the way his face turns red and the veins stand out on his forehead. I half expect him to pull out a knife or a short sword and slit the bartender's throat. Instead, he closes his eyes and starts counting softly in Chinese.

"Yuht, yee, sahm, say . . ."

When he gets to ten, he opens his eyes, takes a deep breath, and smiles at the bartender.

"Okay then," he says, "give me a Bud Light."

As the bartender pulls out a pint glass and puts it under the tap, Genghis turns to me and smiles. "Anger management classes."

I just nod at him and try not to make eye contact.

When his beer arrives, Genghis raises his glass to me. *"Gan bei,"* he says, then downs his beer in one gulp.

How I ended up in Barney's I have no idea. I think this is another memory, but I don't know when this happened. Or even if it's real.

Genghis wipes his mouth, lets out a belch, then slams his empty glass down on the bar. "Give me another!"

"Do you want to open a tab?" asks the bartender.

Genghis pulls out an American Express gold card and gives it to the bartender. "And another beer for my friend here!"

While the bartender pours Genghis another Bud Light and gets me a refill of my Guinness, Jack the Ripper sits down on the other side of me and orders a Bloody Mary.

Go figure.

"Evening, mate," he says to me with a smile.

I smile back to be polite, not wanting to get on his bad side, waiting for someone to fill me in on the joke, but I don't see a punch line in sight.

When I look in the mirror behind the bar, I notice that in addition to Jack and Genghis, the patrons of Barney's Beanery include John Wilkes Booth, Professor Moriarty, Don Juan, Bonnie Parker, Mr. Hyde, Dr. Evil, the Wicked Witch of the West, Al Capone, Lex Luthor, Norman Bates, the Queen of Hearts, Charles Manson, Ed Gein, Marie Antoinette, and Lord Voldemort.

"Where did all of these people come from?" I ask.

"From you," says Jack.

"From me?" I say, looking around. "What do you mean? How did they come from me?"

Genghis laughs and slaps me on the back so hard that he almost breaks one of my ribs, then our drinks arrive and before I can take my first sip, he's downing his beer and asking for another round.

Jack raises his Bloody Mary to me and says, "Cheers, mate."

CHAPTER 56

"What can I get you to drink?" says the bartender, an Asian man in a black short-sleeved shirt who looks like he's been working here since the place opened back in 1934.

I look around and realize I'm at the Formosa Cafe rather than Barney's Beanery, and there's no Genghis Khan or Jack the Ripper in sight. So I've got that going for me. And at least for the time being, I'm still James Bond.

I open my mouth to ask the bartender for a Grey Goose martini. Shaken, not stirred. With two olives. But before the words come out, 007 disappears and JFK takes his place. So instead of a martini, I order a daiquiri.

The bartender gives me a funny look. Not funny like he's never seen a man order a daiquiri before, but more like he's trying to figure out who I am. And I realize he probably saw my face shift when I transitioned from one Ego to another. I glance up and look in the mirror behind the bar, where a semblance of JFK's boyish, good-looking face stares back at me.

"Everything all right?" I ask the bartender with a thick Boston accent.

He just nods once and goes to fix my drink while I take a seat and look around. Most of the chairs at the bar are filled, as are the deep red booths behind me, where the photographs of dead movie stars keep watch over the current clientele. Sitting on my left is a young woman with short, dark hair, luscious red lips, and a nose ring. I smile at her and introduce myself and offer to buy her a drink. She points to her nearly full pint of beer.

"I'm good," she says, then reaches for her drink. "Besides, I'm Republican."

So much for JFK's irresistible charm.

On the other side of me are two gay men sporting stylish hair and artificial tans who keep arguing about truth and wisdom. Down at the far end of the bar, some sleazeball with a ponytail is hitting on a cute little number who looks like Marilyn Monroe. As a matter of fact, I think she is Marilyn and I'm wondering if she'd like to knock one out for old times' sake. She excuses herself from the sleazeball to go to the bathroom and starts walking my way. I'm about to stop her when a car backfires out on Santa Monica Boulevard and I flinch and duck and reach up to make sure my head is still in one piece. It's kind of an automatic response. I can't go anywhere near a parade. And a Fourth of July fireworks show? Forget it.

When Marilyn passes me, I turn to say something to her but JFK slips away and Holden Caulfield takes his place. Not the smoothest of transitions. It's a bit disconcerting to go from being the former president of the United States to a fictional character with mental problems created by a reclusive writer.

"Forget something, pal?" says some five-and-a-half-foot phony with a cheesy mustache who appears in front of me. He's wearing a blue suit one size too small and has enough grease in his hair to deep-fry a goddamned turkey.

"Christ," he says, before I have a chance to answer his first question. "What the hell happened to you?"

I glance at the mirror behind the bar and notice that my face doesn't look anything like me. It doesn't look like JFK or James Bond or Indiana Jones. And although only Salinger knows for sure what Holden Caulfield looks like, I don't recognize the person wearing my suit.

I'm a stranger in my own skin.

A spectator watching a performance.

Truth is, I'm not sure if I'm real or make-believe.

"Last time I saw you, you looked different," says the phony.

"Last time?" I say.

"Yeah." He waves the bartender over. "Not thirty minutes ago. Right over there."

He points toward the end of the bar, where some phony

with a ponytail is checking himself out in the mirror like a goddamned prince.

I don't remember coming in here half an hour ago. Or talking to this phony. Or how I ended up in the alley. Then my gears shift again and Holden Caulfield is gone and it's me.

"Jesus!" says my mustached companion. "What the fuck is wrong with you?"

I look in the mirror and see my reflection. My face. My eyes. My lips. It's good to be back, though I wonder how long I'm going to stay this way. Then I remember the business card in my wallet.

I pull out my wallet and remove the business card. "This is yours," I say to the guy with the mustache.

"No shit." Joey Balsama turns to the bartender. "Jack and Coke. Easy on the Coke."

It all comes back to me: the conversation, the address in Brentwood, and what I could get at that address.

"So did you change your mind?" says Joey. "Or are you looking for someone to hold your hand?"

"No on both counts," I say.

"Good. Now do me a favor and make yourself scarce." He picks up his Jack and Coke. "I'm busy."

I pay the bartender for my daiquiri and leave the drink on the bar without touching it, then walk outside and stand on the sidewalk in the post-dusk gloom as cars drive past on Santa Monica Boulevard. I study the business card in the hollow glow of the streetlights, flipping the card over from one side to the other.

I'm trying to remember when I set this in motion and

how I even met Joey Balsama, but I don't know if I was me when I first met him or if I was someone else. James Bond. Philip Marlowe. Tyler Durden. Whoever I was, it occurs to me that I should probably think about making some travel plans.

CHAPTER 57

"Where would you like to go?" asks the travel agent, her voice soft and inviting in my ear.

I sit at the signal and stare through the windshield of my '59 T-Bird at the traffic passing back and forth in front of me on San Vicente Boulevard, windshields and metal surfaces reflecting the afternoon sun, the travel agent's question replaying in my head.

Where would you like to go?

I'm twenty-seven years old and I've never been out of the country. The only times I've been out of the state were to Tijuana during high school and college and once to Vegas with Nat after we both turned twenty-one. I've never flown on a plane.

Where would I like to go?

My father never asked me that question. Or my mother. We never did anything or took any vacations. At least not together. As I found out later, my father took a lot of "vacations" without us. My parents claimed they took me to Venice Beach once when I was four years old but I don't remember it. And my parents didn't take any pictures, so I'm dubious it ever happened.

Where would I like to go?

There are so many places to choose from. So many places I've never been that I'd like to visit. Portugal. Greece. South America. Australia. Europe. The Caribbean. New York City. Disneyland. I'm not sure I have any idea where to begin.

"I don't know," I say into my wireless headset.

"Well, are there any specific experiences you'd like to have?" asks the travel agent, her voice deep and husky and filled with unspoken promises, like I'm ordering up phone sex. I can almost picture her crawling across a giant map of the world on her hands and knees wearing nothing but a smile, then giving me a coy look over one shoulder. "Anything special you had in mind?"

Her choice of words isn't helping me to focus on picking a destination.

"Someplace out of the country," I say.

"Good." The word comes out like a purr and almost tickles my ear. I imagine her running her tongue across her lips. "Let's start there."

The light turns green and I accelerate through the intersection, thoughts of naked travel agents and all-inclusive resorts running through my head.

"So what kind of vacation were you looking to take?" she asks. "Were you thinking of a tropical destination? An African safari? Or maybe a Mediterranean cruise?"

Someplace tropical sounds tempting. I like the idea of white sand and the ocean and endless mai tais. Maybe Fiji. Or Jamaica. They both sound like a better idea than an African safari. And I don't even know where the Mediterranean Sea is.

The travel agent keeps talking, giving me different options, her sultry voice arousing more than just my curiosity.

"We also have a great deal on a two-week trip through Italy, France, and Spain," she says. "It even includes an optional Disneyland Paris package."

And I'm not getting the phone sex vibe anymore.

I'm also wondering if it was a good idea to call and ask a travel agent to help me pick a destination. I should have just figured this out on my own. After all, it's not like I'm looking to book a travel package or take any guided tours. I just want to go someplace where no one can find me.

Problem is, since I've never been out of the country other than Tijuana, I have no idea where to start. And I don't have the time to sit in front of a computer and try to figure out where I want to go. By this time Christmas day, I need to be wherever I'm going. Starting over. Changing my identity.

Becoming a new and improved version of me.

"I'm thinking something more remote," I say. "Preferably someplace warm with an English-speaking populace that doesn't have an extradition treaty with the United States."

There's silence on the other end of the line. I'm driving along Wilshire Boulevard through Beverly Hills, waiting for a response, wondering if we got cut off.

"Hello?" I say. "Are you still there?"

"Yes, sir." The travel agent no longer sounds like a sex phone worker but more like a pissed-off ex-wife. "I'm still here."

"Did you hear what I said?"

"Yes, sir. Unfortunately I don't think I'm going to be able to help you with your travel plans. But thank you for calling."

And then she hangs up.

CHAPTER **58**

I pull up to the curb and get out of my car and look at the address written on the back of Joey Balsama's business card, then I look up at the corresponding street number on the mailbox.

3070 North Rockingham Avenue.

This must be the place.

Two stone pillars frame the entrance to the driveway, which is blocked by a black, six-foot-high decorative wrought-iron sliding security gate. Beyond the gate, a blue Mercedes sits parked in the circular driveway. Behind the car, the clay-tiled roof of a two-story Mediterranean home rises up above the Japanese maples that obscure the rest of the house from view.

I look up and down the residential street, waiting for JFK or Captain Kirk to make an appearance. Maybe even Holden Caulfield to show up and make some comment about this place being full of phonies. But all of my alternate egos have grown silent. I don't know where they went, but it's good to have myself back. It's good to know that I'm still here. At least for a little while.

I look once more at the address on the back of the business card, then I walk up to the intercom. Above the gate, a video surveillance camera sits on a post inside the property, pointed in my direction. I smile and wave, then I reach out and press the button. Ten seconds later, a male voice comes over the intercom and asks me who I am. So I tell him. Then I hold up the business card for the camera and, acting like Joey and I are old friends, I say:

"Joey Balsama sent me."

Before I put the business card away, the security gate starts sliding back on its track. I drive inside and head toward the front of the house, feeling a little anxious and wishing James Bond would show up. Or Indiana Jones. I'd even settle for Elvis's swagger, though I doubt his appetite for deep-fried peanut butter and banana sandwiches would help right now. Nor would his ability to belt out a solid rendition of "Don't Be Cruel." Besides, I'm too anxious to eat. And there's not a karaoke machine in sight.

The front door is already open. Standing in the doorway and eating a sandwich as big as my head is a gorilla of a man who nearly fills up the entire door frame. He's easily six and a half feet tall, with a shaved head, shoulders like cinder blocks, and forearms so thick he should have heads sprouting from the end of them instead of hands.

And I'm wondering if it's too late to change my mind.

"So . . ." He takes a bite out of his sandwich. "Joey sent you."

I nod. "He told me you were the right man for what I was looking to get."

"That all depends," he says, his mouth full of meat and cheese and bread.

"Depends on what?"

"On what you plan to use it for."

Somehow I didn't think making a black market transaction would require having to explain my motives. I kind of figured it would have a no-questions-asked kind of vibe. Still, I don't think it would be a good idea to tell him the truth, at least not in the absolute sense, so instead I opt for a CliffsNotes version of what I plan to do.

"Let's just say it's for a good cause."

"Good causes are like good art," says the gorilla, then he takes another bite of his sandwich. "It's all a matter of subjectivity."

Funny. I didn't think I'd be getting a lesson in philosophy with my illegal purchase.

"When it comes down to it," he says, chewing, "every terrorist thinks he has a good cause."

Funny. I never thought of myself as a terrorist, either.

Suddenly this is getting a lot more complicated than I'd planned.

But when you're trying to save the soul of humanity, you have to expect things might get a little messy.

I have to admit, saving the soul of humanity sounds a little grandiose, but I don't believe it's hyperbole. After all, when you become someone else, the real you ceases to exist.

If the real you ceases to exist, then the fundamental purpose of *you* also ceases to exist. And if the fundamental purpose of you ceases to exist, then isn't that the essence of the soul?

I believe Big Egos have stolen our purpose. They've stolen our reason for being us. They've stolen our souls. And it's up to me to help get them back.

Truth is, everyone wants to be the hero of their own story.

I realize that after what I've done, I probably don't have much hope for saving my own soul. But I'm hoping it's not too late for all the others who still have a chance to be who they're supposed to be and to play the role they were born to play rather than playing a role that belongs to someone else.

"It's personal," I say. "But no one will get hurt. And it'll end up helping a lot of other people, too."

The gorilla stares at me, measuring my answer, studying me with his dark, unblinking eyes. Then he takes another bite of his sandwich, nods his head once, and steps out of the way.

"Okay," he says. "Let's talk business."

CHAPTER **59**

*D*r. Seuss walks through the room, wearing a striped top hat and a tuxedo with tails and telling everyone how he doesn't like green eggs and ham. Then he starts in with the whole one fish, two fish, red fish, blue fish bit again. He's been doing that for the past fifteen minutes, back and forth from one bit to the other, occasionally climbing up on a chair and telling everyone "I'm the Lorax and I speak for the beer," as he raises his glass to his lips and drains the rest of his pint.

I watch him and wonder how long he's been taking Substance D. And how long it will be before he believes he's covered in bugs.

But he's not the only one at the party who looks like he's high on something.

William Faulkner stands at the entrance to the hallway, taunting Ernest Hemingway, calling him an overrated hack and waving a red table napkin like a matador waving his cape.

Hemingway charges toward him, bent over at the waist, index fingers held up on either side of his head like horns as John Steinbeck and F. Scott Fitzgerald watch, laughing and applauding and stoned on gin-and-tonics. Jane Austen and Charlotte Brontë stand nearby sipping cocktails, acting as if they find the entire proceeding boorish and juvenile.

When Hemingway charges into Faulkner and they both tumble to the ground in a tremendous heap of arms and legs, Fitzgerald laughs so hard he sprays a mouthful of gin-and-tonic all over Jane Austen, who doesn't find the situation amusing and grabs Fitzgerald by the hair before slapping him in the face.

So much for her sense and sensibility.

I walk away from the chaos as Hemingway and Faulkner wrestle on the ground like a couple of drunken fraternity boys and make my way toward the giant stone fireplace, the opening of which looks like a portal to a parallel world, a crack in space, and I wonder what I would find if I crawled through it.

On one side of the fireplace, Bram Stoker sits in a large, overstuffed purple wingback chair with Mary Shelley on his lap, the two of them discussing corpses and the living dead and staring into each other's eyes like a couple of lovesick teenagers. Stoker leans forward and whispers something into Shelley's ear and she smiles and nods, then she stands up and takes his hand and they walk down the hallway toward the back of the house.

Mark Twain and Oscar Wilde, who have been trading amusing insights and quips for the last twenty minutes, observe the two amorous authors as they disappear into the guest bathroom. Twain remarks that it appears Shelley is going to become a Stroker. Wilde gives him a high-five and the two of them decide they should go listen at the bathroom door.

"In the name of research!" Twain raises his glass in the air as he and Wilde stumble down the hallway.

"Hey Phil," says Robert Heinlein, who slaps me on the back on his way to the wraparound couch, where he joins George Orwell, J. R. R. Tolkien, H. G. Wells, and Ray Bradbury in a game of Dungeons and Dragons, with Tolkien presiding as Dungeon Master.

Shirley Jackson and Sylvia Plath sit next to each other on the floor near the couch, smashed on wine, gossiping like a couple of high school cheerleaders, while Mickey Spillane and Raymond Chandler perch nearby like vultures, eyeing the two women and conferring with one another over glasses of scotch.

Several guests converge upon the dining room table, including Aldous Huxley, who is double-dipping tortilla chips into the guacamole, and Charles Dickens, who sits nearby scarfing down a plate of cocktail shrimp with a napkin tucked into his shirt collar. When he finishes, he hands his empty plate to William Shakespeare and asks if he can have some more.

The Bard gives him a look of disgust and mutters something about being eaten out of house and home. Then he takes the plate and walks into the kitchen, passing Kurt Vonnegut, who is making a cat's cradle out of a piece of string. When Vonnegut is done, he holds his hands up to James Joyce, who looks at the cat's cradle and shakes his head and says, "I still don't get it."

In the kitchen, which is connected to the dining room and the great room in an open floor plan, Fyodor Dostoevsky keeps trying to engage Franz Kafka in a discussion of existentialism as Kafka scuttles around on the floor pretending to be a cockroach, much to the delight of Virginia Woolf, who laughs so hard she starts to snort. Shakespeare ignores the lot of them and says, "What fools these mortals be."

Out in the great room, Truman Capote and Jack Kerouac have set up a karaoke machine and Capote is singing "Dancing Queen" while Emily Dickinson and Dorothy Parker whistle and applaud. Dante yells for everyone to shut the hell up as Edgar Allan Poe and Tennessee Williams shout out requests. William Golding stands in the middle of the room, holding up a conch, trying to get everyone's attention, while J. D. Salinger stands in the corner, eyeing everyone, looking awkward and uncomfortable.

I watch everyone and wonder if they're real or if I'm real. If I'm their dream or if they're mine.

If two people dream the same dream, does it cease to be an illusion?

I listen as Kerouac starts singing "On the Road Again," then I meander past Samuel Beckett, who is hanging out by the front door, constantly looking outside and checking his watch, apparently waiting for someone.

Down the hallway, Twain and Wilde stand outside the bathroom trying to one-up each other with clever witticisms while occasionally stopping to comment on the groans and cries of pleasure emanating from behind the bathroom door.

"It's not the size of the cock on the man," says Wilde. "It's the size of the cock in the woman."

Past the bathroom, the hallway branches off into two separate hallways, each of them with a couple of doors, and I wonder if one of them leads to the penultimate truth.

The first door I check is closed but not locked and when I open it, I find Emily Brontë on her hands and knees on the bed *with her dress pulled up and her panties on the floor while Ian Fleming stands at the edge of the bed with his pants around his ankles, jackrabbiting her.*

For a moment I see Indiana Jones having sex with Mary Magdalene and it's like I'm looking through a portal into another reality, experiencing parallel lives at the same moment. Then Fleming and Brontë return and Fleming asks if I would be a sport and give them some privacy.

I close the door and continue to the next room, where the door stands open to reveal Victor Hugo, Sir Arthur Conan Doyle, and Robert Louis Stevenson smoking cigars and ripping on American authors. In another room, Lewis Carroll and C. S. Lewis are standing in front of an open wardrobe, sharing a joint, completely stoned, laughing and daring each other to climb inside.

Eventually I find my way to the study, where Leo Tolstoy and Herman Melville are snorting cocaine on a framed photo of a family of four. Both Tolstoy and Melville look up suspiciously when I enter.

"Mind if I join you?" I produce a small plastic bag containing half a dozen capsules filled with white powder and set the bag down on the table.

"What is in capsules?" asks Tolstoy in a thick Russian accent.

"It's called Can-D," I say.

"And what does this candy do?" asks Tolstoy.

For a moment I see a beam of pink light in the glass, reflecting up into my eyes, transmitting information directly into my consciousness, allowing me to see the world as it truly exists: a fake. A cardboard facade. Then the beam is gone.

"It makes everything seem better than this reality," I say with a smile. "It's like no experience you've ever had before."

Melville gives me a smile and a nod and tells me how Moby-Dick *was really just a euphemism for his cocaine habit and that he's been chasing the great white whale most of his life. The entire time he grinds his teeth and wipes his nose as Tolstoy grabs my offering and starts emptying the contents of the capsules onto the framed photograph.*

I notice that Tolstoy and the man in the framed photo have the same head of hair.

"So what is your story?" Tolstoy asks as he starts to chop up the white powder into six lines.

I introduce myself and Tolstoy says he's never heard of me.

"I'm pretty famous in the science fiction community," I say. "I didn't have a lot of commercial success while I was alive but I've been called the Shakespeare of science fiction. Over a period of twenty-seven years I wrote more than one hundred and twenty short stories and forty novels, with nearly a dozen of my stories adapted into films."

"Forty novels?" Tolstoy cuts up the powder while Melville watches the lines form like a ten-year-old kid watching a confectioner drizzle hot fudge across an ice-cream sundae. "I do not believe anyone could write so many books. Is ridiculous."

I tell him it's true. I also tell him that one of my books was named as one of the 100 greatest English language novels of the last century.

"What are some of the titles of these novels?" asks Tolstoy.

I tell him a dozen or so. He laughs and dismisses me with a shake of his head. "Counterclock World? The Cosmic Puppets? Do Androids Dream of Electric Sheep? *I do not believe anyone would pay money for books with titles such as those."*

"Me either," says Melville.

"*Those are not literary titles,*" *says Tolstoy.* "*Those are names of children's books.* War and Peace. Anna Karenina. *Now those are real titles.*"

"*And* Moby-Dick." *Melville grabs a rolled-up hundred-dollar bill and tightens it.* "*Don't forget* Moby-Dick."

"*That is not a real title, either.*" *Tolstoy takes the rolled-up Franklin from Melville.* "*It is the title of a pornographic magazine for women who like large penises.*"

"*Or men who like large penises,*" *I say.*

"*Yes.*" *Tolstoy gives Melville an appraising glance.* "*Or men.*"

Tolstoy leans over the framed family photo and snorts one line with his left nostril, then another with his right before handing the Franklin to Melville, who takes it like a dog accepting a piece of cooked bacon. Melville snorts up his two lines so fast he doesn't have time to blink.

"*You amuse me,*" *says Tolstoy,* "*with your talk of excessive novels and ridiculous titles. Even your name is ridiculous. Not the name of a serious writer.*"

Melville nods his head in obedient agreement, even though my last name and the title of his novel share some common ground.

I just shrug and say I can't choose the name I was born with.

"*No,*" *says Tolstoy.* "*You cannot. But your name chooses you. And your name is a barometer of the vocation at which you were born to excel. Tolstoy. Dostoevsky. Chekhov. Those are names of literary giants.*"

"*And Melville,*" *says Melville.*

Tolstoy ignores him. "*It is not possible for you to be successful writer with last name such as yours.*"

"*Yeah,*" *says Melville.* "*It's presumptuous.*"

"*I think you mean preposterous,*" *says Tolstoy.*

"*Right,*" *says Melville.* "*That's what I meant.*"

A moment passes where both Tolstoy and Melville watch me to see what I do next. My initial reaction is to tell Tolstoy to take his discriminating self-importance and shove it. Or else go fuck himself. Either one of which would be much more satisfying than taking the high road. But I don't want to make a scene. The last thing I want is for someone to mention any kind of confrontation. As far as everyone else at the party knows, I was never in this room.

So I decide to take a different approach and hope the Pre-crime unit isn't watching.

"*Why don't you each take one of mine.*" *I indicate the two remaining lines on the photograph.* "*As a show of respect. And to show there's no hard feelings.*"

Melville doesn't wait to give me a chance to retract my offer and snorts up one of the lines faster than you can say "Que-equeg."

Tolstoy eyes me a moment, then nods. "*I may have misjudged you.*" *He takes the rolled-up hundred and snorts his extra line in a much more leisurely fashion, almost savoring it. When he's finished, he closes his eyes and presses an index finger to the side of the opposite nostril and inhales.*

He opens his eyes and smiles at me and starts to say something, more than likely another condescending remark. But before he can form any words, his smile falters and his eyes roll up and he drops face-first onto the framed photo, the glass cracking on impact. A moment later, Melville falls off his chair and collapses on the floor.

I grab the empty Baggie, then walk to the door and crack

it open to make sure no one is around. I don't see any sign of the Precrime police or the adjustment team or anyone from the party, so I close the door and head back down the hallway past the bathroom, where Twain and Wilde are still standing with their ears to the door, listening to Shelley and Stoker.

"I do believe Santa Claus is coming to town," says Wilde.

Twain nods. "Or he's about to come upon a midnight clear."

"Or upon something else," says Wilde.

"Either way," says Twain, "I'm guessing someone is about to have a white Christmas."

CHAPTER **60**

I'm standing in my bathroom trying to keep from passing out. My thumb keeps bleeding, no matter how much pressure or gauze I apply, so I hold my hand over my head to try to stop the flow but all that accomplishes is to cause blood to run down my wrist and drip onto my vintage Ramones T-shirt.

I'm thinking I probably shouldn't have worn one of my favorite T-shirts. And that I should have been a little better prepared before I attempted this.

On my Sirius satellite radio, Elvis is singing "White Christmas."

It's an Elvis holiday channel. All The King, all the time. When I look in the bathroom mirror, I realize I look like Elvis. I don't remember injecting him, but then, I don't remember a lot of things I've done lately.

But right now, I'm more worried about bleeding to death.

I put my thumb back under the cold water running out of the bathroom faucet, but the blood just keeps flowing. My thumb is throbbing and my vision is dimming. The longer I stand there, the more I feel like I'm going to pass out. Or throw up. Or both.

Trying to get a pint of blood out of myself without a trained technician isn't as simple as I thought it would be.

Initially I was going to go to a Red Cross center and donate a pint and then rob the phlebotomist at gunpoint before she could ferry away my blood. But that scenario posed too many problems, not the least of which is that I don't own a gun. Even if I used a knife or a can of pepper spray, I'd end up making a scene and people would notice me and the last thing I want is to draw attention to myself. Or end up in jail.

Plus I found out that the plastic bags they use to collect the blood contain sodium citrate, phosphate, and dextrose to keep the blood from clotting and preserve it during storage. I can't have that. My blood has to be clean. Pure, 100 percent me with no additives or artificial sweeteners.

So I scratched that idea.

I thought about calling Emily or Vincent to help me, but I still don't know if I can trust them. It's probably just me being paranoid, but lately that's the status quo. The last thing I want is either Emily or Vincent asking me why I'm draining a pint of my own blood. The less they know the better.

Last I heard, Emily, Vincent, and Kurt were still working at EGOS, though apparently after the death of Bill Summers, there was some question as to who would oversee Investigations or even if it could function with half its crew having been patched together from other departments. The deaths of the executive vice president and the chairman of the board have thrown the entire EGOS operation into a state of chaos.

Even if I could trust Vincent or Emily, I can't risk the chance of a stray hair or dead skin cells from anyone else getting mixed in with my blood.

I realize I'm probably being anal retentive, but I don't want to take any chances.

So I decided the only way to do this safely and without contaminating my blood or arousing any suspicion was to do it at home alone.

My first attempt was with a needle and syringe. I wrapped an elastic tourniquet around my arm and sterilized the soft flesh just inside my left elbow with rubbing alcohol and iodine, then I sat down in the guest bathroom with my arm on the counter and I went to work. Problem was, I couldn't manage to hit the median cubital vein, and after half a dozen unsuccessful attempts I gave up. Which is just as well, since the syringe is only ten milliliters and I would have had to draw fifty samples to get a pint of blood.

I probably should have thought this through.

Eventually I decided to slice open my left thumb and drain the blood into a sterile, one-pint container. Which is fine in theory and when you see it done on television or in the movies, but taking a knife to your own flesh isn't something you can do without giving it a second thought.

Or a third thought. Or a tenth thought. I placed the blade against my left thumb more than a dozen times, taking a deep breath each time and closing my eyes, which probably wasn't the smartest idea I've ever had, only to open my eyes and set the knife down.

Finally, I took one more deep breath, picked up the knife, kept my eyes open, and sliced.

The normal time for donating a pint of blood using a needle and a plastic bag in a controlled environment runs ten to fifteen minutes. That's not counting the time for juice and cookies afterward. But when you slice open your thumb with a fillet knife that you sterilized with alcohol and iodine and the blood starts dripping out of your self-inflicted wound into a sterile plastic specimen container, you begin to appreciate just how fast blood can flow out of you and how light-headed you can get watching yourself bleed.

I didn't realize the extremities bled so much.

Once I had the one-pint container filled, I grabbed my thumb and rinsed it off beneath the faucet, then wrapped it up and applied pressure, taking deep breaths and sitting down because I felt like I was going to pass out. By the time I finally raised my hand above my head and ruined my Ramones T-shirt, I'd lost another quarter pint of blood.

I'm thinking I probably need stitches.

But the last thing I want is for someone to file a hospital report with my name on it. And since I'm not good with a needle and thread and I don't think a staple gun would be a good idea, I go into the kitchen and rummage around in drawers until I find a tube of superglue. Back in the bathroom I unwrap my thumb, rinse it off in the sink, then I apply a ribbon of glue to the wound before the blood can start flowing again. I didn't realize how much superglue would burn. It feels like I dipped my thumb in acid, so I let out a scream that nearly causes me to black out.

This isn't something you should try without adult supervision.

On my Sirius satellite radio, Elvis is singing "Merry Christmas Baby."

After about a minute the pain starts to subside and the glue seems to be doing the trick: the blood has stopped flowing. I wrap my thumb in gauze and tape, screw the lid on the one-pint specimen container filled with my blood, and put it in the refrigerator. As I'm closing the door, James Bond shows up, so I grab the jar of pimento olives, get out the vodka, vermouth, and a martini glass, and sing along with Elvis.

CHAPTER **61**

J ames Bond and Elvis Presley are drinking martinis in my living room.

They're sitting on the couch, sharing a laugh. When they catch me looking at them, 007 leans over and whispers something to The King, who sprays a mouthful of vodka and vermouth across the room and starts coughing.

Ace Ventura, who catches the brunt of Elvis's spray, calls The King a loser and challenges him to an ass-talking contest. Leo Tolstoy stands nearby stirring his cocktail with a straw and shaking his head while Herman Melville snorts some cocaine out of a bullet. David Cassidy is across the room telling Jayne Mansfield that he thinks he loves her as Tarzan lopes past them and through the crowd of partygoers.

I'm not Morrison or Marlowe or Indiana Jones. I'm not Elvis or Captain Kirk or Holden Caulfield. I'm not anyone else, just me. But I'm wondering what all of these other people are doing in my house. And who invited them.

There's Bob Marley, Walt Disney, and Napoleon Dynamite.

Ingrid Bergman, Rita Hayworth, and Lara Croft.

George Harrison, John Wayne, and the Fonz.

I feel like Miss Mary Ann on *Romper Room,* looking into her magic mirror and seeing all of her friends who are having a special day. Except none of these people are my friends, and most of them don't actually exist.

I see Don Draper and Abraham Lincoln and Bridget Jones. I see Elmer Fudd and Rocky Balboa and Louis Armstrong. I see Ellen Ripley and Ferris Bueller and Hunter S. Thompson.

Romper, bomper, stomper boo.

I look at all of them and try to understand what they're doing in my kitchen and my living room and my hallway, though I realize no one's really here. This is all in my head. My first thought is that I'm projecting all of the Egos I've used over the past three years, but I was never Bridget Jones or Ingrid Bergman. And we never offered The Hunter S. Thompson because it was too unstable.

It takes me a few more moments of looking around before I realize that my houseguests are all of the black market Egos to whom I gave the antidote. All of the people I thought I was helping. All of the people who died as a result of my actions.

Though not all of them were an accident.

I see Bill Summers and David Cook. I see the chairman

of the board and his wife. I see the black market dealer and his partner, Eddie. I see the CEO and president of EGOS. I see all of them here with me on this fucked-up version of *Romper Room*.

And none of them is having a special day.

CHAPTER **62**

I'm standing alone in my living room. My houseguests have all gone, though Elvis is still on the radio singing "Santa Claus Is Back in Town" as I sip my martini and read the front-page headline of the *Los Angeles Times* on my iPad Platinum:

CEO and President of EGOS Found Dead

According to the article, Alistair Moore, the CEO of Engineering Genetics Organization and Systems, and Paul Lawson, the company's president, both died from an apparent cocaine overdose during a private Ego holiday party held at Moore's Beverly Hills home. Unfortunately, with the nature of Egos, eyewitness testimony is not always dependable, so the police don't expect to learn much from those in attendance.

Moore and Lawson were pioneers who together turned EGOS from a struggling midlevel bioengineering company into the leader in molecular cloning.

Investigators are looking into the possibility that both Lawson's and Moore's deaths were caused by the use of Big Egos rather than recreational drugs. Along with the recent fatalities of Bill Summers, David Cook, and several other executives and board members, the deaths of Moore and Lawson—the company's chief innovators—have caused EGOS's stock to drop by more than 40 percent.

On my satellite radio, Elvis is singing that it's Christmas time and the snow is falling down.

I finish reading the article, then I walk into my bedroom and strip down to my boxers and stand in front of the full-length bedroom mirror, studying my reflection as I sing along with Elvis, channeling The King even though I haven't injected him in more than a month.

The boxers I'm wearing are cotton. From the Gap. Or maybe Banana Republic. At this point it's all just speculation. But Delilah bought them for me last Christmas, of that I'm fairly certain. As I am of the fact that Delilah isn't home. I don't know where she is. Maybe she went out to do some last-minute Christmas shopping. Either that or she left me altogether, which seems more likely. I'd probably leave me, too, except I don't have much of a choice.

My boxers are white with smiley faces all over them. Big smiley faces and small smiley faces. Yellow circles with black dots for eyes and black curved lines for mouths. Some of them have big smiles. Filled-with-capped-teeth smiles. Cheshire Cat smiles.

Like an emoticon on crack.

I can almost hear them laughing at me—in my head, in the room, lots of high-pitched laughter. Only I don't get the joke because I'm not laughing with them.

I stare at my boxer shorts in the mirror, at the Cheshire Cat grins floating around my groin and upper thighs, and I feel like I've fallen down the rabbit hole, only instead of making me larger or smaller my pills are making me someone else. And instead of Alice, I'm the Mad Hatter. And I've misplaced my hat. Either that or someone has stolen it. Doesn't matter. But eventually I'm going to need to find something to wear on the top of my head.

My attention moves from my boxer shorts to my flat stomach, then to my chest and my shoulders, then finally up to my face. I look back at myself, not smiling or frowning but wearing an expression that's devoid of emotion. I'm like a mannequin. Or one of those really expensive lifelike sex dolls. Either way, no one's coaxing more than a blank stare out of me.

My face isn't my face. Not the one I grew up with. Not the one I remember. It belongs to somebody else now. Someone famous. Someone fictional. Someone other than me.

It belongs to Elvis. It belongs to Indiana Jones. It belongs to James Bond.

It belongs to each of them and to all of them.

Actors and characters and celebrities.

All of these people I've pretended to be. All of these Egos I've been at one time or another. More times than I can count. More times than I can remember.

All for one and one for all. Though as far as I know,

I've never been one of the Three Musketeers. Or even d'Artagnan.

I cock my head and so does my reflection. Then I cock my head the other way and my reflection follows suit. The image in the glass that's me but isn't me. My legs and arms and torso with someone else's head. About the only part of my face I still recognize is my eyes.

My reflection stares back at me, and for a few moments I lose track of which one is the reflection and which one is me. Then I reach up to scratch my head and realize both of us are holding something in our hands.

In my right hand is a pair of electric clippers. In my left hand is a nearly empty martini glass. I don't recall how either one of them got there. Or why my left thumb is throbbing and wrapped in a bunch of tape and gauze. Or how I ended up in front of the mirror in my boxers. But I'm suddenly thinking of David Cassidy and I'm pretty sure I understand what I intended to do with the electric clippers.

I just have to trust that whatever part of me brought me here knows what I'm doing.

On my satellite radio, Elvis is singing that Santa Claus is back in town.

I raise the martini glass to my reflection and give it a smile, down the rest of my cocktail, toss the glass aside, and turn on the clippers.

CHAPTER **63**

Two dozen Christmas carolers are singing "Joy to the World" as they march back and forth in front of the security gate. Except they're not really Christmas carolers. They're protesters. And some of them are getting the lyrics to the Christmas hymn about Christ's triumphant return confused with the Three Dog Night version of the song.

Jeremiah might have been a bullfrog, but I don't think he had anything to do with the birth of the Savior.

Of course, everyone has their own version of salvation.

Jesus. Muhammad. Buddha.

Truth is, no one really knows what the truth is.

As I approach the entrance, the protesters stop singing and gather in a poorly rehearsed protest formation, splitting up on either side of the road and shouting over one another while holding up their protest signs.

No More Egos!
Let Go of My Ego!
What Would Jesus Do?

I'll tell you what Jesus would do. He'd probably wonder why all these people are out here protesting against a consumer product rather than preparing for the celebration of his birthday. Never mind that astronomers and scientists have determined that Jesus wasn't actually born on December 25 and that the celebration of his birth has been turned into the biggest commercial holiday in history.

It's 8:02 p.m. on Christmas Eve. These people should be home with their families in front of a fire, drinking eggnog and eating fruitcake and watching *It's a Wonderful Life*. Instead they're marching back and forth in front of the EGOS laboratory in Los Feliz, singing Christmas carols and shouting out protests, their breath releasing in smoky plumes that vanish into the unusually cold Southern California night.

These people really need to get a life.

As I drive past them, the protesters start screaming at me, calling me a corporate whore and a capitalist pig and an identity rapist. Only they're not screaming at me. Not really. They're screaming at a concept, an ideology, at who and what I represent.

Or at least what they think I represent.

Once I reach the security gate, I roll down my window.

"Evening," I say to the security guard, who slides open the security booth door and steps out. The guard is wearing a uniform with the EGOS name and logo. The ID card clipped to his uniform identifies him as WILLIAM BLAKE.

For a second I look at him and wonder if he's actually the English poet or if he's injected William Blake's ego and likes wearing the name tag for fun. But then I realize he's probably just a security guard with the same name. Of course, nowadays, you can never be sure.

Still, a line from Blake's "The Marriage of Heaven and Hell" goes through my head:

If the doors of perception were cleansed, every thing would appear to man as it is—infinite.

That's what I'm here to do. Cleanse the doors of perception. Make everything clear to my fellow man. Though infinity is a little bit above my aspirations. I'm not that ambitious. I'm just shooting for the present moment.

"Evening," says William Blake.

I hand him my official EGOS identification card, which should be valid since I'm still an employee. I'm just on a paid sabbatical. With any luck my ID hasn't been flagged or doesn't require authorization for admittance; otherwise I'm going to have to go to Plan B, which is a problem since I don't have a Plan B.

William Blake takes the ID card from me and studies it, then gives me a good, long look. I give him a smile and hope he doesn't notice that I'm wearing a wig. And that he doesn't want to check the trunk of my car.

I can sense one of the dozens of Egos I've injected over the years wanting to slip to the surface but I can't let that happen. Not now. So I clench my fists and take deep, measured breaths and focus all of my energy on holding tight to my own identity.

"So what brings you out tonight?" asks the security

guard. "I thought I was the only one working here Christmas Eve."

"The VP of marketing wants additional testing done before product hits the shelves, so I have to pick up some of the prototypes for the new line we're supposed to launch," I say, trying to sound cool and calm, which isn't easy when Jim Morrison is howling at the door like the Big Bad Wolf.

Little pig, little pig, let me in . . .

The security guard gives a knowing nod. "I guess even with everything that's happened lately, the show must go on."

"I hear the CFO is trying to keep things together," I say, even though I've heard no such thing, but it sounds good. "And even without a president, a CEO, or a chairman, there's still a Board of Directors, so someone has to try to keep the stockholders happy."

My father always said that if you act like you're supposed to be somewhere and exude an aura of confidence, most people accept that you're who you say you are and that you have the authority to be doing what you're doing. The trick is to make people believe you are who they think you are. Or at least who they think you're supposed to be. Play your role and everything will fall into place.

"So how's the protest going?" I ask.

William Blake looks out at the protesters. "They're a pain in the ass. Been out here all day long. I wish they'd go home. Although they do provide some entertainment value."

Behind us, the protesters are shouting out insults and singing "Rudolph the Red-Nosed Reindeer."

"You have to deal with them all night?" I ask.

"Just for another hour," he says.

"At least you don't have the graveyard shift."

"You're telling me," he says, then steps back into his booth to write something down.

I glance inside, where a single video monitor shows my car sitting at the security gate. I have an impulse to lean out my window and smile and wave but common sense prevails. Then William Blake steps out of the booth and hands my ID card back to me.

"Have a Merry Christmas," he says.

"Thanks. You do the same."

He presses a button and the gate starts to slide open. I give William Blake a final wave, then drive through the gate and turn left and head around the back of the building. Once I reach the rear corner of the parking lot, where I'm out of the line of sight of the security gate, I park the car and take several deep breaths to try to keep Morrison and the rest of my Egos in check, but I know it won't last much longer. Eventually they'll break through and I won't be able to stop them, so I pop the trunk and get busy.

From inside the trunk I pull out a nylon backpack and set it on the ground next to the car, then I remove a duffel bag, a rolled-up nylon emergency escape ladder, and a compact, telescoping extension ladder that extends to fifteen feet. Once I have everything I need, I close the trunk, slip the backpack over my shoulders, pick up the ladders and the duffel bag, then walk toward the back of the fence, which is made of twelve-foot-high, heavy gauge metal privacy storm fencing with coiled razor wire running along the length of the top. It has all the charm of a prison. Or a concentration camp.

When I reach the fence, I set down the extension ladder, lean it against the storm fencing, and extend it above the razor wire to its full height. Then I climb to the top with the rolled-up nylon ladder, which I hang from the top rung of the extension later and drop down the other side of the fence. Once I'm finished with what I came here to do, I'll be able to climb over the fence without getting caught up in the razor wire. I still haven't figured out how I'm going to get the extension ladder from this side of the fence over to the other side so I can take the ladder with me, but at the moment it's taking all of my concentration just to focus on what I'm doing now.

As I descend the ladder, I notice the back of a metal sign attached to the fence. If I were on the outside the sign would say NO TRESPASSING and tell me this is private property and that violators will be prosecuted to the full extent of the law. The protesters out by the security gate aren't trespassing. They're obeying the law while trying to get their message across.

Me? I'm choosing a different course of action.

Except suddenly I'm not me. I'm Ethan Hunt from *Mission: Impossible,* the movie not the television series, and I'm channeling Tom Cruise, the theme song running through my head.

Bum bum bum-bum, bum bum bum-bum . . .

On the other side of the storm fencing, the Santa Monica Mountains rise up into the night, bordering the back edge of the factory. A little less than a mile away, in the parking lot next to the Roosevelt Municipal Golf Course in Griffith Park, sits a Ford Taurus that I bought with cash for three grand from some guy on Craigslist. I used the fake identification I got from the gorilla in Brentwood, so I'm hoping no one will be able to trace the transaction back to the real me.

Whoever that is.

This pretending to be someone else has become a lifestyle.

By the time I've finished setting up the ladder and I'm walking toward the back entrance of the factory, Ethan Hunt is gone and I'm James Bond, channeling a young Sean Connery, scanning the grounds for snipers, expecting to see General Orlov or Dr. Kananga, but apparently they had other plans.

I glance at my watch. I should be in and out of here in less than thirty minutes, which gives me plenty of time to get to my car before Griffith Park closes. After that, it's a four-hour drive to Mexico. Then another two day's drive to Cancún. I can already see myself at a beachside bar, enjoying the sun and ordering up a nice, cool tropical drink. Then Bond is gone and I'm Elvis and I have a hankering for an ice-cream soda.

Out by the security gate, the protesters are singing "Winter Wonderland" as I reach the rear entrance. I use my ID badge to activate the electronic entry, channel The King, and sing along with them.

CHAPTER **64**

Elvis sings "Winter Wonderland" on the stereo as a fire crackles in the fireplace and I sit next to the Christmas tree in my pajamas, my glass of eggnog untouched, wondering if other kids are having as much fun as me.

Where I am is home on Christmas Eve with my mother and my father. I'm seven years old. This is after my father dropped the bomb about Santa Claus and the Easter Bunny and the Tooth Fairy. Only my father isn't my father. He's Christopher Walken.

"I know you're disappointed," says Walken. "But this is a lesson in what you need to understand in order to survive in the world. This is a lesson in truth."

I want to tell my father that this is more like a lesson in dream-crushing, except I don't have the courage to talk back to my father. It's bad enough when he's him, but Christopher Walken scares the hell out of me. So instead I'm sitting here playing Santa Claus, wrapping my own Christmas presents and stuffing my own stocking, while Walken explains how other parents foster the misconceptions of their children and cause them to grow up delusional.

"Children should know what's real and what's make-believe," he says. "No one succeeds in life by believing in supernatural beings that don't exist."

And I'm wondering about all of the people who believe in God.

My mother, who looks like Marge Simpson, complete with the tower of blue hair, finishes wrapping one of my presents and puts it under the Christmas tree, then stands up.

"Would anyone like some more eggnog?" she says.

Walken hands her his glass. "A little more rum this time."

"How about you, honey?" she asks, as if nothing is wrong. As if the death of her son's naïveté happens every day.

I look at my untouched glass of eggnog. "No, thank you."

She gives me a kiss on the top of my head and then walks away into the kitchen.

"You know, son, you're lucky," says Walken as he continues to rationalize the raping of my childhood innocence. "You're getting to experience a reality that most children in this country at your age don't know exists. You're living the truth while the rest of them are living a lie. And in the long run, you'll be better prepared because of it."

Yes, that's what I want to be. Better prepared for life by being denied the joy of waking up on Christmas morning and racing out of my room to see what Santa left for me beneath the tree. Staying up with my parents and wrapping my own presents is so much more rewarding.

"And I'd advise you to wipe that expression off your face."

Expression? What expression? The one that looks like someone has taken a jackhammer to my favorite night of the year?

"I know this isn't what you were hoping for, son, but sometimes you have to make the best of what you have." Walken pulls out a .38 Special and holds it up for emphasis. "So I suggest you stop with the pouting before I give you something to pout about."

"Yes, sir," I say. And he puts the gun away.

I'd wish for Santa to come down and rescue me, take me away with him on his sleigh to live with him at the North Pole, but apparently that's not an option anymore. So instead I wish that I were Santa Claus. At least that way I could enjoy my Christmas.

Marge Simpson returns with my father's eggnog and sits down near the fireplace. I look to her for help, but she's too busy wrapping another one of my presents to notice my suffering.

Buddha said that desire is the root of all suffering. That if you stop seeking pleasure, then happiness will be yours. So that means if I don't have any desire for an enjoyable holiday experience, if I accept this as my truth and embrace the concept that everything I want is already mine, then I should have a merry Christmas.

I bet Buddha never had to stuff his own Christmas stocking.

"Here," says Walken as he hands me my Christmas stocking along with a comic book, a small rubber monkey, a box of crayons, and a candy cane. "Make yourself useful."

CHAPTER **65**

I pull off my wig and run my hand across my shaved head, then I shove the wig into my backpack. From inside the duffel bag I remove the rest of the forty pounds of C4 I bought from the gorilla in Brentwood and place it at strategic points around the lab, channeling Sean Connery from *Thunderball* and *You Only Live Twice* as I insert the wireless detonators. I've always been partial to Connery's Bond. He had a certain sophisticated, womanizing charm about him that I admire.

It's been more than a week since I injected James Bond, but I'm still feeling the effects as if I'd injected him just hours ago. Of course, there's no telling how long I'll be Bond before I shift to someone else. My alternate personas have taken to sticking around like lingering houseguests, refusing to leave. It's as though they're all staying in my system, blending together, becoming part of me.

Truth is, I'm not completely sure who I am anymore.

I realize I might be like this for the rest of my life. That wouldn't be so bad if I could stick with one Ego, if I could be James Bond or Indiana Jones or JFK forever. But this constant shifting from one Ego to another makes it difficult to focus on clipping my fingernails, let alone wiring detonators into plastic explosives. And it's not like I've ever done this before. But with James Bond channeling through me, I have the confidence that I know what I'm doing.

For a moment I become Indiana Jones and I'm suddenly losing my focus on the plastic explosives and looking around for stolen artifacts and wondering what the hell happened to my hat. And my whip. Where the hell's my whip? Then in a flash Bond returns, only this time I'm getting a Roger Moore vibe from *Moonraker* and *The Spy Who Loved Me* and I'm hoping Richard Kiel isn't anywhere around with his mouth full of metal teeth.

The security cameras in the corners watch me, the lights on top blinking red, though the can of black spray paint I brought with me has rendered the cameras useless. The fact that no security guards or a SWAT unit has burst in to arrest me is a good sign. But it calms my nerves to know that Big Brother isn't watching. Or at least if he is, all he's seeing is a lot of black. Fortunately the videos in here aren't on a live feed. They're just set up to catch an employee ignoring proper protocol or trying to get away with something that's against company policy.

Like trying to blow everything up.

Once I finish wiring the last of the C4, I set the timers

on the detonators for ten minutes each, then I reach into my backpack and remove the specimen container filled with a pint of my blood, which has now warmed up to room temperature. I don't know if it's starting to clot or if that will even make a difference, but at this point it's too late for me to be worried about whether I should have used an anticoagulant.

I open the container and toss most of the blood around the lab in a splattering spray, then I dump the last of it on the floor. After screwing the lid back on and shoving the empty container inside my backpack, I pull out the one-gallon Ziploc plastic bag filled with my freshly shaved hair and scatter it around the room, making sure to get some stuck in the blood pooled on the floor.

Once I'm done, I put the empty bag in my backpack, then pick up the remote control for the timers and look around at my handiwork and nod. Sure, it looks like Charles Manson stopped by for a visit and then gave himself a hair-cut, but with any luck they'll find enough traces of my DNA that they'll think I died in the explosion. The fact that I paid cash for my flight probably won't matter, considering the feds can run my name through an airline database search and find out that I booked a flight to Vietnam. But I'm hoping the fact that my car and my blood and my hair are all still here will buy me enough time to get out of the coun-try. And that if they figure out I didn't die in the explosion, they'll be looking for me in Southeast Asia rather than in the Caribbean.

Is it a perfect plan? No. But it's the best I could come up with on short notice. I'm just hoping the crime scene investigators won't be able to tell that my blood and my hair were removed from my body twenty-four hours before any of it ended up in the lab and that they'll believe I was still in the building when it blew up.

I'm thinking I might have overdone it a bit with the hair and the blood, but my father always taught me that if I'm going to do something, never do it half-assed.

Part of me wishes I'd done more research on criminal forensics, but I didn't really have the time. So I just watched a bunch of *CSI* episodes and purchased a black market Ego of The Dana Scully. That was kind of erotic, in an *X-Files* kind of way.

I'm suddenly getting a Fox Mulder vibe, which is weird because I only injected his Ego once during testing and that was nearly a year ago. The last thing I need right now is paranoid neurosis and borderline psychological obsession about aliens dancing around in my head, but I can't help wondering if any of this laboratory equipment is being used to test for the existence of extraterrestrials.

Before I have a chance to investigate, Mulder is gone and I'm back. Not just my consciousness hovering beneath all the other Egos, but me. No James Bond or Captain Kirk or Jim Morrison in sight.

Even though I have occasional moments of clarity, it feels like it's been years since I've been myself, since I've glimpsed the person I used to be before I became all of these other people, so I grab hold and I try to hang on to me, to keep me present in the hopes that I can stick around and push all of these other identities out. Then my grip falters and my hand slips and I'm gone and Ethan Hunt from *Mission:*

Impossible is back, the Tom Cruise version, filling me with the confidence that I need to finish the job.

I don't know if blowing up the lab and the factory and the records is going to change anything. All of the important backup files and formulas and documents are most likely stored on a secure off-site server somewhere. But with the CEO, chairman of the board, and the president of EGOS gone, and with all the recent negative publicity I've helped to create, I'm hoping this will be the end of Big Egos and allow people to stop spending so much time trying to be someone else and get back to playing the roles they're supposed to play.

After all, it's never too late to be the person you were meant to be.

I take one final look around to make sure I haven't forgotten anything, then I slip my arms through the straps of my backpack and walk out of the lab, the door closing shut behind me. Once I reach the hallway, I go over my exit strategy.

According to the gorilla, the remote detonator has a limited range of one hundred feet and requires line of sight. Since I wired C4 in the main storage room as well as in the lab and the computer server room, I have to factor in multiple walls and doors and more than two hundred feet from here to the back of the parking lot. That's why I set the timers on the wireless detonators for ten minutes, so I would have plenty of time to go from room to room activating the timers and get out of the factory and safely away from here before the C4 explodes.

By the time the detonators go off, I'll be over the fence

with the ladder and my backpack and any proof that I made it out of here alive. After getting rid of the ladder and any incriminating evidence, I should be across the border and into Mexico before Santa Claus has finished visiting all of the good little boys and girls.

I do one final run-through in my head, hoping that all of my various identities are on the same page. As far as I can tell, everyone's in agreement. Still, I have this nagging feeling that there's something I've overlooked, but I don't have time to worry about the details now.

I take a deep breath and depress the button on the hand-held remote to start the first detonators on their countdown. It's not until that moment I realize I set all of the wireless timers for one minute instead of ten.

CHAPTER 66

I'm running as fast as I can, breath bursting out of my mouth in white clouds and disappearing into the cold December night. White LED parking lights illuminate the ground as I race across the asphalt toward the back of the perimeter fence, toward the extension ladder leaning against the chain links and the razor wire.

My arms and legs pumping like pistons, my expression set and determined, I'm Tom Cruise in *Mission: Impossible*. Or *Minority Report*. Or *The Firm*. Except I'm not running from Wilford Brimley or the Precrime police. And I'm wearing Nikes instead of Kenneth Coles. I always wondered how Tom Cruise could run so fast in oxfords. No one has ever run better in movies than him. You ask me, he should win a lifetime achievement award for Running in Films.

The next thing I know I'm James Bond, my theme song playing in my head, the thrill of being the world's greatest secret agent surging through me. Mostly Roger Moore, with a hint of Sean Connery and Pierce Brosnan, but no Daniel Craig or Timothy Dalton.

More than a hundred yards behind me across asphalt and commercial landscaping, the protesters march back and forth, singing Christmas carols. I glance back to see if anyone sees me, if I'm being followed, looking for any signs of General Orlov or Hugo Drax or Mr. Big. The next thing I know, I'm tripping over my own feet and stumbling to the ground. When I get back up, my palms are raw and bleeding and my left pant leg is torn open, my left knee throbbing. I could use some hydrogen peroxide and some sterile gauze, maybe a nice hot bath with some essential mineral oils.

So much for James Bond.

Right now, it feels more like I'm channeling Miss Moneypenny.

I take off, sprinting away from the building, the clock ticking down in my head. No James Bond. No Ethan Hunt. No theme songs to give the scene some ambience. It's just me, myself, and I.

The protesters sing "Silent Night" as I close in on the fence, less than twenty feet away, and I think I'm going to make it. But just before I reach the fence there's a *whump* and a flash, the night suddenly bright and glowing and hot behind me, the sound of glass and concrete and metal exploding up and out, and I'm thinking I should have really double-checked the timers.

The concussion from the blast lifts me off my feet and throws me into the ladder and the fence, chain links and razor wire collapsing around me. Hot air roars past, sucking the air from my lungs. My head hits something hard and metal. Something else slices into my right leg. My left arm gets caught in the ladder as the extension safety disengages and two metal rungs going in opposite directions slam down on my arm, snapping it at the elbow.

I let out a scream as another explosion sends debris raining down on the asphalt around me and lights up the night. Not that it needs any more lighting. What's left of the building is already engulfed in flames. Fire and smoke billow out of empty windows. Half the building is gone. Voices shout out, some of them in shock, others in celebration. Someone keeps shouting "That's right!" over and over again. Several others are singing "Deck the Halls."

Or at least that's what it sounds like. But I'm not sure I can put much stock in my ability to process information at the moment.

When you're wrapped up in razor wire, your left arm broken and your back blistered from the heat of an explosion, blood dripping from a head wound and the curtains of a concussion closing across the screen of your thoughts, you tend to lose your ability to think rationally.

I lie on my back with the ladder on top of me and stare up into the sky filled with heat and smoke, my head and arm throbbing, tears pouring out of my eyes. I know that in spite of my injuries I need to get up and get moving, but extracting yourself from storm fencing and razor wire when you're pinned to an extension ladder isn't as easy as it sounds. The trick is pushing up on the top rung of the ladder with your good arm while pushing down on the bottom rung with your broken arm, all while trying to keep the razor wire from slicing into your femoral artery.

From what sounds like the bottom of a well, I hear the protesters shouting, some of them cheering and applauding and singing "We Wish You a Merry Christmas" at the top of their lungs.

It's good to know someone's in the holiday spirit.

I reach over with my right arm and grab a ladder rung and pull, pushing down with my left arm in the opposite direction and screaming until I'm finally free. Then I'm rolling over and cradling my arm, passing out for I don't know how long. When I regain consciousness, I'm curled up in a fetal position in a tangle of chain-link fence. I have razor wire wrapped around my right leg. Something warm is running down my face. My back feels like it's on fire.

I push myself up and see blood pooled on a dented NO TRESPASSING sign. My breath comes out in short, ragged puffs of smoke as I try to figure out a way to untwist myself from the fencing and razor wire.

This isn't exactly how I saw things playing out.

Though to be honest I'm not sure what I expected to happen, but I was hoping for something a little different than this. Something easier. Something less painful. Something that included beaches and bikinis and rum drinks with tiny umbrellas.

Off in the distance I hear sirens. Through the smoke and the heat drifting off the burning rubble, lights flicker in the darkness. For a moment I think I'm looking into the night sky, at constellations I don't recognize, at stars that no longer exist, burned out aeons ago, their light just now reaching us. Then I realize I'm looking toward the city, at the lights of Los Angeles, at the convoy of emergency vehicles heading this way, bringing paramedics and ambulances and medical assistance.

And I'm thinking I should probably get out of here.

When I try to move, the razor wire bites into my flesh and the curtain starts to drop again on my consciousness, so I slap myself once across the face. The slap doesn't hurt compared to the rest of my injuries but it does the trick and keeps me from passing out.

Holding my left arm against my stomach, I reach down with my right hand and start to unwrap the razor wire from my leg. There's a lot of blood. Not so much that I think it's sliced through my femoral artery, but it's more blood than I want to see coming out of me. Especially since I already drained a pint last night.

Although I manage to unwrap most of the razor wire from my leg without making things worse, several of the barbs have sliced their way under my skin to the point that I realize I'm probably going to do more damage getting them out than they made going in. Which I guess is the point. Once you get caught in this stuff, you're not supposed to just get up and walk away.

My heart is pounding and emergency lights are flashing. If I don't do something quick, someone is going to come along and find me here and I don't think they're going to throw me a party or give me a medal or make me a saint. So I take hold of the razor wire and close my eyes, then I hold my breath and count to three. Then I count to three again. Then I decide to give myself a little more time and I count to ten.

One . . . two . . . three . . . four . . . five . . .

Another explosion goes off and I flinch, pulling the razor wire free before I'm ready.

I black out.

The next thing I know I'm walking through some trees out behind the factory, my back warm and my left arm heavy and throbbing. Blood trickles from the scalp wound past my left eye. More blood runs down my leg into my sock, pooling in my shoe, so every other step I take sounds like I'm walking in mud.

I turn and look back at the fire and the chaos and the destruction I've created. Part of me doesn't believe I was actually responsible for all of this, that I'm just dreaming or imagining everything in some altered state of consciousness. Except I realize there's nothing altered about my consciousness. No other identities are in my head. There's no VACANCY sign out front. I'm thinking as clear as I've ever thought. I'm the most me I've been in months.

I'm not Indiana Jones or James Bond.

I'm not Jim Morrison or Captain Kirk.

Truth is, for the first time since I can remember, I feel like myself.

I take several deep breaths as I look around at the city lights in the distance, bright and colored and blurry. Something swirls around me, drifting out of the darkness and falling to the earth. At first I think it's snow, which doesn't make any sense because it never snows in Los Angeles, until I realize it's ash from the fire.

Part of me wonders how the hell I ended up like this. What happened to the path I started down?

But I guess that's life. You start looking for answers and making decisions and creating inertia and before you know it, you're twenty-seven years old and working for a bioengineering company, blurring the lines between fantasy and reality and blowing up buildings.

This definitely isn't the future I envisioned for myself twenty years ago, though I don't know for sure what I thought my life would be like. What seven-year-old kid thinks that far ahead? But I guess I expected something more. Something that mattered. Something that gave me a sense of purpose.

On the other side of the burning factory, the protesters are singing "Let It Snow! Let It Snow! Let It Snow!"

As the ash falls to the ground around me like snow and the city lights twinkle in the distance, I can't help thinking about Christmas—the lights decorating the houses, the brightly wrapped packages, the smell of a freshly cut pine tree, the sound of Nat King Cole singing about chestnuts roasting on an open fire.

I look out at the city and think about all the children who are tucked away in their beds, dreaming of Santa Claus or too excited to sleep, looking out their windows hoping to catch a glimpse of a sleigh being pulled across the sky by reindeer, anticipating the magic and the joy of Christmas morning. I think about how my father denied me the thrill of believing in the holiday magic. How he robbed me of the excitement and anticipation of Christmas Day. How he ended my dreams of reindeer pulling a sleigh across the heavens.

I look up into the sky through the swirling ash and think about how I spent Christmas Eve wrapping my own presents, stuffing my own stocking, playing the role of Santa.

A smile touches my lips as a thought occurs to me that I've never had before. A thought that makes so much sense because it's been there all along, waiting for me to find it, to discover it.

The role I was always meant to play.

Sometimes you don't realize who you're supposed to be until the moment comes.

I turn back around and continue to walk through the trees at the base of the Santa Monica Mountains, heading toward Griffith Park, excited about my future. After a few steps, I stumble forward and fall down. Pain flares up in my broken arm as I land on it and I black out again, coming to I don't know how much later. Maybe seconds. Maybe minutes. Maybe hours. Except I still hear sirens and people celebrating, so I'm guessing I wasn't out too long.

The protesters are now singing "Here Comes Santa Claus."

Somehow I get to my feet. I don't remember doing it but it must have happened because I'm standing up, my vision going in and out. I close my eyes hard, struggling to focus, and when I open them again, everything's a little clearer. More crisp, like the night sky.

I take in another deep breath and hold it, filling my lungs with the cold December air, and then exhale. I do this a few more times until my head is clear and I feel like I can walk without passing out, which is about the best I can hope for at this point. Eventually I'll need to find some medical attention, but not until after I get away from here. In the meantime, I have a lot of decisions to make.

The sirens grow louder and another explosion fills the night as I limp through the trees, thinking about what I have to do—making plans, calculating expenses, anticipating obstacles. I wonder if I should head north or if I can set up shop in Mexico. The labor would probably be cheaper south of the border, but I don't know the going rate for elves. Or if I have to deal with a union.

Behind me the protesters are still singing, so I sing along with them.

"Here comes Santa Claus, here comes Santa Claus, right down Santa Claus Lane . . ."

I wonder if I should grow a beard. If I need to gain weight. If there's any real estate for sale in the North Pole.

I wonder if reindeer really know how to fly.

ACKNOWLEDGMENTS

Even though I write fiction, I do quite a bit of research to ground my stories in reality. For example, during the writing of *Big Egos* I read up on Carl Jung, Sigmund Freud, Buddhism, 1970s pop culture, Philip Marlowe, Jim Morrison, James Bond, DNA replication, remote detonators, Shakespeare, Santa Claus, Greek mythology, silverback gorillas, karaoke, *Star Trek,* obsessive-compulsive disorder, Starbucks, Pink's Hot Dogs, the Formosa Cafe, Indiana Jones, donating blood, *The Catcher in the Rye,* Oscar Wilde, Philip K. Dick, countries that don't have extradition treaties with the United States, and Elvis Presley's favorite snacks.

Just to name a few.

However, I didn't interview anyone or use any academic articles or text that required permission, so there's no specific person or persons to thank for helping me with my research. Instead, I'll thank everyone who compiled the information that enabled me to write this book. Whoever you are.

As for the less anonymous people I'd like to thank, there are a few of the usual suspects. My editor. My agent. My writing group. But I'd also like to acknowledge some of the unsung heroes—not for their help in the creation of this particular novel but for their own unique contributions to my success over the past five years.

Jon and Ann Bibler, Guy and Jenn Genis, Ed and Barbara Goff, Eunice and Greg Magill, Jeff Bibler, Shannon Page, and Lori Stein (aka Party Radar). Thank you for your hospitality and your generosity and for providing me a home away from home. I had keys made.

Alan Beatts, Jude Feldman, Maryelizabeth Hart, Nathan Spradlin, and Del and Sue Howison. Thank you for your love of authors and books. You complete me.

Bill Breedlove, David DeSilva, Jim Saltzman, Kelly Young, and JX Bell. Thank you for massaging my ego, listening to me complain, and supporting my habit. Man-hugs all around.

Clifford Brooks, Ian Dudley, and Keith White. Thank you for your insight and feedback on the early drafts of *Big Egos*. Does it work now?

Jennifer Seis (aka Miss Friendly). Thank you for your glimpse into corporate culture and for just being you. I owe you dinner.

The team at Gallery Books and Simon & Schuster. Thank you for all that you do to get me out there in front of readers. Without you, I'm just shouting in an empty room.

My editor, Ed Schlesinger. Thank you for your enthusiasm and your trust and for making me look good. Nobody does it better.

My agent, Michelle Brower. Thank you for finding me a home, giving me advice, and for just being you. You are marvelous.

My friends and family. Thank you for helping me to keep my own ego in check. I couldn't have done this without you.

And finally, a big thank you very much to Elvis Presley, Raymond Chandler, Ian Fleming, Gene Roddenberry, J. D. Salinger, Jim Morrison, and Philip K. Dick. Without you and your creations, this novel would not have been the same.